The Shadow Keeper

Also by Abi Elphinstone

The DreamSnatcher

The Shadow Keeper

Abi Elphinstone

SIMON & SCHUSTER

First published in Great Britain in 2016 by Simon & Schuster UK Ltd
A CBS COMPANY

7 9 10 8 6

Simon & Schuster UK Ltd
1st Floor
222 Gray's Inn Road
London WC1X 8HB

www.simonandschuster.co.uk

Simon & Schuster Australia, Sydney
Simon & Schuster India, New Delhi

A CIP catalogue record for this book
is available from the British Library.

PB ISBN 978-1-47112-270-5
EBook ISBN 978-1-47112-271-2

Typeset in Goudy by M Rules
Printed and bound by CPI Group (UK) Ltd, Croydon, CR0 4YY

To Mum, Dad, Will, Tom and Charis

For being such a loyal and loving Tribe

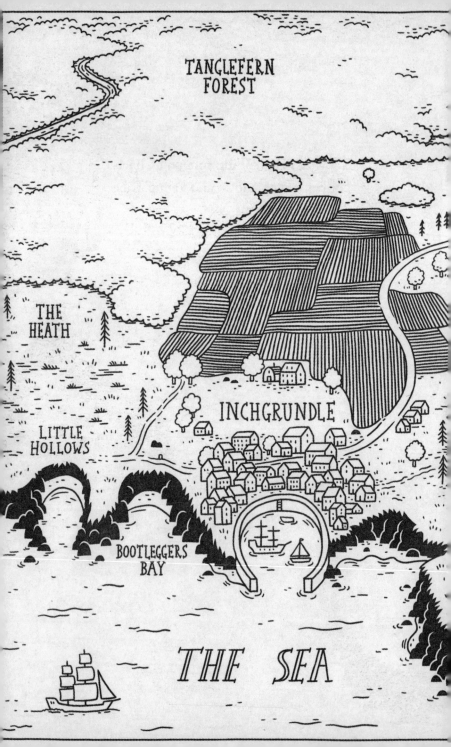

Prologue
The Crooked Cave

The sea breathes quietly tonight, a sprawled darkness rolling in and out. It slips over beaches and laps at harbour walls. But further along the coast, where the cliffs turn ragged and shards of rock jut into the water, strewn like broken gravestones, the current is stronger. It moves with a strength all of its own here, heaving and churning, smashing and pounding. This is a place few men or women brave, and none on a night as dark as this.

And yet there is a light moving between the shards of rock, a lantern fixed to the front of a rowing boat, and, though the waves swell and suck and crash, the boat weaves a way through. The moon slides out from the clouds for a moment, scattering silver on the sea, and then it is gone. But the lantern still shines, splaying light on the snakeskin mask of the figure in the boat. He wears a cloak, the hood pulled high, and only his tongue moves – forked and flickering. His arms stay folded in his lap – he has no use for oars to propel the boat forward. It moves of its own accord, drawn by magic towards the opening in the cliff face.

Carving a channel through the last of the rocks, the boat disappears inside. The passageway of water within is still, a snake of black beneath arched walls of rock. The boat glides on, winding into shadows, then it nudges to a halt as it meets a metal grate stretched the height of the passageway. The figure drops his hood, his tongue quivers over his lips and he speaks.

'It is Ashtongue who enters the Crooked Cave. I've come to you, Darkebite, as you commanded.'

A hiss escapes from Ashtongue's lips, scratching at the silence, then there's a grinding noise, like a chain being pulled, and the grate lifts. The boat noses through, into a wider cavern, and Ashtongue steps out on to a beach littered with bones. He looks at the glass bottles and metal cages arranged on ledges of rock surrounding the beach. They glint under the light of his lantern and each one is filled with animal parts: moth wings, fox teeth, owl talons, bat claws . . . Ashtongue smiles and turns to the cauldron standing in the middle of the beach. A burst of green erupts from inside it and a cloaked figure emerges from the shadows, plucking the wings from a dead moth as it crunches over the bones.

Ashtongue dips his mask. 'Greetings, Darkebite.'

Darkebite's cloak slips to the ground and, where shoulders should be, two enormous black wings flex, rising up like crooked sails. 'Skull and Hemlock failed.' The voice bristles with anger. 'The child and the beast still live.'

Ashtongue stiffens. 'The girl and her wildcat defeated *two* Shadowmasks?'

Darkebite's mask of charcoaled wood is absolutely still, the jet-black hair wild around it. 'With the help of their friends.'

Ashtongue shakes his head. 'But Skull had the girl locked in a cage in the forest – he had hounds trained to track her – and Hemlock conjured poison to make sure she wouldn't survive!'

'It wasn't enough.' Darkebite's wings twitch. 'The children found the first amulet and used its power to destroy both Skull and Hemlock. I saw it happen and was forced to flee. We must kill the girl and her wildcat before they find the second amulet. Only then can we shatter the old magic and conjure an evil to take its place.'

Darkebite walks towards the cauldron, veined wings trailing through the bones. Ashtongue follows and the two Shadowmasks stand in silence for several minutes, watching the green liquid bubbling inside the cauldron.

'You must call upon the spirits of the Underworld,' Darkebite says. 'Use them to wreak havoc on the old magic.' Picking up a glass bottle, the witch doctor tips an owl talon into the cauldron; the liquid hisses and green smoke fizzes upwards. 'I'll conjure the night creatures; Molly Pecksniff and her wildcat won't escape.'

There is a pause.

'No one escapes the Shadow Keeper's curse.'

Ashtongue nods, his snakeskin mask glimmers, then he watches as Darkebite strips the barbs from an owl feather and lets them flutter into the cauldron. The liquid swirls, sucking the broken feather into its clutches, then a talon bursts

3

through the surface, snatching at the air before slipping silently down.

The Shadow Keeper smiles because inside the cauldron something hideous is stirring . . .

Chapter 1
Visitors in the Cove

It was Gryff who heard it first. A sound that didn't belong in the cove – sudden, rasping, like paper being torn. He looked up from the rocks where he had been resting, ears cocked, whiskers twitching. The others hadn't heard the noise, but a wildcat's ears miss nothing. Gryff scanned the towering grey cliffs that curved round the beach, closing it off into a secluded bay.

But nothing seemed amiss. Seagulls were still squawking from jutting crags and tussocks of grass, the beach was deserted and beyond it the sea stretched out to the horizon, glittering in the early morning sun. Gryff slunk between the rock pools, away from the cave, before leaping down to the sand.

Then the noise came again, shivering the air like a sheet being ripped in two. It was louder this time, closer, and its echo hung in the cove. A cluster of seagulls on the highest crags launched themselves into the sky, white arcs carried out over the sea. As if pulled by invisible strings, the rest of the gulls followed, leaving the cliff face still and grey. Only the grass and sea thrift moved, fluttering in the wind.

Still Gryff watched, waiting. And then his fur prickled. There was a shadow out of place behind a clump of grass – something dark shifting among the rocks. Then it was gone, lost in the gorse and bracken that spread down one side of the cliff face and partly obscured the path zigzagging towards the sand. But the air felt different somehow, as if it might shatter into pieces at any moment. Gryff's muscles stiffened.

Gathering speed, he ran across the beach, past a wigwam of washed-up driftwood, round a battered rowing boat, on towards the rocks at the other side of the cove which cut into the sea and closed the bay in from the rest of the coastline.

On the furthest rock stood a girl, her long, tangled hair as black as the tip of a jackdaw's wing. She drew herself up and the wind roared in her ears, rippling through the old swimsuit she was wearing and clinking the gold boxing fists that hung around her neck on a chain.

'You won't manage it,' said a boy, treading water just beyond the rocks. 'You'll slip and mash your head.' A strand of seaweed had twisted itself round one of his sticking out ears. He shook it off and turned to the boy in the sea beside him. 'Alfie, you tell her. She's mad to try this!'

Alfie squinted against the sun, his jay feather earring flapping against his neck. 'Sid's right, Moll. Just get a move on and jump in like we did; all this hanging around is making us cold.'

Moll wrinkled her nose and shuffled down to the edge of the rock. The sea slapped against its marbled base before foaming over the limpets and splashing up on to her anklet. She looked across at Alfie and Siddy and tried to raise one eyebrow to show she meant business – but when both started wriggling she flared her nostrils instead.

Siddy rolled his eyes. 'Don't expect anyone to come and mop you up when you go back to the cave with cuts and bruises. Mooshie's still tempered up because we put seaweed in her hammock.'

Married to Oak, the head of the camp, Mooshie was in charge of cooking meals and tending to injuries; she was like a mother figure to the rest of them. It hadn't been wise to provoke her with seaweed, Moll knew that, but it had been necessary. Because, in Moll's eyes, Mooshie had offended the Tribe – the secret gang comprising Moll, Gryff, Siddy and Alfie that was dedicated to breaking rules and causing havoc.

Moll shrugged. 'Mooshie should've known better than to force us to eat sea slugs – hardly surprising the Tribe rebelled. I'd say she was lucky it was just seaweed we punished her with. It would've been eels if I'd had more time.' She steadied herself on the rock, then looked up and smiled. 'Watch and learn, boys. This is exactly the kind of behaviour the Tribe needs to see more of.'

Alfie, half amused now, flicked the water from his fair hair and kicked up his legs so that he was floating on his back. 'There's not a chance you'll pull off a somersault into a dive; your last four jumps have been bellyflops.'

Muttering a last-minute prayer to the sea spirit in charge of crash landings, Moll bent low. Out of the corner of her eye she glimpsed Gryff hastening across the rocks towards them, but, thinking nothing of it, she gripped her boxing fist talisman for luck and launched herself into the air. The tuck that was meant to follow never did. Instead, Moll's legs punched out at extraordinary angles, her arms flapped like a demented bird and she plunged belly first towards the sea. There was an almighty slap, the loudest one yet, as Moll's skin smacked into the water.

She surfaced with a scowl, hair plastered across her face, then raised a fist, ready to take on Siddy and Alfie's abuse. But it never came.

Gryff's growl cut a channel through the waves towards them. '*Urrrrrrrrrr.*'

Moll, Siddy and Alfie met his yellow-green eyes. Then they heard it too: a noise from the cliffs, curdling the air, like silk tearing again and again. But there was no movement among the rocks – just a wall of ragged stone and gorse staring back at them.

'What – what was that?' Siddy asked.

The sea around Moll felt suddenly cold and she narrowed her eyes at the cliffs. 'I don't know but it doesn't sound right. We should get back to the cave and—'

'The seagulls,' Alfie interrupted. 'They've all gone . . .'

'And – and the gorse,' Siddy stammered, pushing dark curls back from his face and straining his own eyes towards the cliffs. 'It's rotted through!'

Moll blinked several times. Siddy was right; the gorse lining the path down the cliff face wasn't green with bright yellow flowers any more: the bushes were bare, a dull grey-brown, like clumps of rusted wire. Moll flinched. Mooshie had taught her about the plants, herbs and weeds down in the cove and how they changed with the seasons. But no plant shed its flowers and leaves this quickly – and gorse didn't lose its flowers in autumn. Something was amiss.

It was then that the cliff face started to move. A swarm of black shapes crawled out from behind rocks and withered gorse bushes, spreading down the cliff like spilled ink. The creatures called to one another in low, crooning hoots.

'Owls in the daytime?' Moll whispered in disbelief. 'Dozens of them . . . and they're *black!*'

Gryff's hackles rose. Moll's shoulders tensed. She knew a bad omen when she saw one; every gypsy did. She glanced to the rocks for her catapult, then realised she'd left it in the cave.

The birds sprang from the cliffs into the air as one, swarming together in a darkened throng, before flying towards the rocks jutting out into the sea.

Moll, Siddy and Alfie kicked backwards, away from the cove.

And the owls loomed closer, just twenty metres away now, a curtain of black closing over the sea, their calls deep and hollow. They were larger than ordinary owls and their enormous wings beat towards the children above scaled talons. They drew nearer still and Moll gasped as they massed high above their heads in a pulsing cloud. Then a bolt of black screeched before plummeting down, its hooded yellow eyes fixed on Gryff.

'Watch out, Gryff!' Moll screamed.

The owl splayed its razor-sharp talons and Gryff leapt aside, narrowly dodging them. Shrieks from above juddered against the wind, but the owl raced on, swiping at the towel on the rocks and ripping a large scrap of material clean off. The bird circled upwards to rejoin the others.

'Jump, Gryff!' Siddy roared.

'But – but he hates the sea!' Moll cried.

Owl after owl dropped from the sky. Gryff sprang across the rocks, snarling and spitting, avoiding their clutches by a whisker. They spiralled upwards again, black stains blotting out the sun, calling together in ghostly hoots.

'Run, Gryff!' Moll shouted. 'You'll outpace them on the beach—'

An owl swivelled its disc face round, blinking narrow yellow eyes at Moll, then it bulleted down, straight for her. Moll ducked beneath the surface and, without a second's hesitation, Gryff leapt from the rocks and plunged into the sea after her.

Underwater, the sea muffled the owl screeches, but Moll kicked deeper, away from the talons that scratched at the surface. Gryff clawed through the water towards her, bubbles spraying out behind him. Sensing the wildcat's presence, Moll twisted round, her breath caged inside her, and opened her eyes. Her heart surged. Gryff could have outrun the owls on the beach; Moll knew the speeds he could reach. But he'd followed her – as he always did – into the deep unknown. They swam on together, pulling themselves through the water after Alfie and Siddy.

But, above the surface, a dark shape followed.

Moll reached out to Siddy and Alfie, her eyes bulging, her chest ready to burst if she didn't take a breath. Alfie pointed upwards and both Siddy and Moll nodded; they'd have to brave the owls for air.

They kicked up, fingers stretching towards the sparkling surface, but the second they broke the water they met with a wall of sound. The owls shrieked and a cluster broke free, nosediving towards Gryff and the children. They drank in a lungful of air, then shot down beneath the surface, hauling themselves on through the water.

The sea was darker and deeper now and the sandy bottom had sunk out of sight. Small fish darted away, melting into the depths beyond, but still the children kicked for all they were worth, back towards the safety of the cave at the far side of the bay. Moll glanced at Gryff beside her, his grey-black striped fur moving with the sea's pull, his paws working as fast as they could. She blinked at him, her head throbbing as the last of her breath seeped from her lungs. *One more breath and I think we'll make it, Gryff.*

Moll surged upwards, surfacing next to the others, and gasped the air hungrily. Owl squawks clattered in her ears, then the birds thundered down all together. Moll caught the yellow glint of one owl's eyes, saw its talons spread out towards her face, then she plunged beneath the surface again.

She'd only taken one stroke when she heard the scream and, though it was stifled by the sea, Moll knew who it belonged to. Siddy. She swerved back up to the surface to find Gryff lashing out with his claws; they clashed against grappling talons and wings. Alfie was trying to drag Siddy under the waves, but Siddy was choking on water, his face scrunched up in pain at the sight of the bloodied cut across his forearm.

'Get him down!' Moll shouted to Alfie, beating through the water towards the two boys. 'Just a few more strokes and we're there!'

Together they dragged Siddy beneath the surface while Gryff swung wildly at any owls that came close. And then they were all underwater again, Moll and Alfie heaving Siddy on. The sound of the owls grew fainter as the sandy seabed rose back into sight. Clumps of seaweed swayed below them and the children kicked harder, water-blurred eyes seeking out the rocks that shielded the camp's cave.

A couple more strokes and the barnacled boulders rose up before them. A crab scuttled out from a dark hole that was a metre wide and high, tucked just below the surface of the sea. Then the creature slipped beneath the seaweed as Alfie and Moll pushed Siddy up towards it. The shallow water carried him into the hole and, one by one, Alfie, Moll and Gryff followed. Moll felt the last of her breath ebbing away as they swam into the tunnel, and then, moments later, the rocks above them opened up slightly.

The children's heads burst through the surface, spluttering water and gulping the air back into their lungs. Dark, wet rock arched just above them and water slopped against the sides of the tunnel, draining with a loud sucking noise as the tide pulled back. But the owls hadn't followed; this was a place only Oak's gypsies knew about.

Siddy glanced at his arm and moaned.

'Quick,' Alfie panted, turning to Moll. 'Get him inside.'

They pushed Siddy further along the tunnel. Moll's knees knocked against the rocks beneath her and they scraped at her skin, then the tunnel veered left, inland for a while, and before long the scalloped rocks above them widened, opening up completely to reveal a large cavern.

They called the cave Little Hollows and it spread out before them now, its marbled roof curving grey and silver far above the sandy bottom. Candles flickered on every shelf of rock jutting from the sides of the cave, lighting up the dried lemon peel, shards of mirror and horseshoe nails that the gypsies had balanced on ledges and in fissures as good-luck omens. And a fire crackled in the middle of the cave, its smoke curling upwards, seeping away through unseen cracks. It had been the gypsies' base for two weeks, ever since Oak had left his son, Wisdom, in charge of keeping the clearing and the other gypsies in Tanglefern Forest safe and a smaller group had broken off to hide from the Shadowmasks.

Here in Little Hollows, Cinderella Bull, the camp's fortune-teller, had taught the Tribe about the sea spirits and mer creatures lurking beyond the cove – about kelpies, sirens and mer ghosts. Mooshie had shown them how to spear mackerel, pot lobsters and cook seaweed, and she'd pointed out which herbs could be used and which ones to avoid: nettles worked in tea, but poppies from the fields above the

13

cliffs would knock you out cold. And Oak had showed them where the currents were at their strongest in the bay and the best spots for diving.

The Tribe had flourished in the cove – the sea was something new and full of adventure – and Moll was almost able to forget that back in the forest only a month ago the Shadowmasks had used hounds, poison and fire to hunt her and Gryff. But now their threat was all too real.

Panting, Alfie and Moll hauled Siddy up on to the slabs of rock that spilled down from the tunnel into the cave. Gryff clambered out after them, his eyes alert for help.

Dripping with water, Moll stepped over the collection of home-made fishing rods – their lines strung from nettle fibres – and jumped down into the cave. Siddy rocked his arm and whimpered and Moll glanced at the sheets tied back by colourful ribbons from the four alcoves at the far end of the cave.

'Mooshie!' she called.

A woman's plump face poked out from an alcove: two dimpled cheeks framed by a purple headscarf and a sparkling brooch at the neck of a shirt. Glowering, she raised a tea towel in her ringed hand and stormed towards the fire. 'I thought I told you lot to use the beach entrance; that tunnel's dangerous! You'll—' Her words were cut short as she noticed Siddy. She bustled closer, her colourful petticoats bouncing round her ankles. 'What happened?' she asked, her face suddenly pale.

Moll glanced back towards the tunnel. 'I think Darkebite's back.'

Chapter 2
Inside Little Hollows

Mooshie knelt before Siddy by the fire, dabbing his arm with a dressing she'd mixed from woundwort leaves bound in wetted cotton.

'Will he be OK?' Alfie asked. He sat down on a stool carved from driftwood, then reached for a blanket and wrapped it round himself.

Mooshie nodded, but she didn't look up from what she was doing; her cures required her absolute attention. Moll stood by the fire, letting its warmth burrow inside her bones, and felt suddenly glad to be among the familiar jumble of objects Mooshie had made to sell up at Inchgrundle, the fishing village a few miles along the coast: lobster pots made from washed-up rope and twine, woven then bound round hazel, and wooden flowers carved from elder.

'Owww,' Siddy moaned as Mooshie pressed down the dressing.

Moll bit her lip and watched as Gryff prowled further into the cave, away from the cluster of people. He stopped before the alcoves, shook the seawater from his fur, then hissed as a dribble snaked into his mouth. Moll hurried over to him.

'Thank you for jumping in after me,' she whispered. 'And for beating the owls away from Sid.'

Gryff grunted, then spat seawater on to the sand. Moll smiled and ran a hand over his back. She didn't need to bend down to touch the wildcat – he was large and she was by far the smallest in Oak's camp – but Gryff had singled Moll out as a young child and he'd been by her side ever since; he'd left the northern wilderness to help her fight back against the Shadowmasks, he'd let her – and *only* her – touch him for the first time just over a month ago and he'd never let her down. And yet Gryff was no pet. He was secretive, often solitary, and as Moll faced him she felt his wildness and sensed the fierce courage buried inside him.

She glanced behind her to ensure she was out of Mooshie's earshot. 'I saved you some of the cod we fried up at breakfast,' she told him. 'It's in our alcove.'

Gryff wrinkled his nose, sniffed and slunk off into the furthest corner of the cave.

Little Hollows was shaped like a giant's hand. Four narrow alcoves at the far end of the cave, like enormous fingers, where the gypsies slept in hammocks bunched high with patchwork quilts, pillows and cushions; the central cave, like a huge palm, where they cooked around the fire and ate; and the tunnel leading into the cave, like a long, crooked thumb, an access point the Tribe had discovered when Moll and Siddy had dunked Alfie in the water there as the last

16

part of his initiation into the Tribe. But the only place Gryff went when he was inside Little Hollows was Moll's alcove – slinking in now and again to ensure she was safe or to devour the leftover food she had sneaked for him.

Moll walked back to the fire, the light from the flames dancing up and down the cave walls around her. Alfie was holding a bandage in place over Siddy's arm while Mooshie busied herself over a rock near the tunnel where dozens of jam jars had been arranged, each one filled with herbs.

Moll plucked at her swimsuit. 'I'm so sorry, Sid. It should've been me this happened to – not you.'

Siddy tried to smile, but it was more of a grimace and Moll just ended up feeling even worse.

Alfie looked up at her. 'It's not your fault, Moll. We all know that.'

Moll sat on a stool, her nails dug hard into her palms. 'There's enough anger inside me to defeat an army or – or – bring down a mountain.'

Mooshie hastened back over. 'Or get you into a serious amount of trouble with my tea towel.' She sprinkled small purple flowers inside each fold of Siddy's bandage. 'Lavender. It'll soothe the pain and calm your nerves.' She looked at Moll then Alfie. 'What happened out there?'

Alfie fiddled with the knot of black horsehair hanging around his neck. It was his talisman – a lock of hair from Raven, his stallion cob, who now roamed the heath above the cliffs. 'It was fine at first,' he said. 'We were just waiting for Moll to bellyflop off the far rocks.'

'I was diving, Moosh,' Moll muttered. 'Teaching the Tribe a thing or two about somersaults.' She buried her feet in the sand. 'Then we heard noises – ripping, tearing sorts of sounds.' Moll noticed Mooshie's hand hover over the bandage. 'And these owls came out of nowhere and bolted down towards us so we dived underwater and swam to the cave.' She looked into the fire. 'It felt like witch-doctor magic, as if the Shadowmasks had found us at last. I kept thinking the owls would swarm together and *become* one of them – like the bats did with Darkebite back in the forest – but they never did . . .'

Mooshie twisted the amber ring round her thumb three times, a habit she'd got into when she wanted to thank the sea spirits for keeping her loved ones safe. 'The owls were just messengers,' she said quietly, 'part of the magic Darkebite and the rest of the Shadowmasks are conjuring to find you and Gryff. We knew this would come – that sooner or later they'd find you. They'll know for sure that you and Gryff have left the forest now.'

Mooshie picked up a penknife from a wooden box by her feet and used the blade to cut Siddy's bandage. 'You were lucky, Sid. This'll heal quickly once the herbs start working, but it could've been a lot worse.'

Siddy huddled inside the blanket. 'Where's Hermit?'

'Cowering in your flat cap. He's been in there all morning.' Mooshie stood up, walked round the fire to the other side of the cave, then stooped beneath the colourful pinafores, shorts and shirts dangling from a washing line fastened into

18

the cracks. She unpegged a flat cap and brought it over to the fire.

'Hermit!' Siddy cried, reaching inside the cap and stroking the crab's shell.

Hermit was Siddy's latest pet. He had an earthworm too, called Porridge the Second (Porridge the First had rather unfortunately been eaten by a cockerel in the forest earlier in the year), but he had failed to show any sort of enthusiasm for beach life so Siddy had been forced to leave him behind. The Tribe had organised a farewell ceremony though – they'd dug up a few more worms to keep Porridge the Second company and carved messages into an oak tree for him: 'Keep Wiggling' from Siddy, 'Cheer Up' from Alfie and 'Don't Get Squashed' from Moll, which Siddy thought pretty morbid given the parting was so emotional anyway. And then Hermit had come along – a crab who was terrified of absolutely everything, even his own pincers, which meant that more often than not he spent his days scampering backwards into his shell.

Moll watched as Hermit stuck out one trembling pincer towards Siddy. 'I'm so lucky I ended up with a wildcat,' she told herself.

Siddy pretended not to hear. 'What were the ripping sounds we heard, Moosh? Before the owls came after us. Like – like paper tearing ...' His voice trailed into silence and Hermit, catching a glimpse of his own pincers, shot off Siddy's knee and clattered into a lobster pot.

Alfie nodded. 'What kind of bird makes a sound like that?'

'Birds made from dark magic, I'd wager,' said a voice from one of the alcoves at the far end of the cave.

Cinderella Bull's hunched figure hobbled towards them, the gold pennies on her shawl jangling together as she walked. On approaching the fire, she lifted up a fortune-telling ball and held it out between fingers sparkling with rings.

'I've seen it, Moll – just seconds ago.'

Cinderella Bull was the oldest gypsy in the gang and her visions from the crystal ball were never wrong. 'Darkebite appeared in the form of a bat when you encountered the witch doctors in the forest. Only a Shadow Keeper can take the form of a nocturnal animal and curse and command night beasts. It seems Darkebite is a Shadow Keeper who sent cursed owls to find you and Gryff – to wound you so that the other Shadowmasks had time to gather close with their Soul Splinter.' She paused. 'My vision was of Darkebite meeting with a figure – another Shadowmask perhaps. They're on to us now.'

Moll faced the words straight on, but her heartbeat quickened. No one had mentioned the Soul Splinter – the deadly shard of ice that held the Shadowmasks' souls and had killed her parents ten years ago – since the small group had left the forest. Some things were best not talked about.

Cinderella Bull's voice dropped. 'Those ripping noises – it's just as the Bone Murmur foretold . . .' She beckoned with a crooked finger and Moll knew better than to ignore the fortune-teller's command.

She stood up with Alfie, leaving Siddy under Mooshie's watch, and followed Cinderella Bull to the cave wall beyond the washing line, near the rocks that masked a gap out on to the beach. There, written by Moll in messy chalk, was the Bone Murmur, the words of the old magic read in the Oracle Bones and handed down to Moll from her ancestors:

There is a magic, old and true,
That shadowed minds seek to undo.
They'll splinter the souls of those who hold
The Oracle Bones from Guardians of old.
And storms will rise; trees will die,
If they free their dark magic into the sky.
But a beast will come from lands full wild,
To fight this darkness with a gypsy child.
And they must find the Amulets of Truth
To stop dark souls doing deeds uncouth.

For a while, Cinderella Bull said nothing, and Moll listened to the sea murmuring beyond the cave, then the fortune-teller pointed a gnarled finger at one of the lines: '*If they free their dark magic into the sky.*' She paused. 'The ripping noises you heard, that was the air tearing, thresholds opening up. The Shadowmasks' dark magic was pouring in from the Underworld.'

Moll blinked at Alfie, started to say something, decided against it, then mumbled, 'Are you *sure*? Because I get things wrong the whole time and—'

Cinderella Bull put a hand on Moll's shoulder. 'I'm sure, Moll.' She slipped her crystal ball into the pocket of her pinafore. 'Though we may not see them, there are worlds out there beyond our own. Our ancestors believed in a world where the old magic lies, where one day our souls will go to rest. We call that place the Otherworld.'

Alfie glanced at Moll, who shrugged. She'd never heard anyone talk about different worlds before.

Cinderella Bull went on. 'They say that in the Otherworld the wind spirit whispers life into mountains so huge they're lost amid clouds where griffins roam – and there's talk of unicorns living behind thundering waterfalls and seas filled with mer palaces.'

Alfie squinted at Cinderella Bull. 'And the other place – the Underworld?'

Cinderella Bull lowered her voice. 'A place where dark magic brews. Though no one can be sure, there are rumours of werewolves stalking rotten forests and giant spiders that crawl through tunnels.'

Moll groaned as she thought of the seaweed she'd dumped in Mooshie's hammock recently. 'I'm bound to end up there.'

Cinderella Bull ruffled Moll's hair. 'The Shadowmasks' magic is gathering strength. We thought we had you safe, but those owls managed to track you – they could only have been conjured from the darkest corners of the Underworld.' She pointed to another chalked line on the cave wall and read the words aloud: 'And storms will rise; trees will die . . . If

22

we don't stop them opening these thresholds, our lands will be destroyed.'

Alfie gasped. 'The cliffs – when we looked up and noticed the owls, we saw the gorse and bracken had died!'

Cinderella Bull nodded gravely. 'So it has begun already. And, as long as Darkebite holds the Soul Splinter, the Shadowmasks will have enough power to open these thresholds. It's time to look for the next amulet.'

Before anyone could reply, there was a moan from one of the alcoves at the far side of the cave. They walked back to the fire and looked up as an old man, bent over like a coat hanger, came staggering out towards them. He was wearing a spotted bow tie, a pair of maroon swimming trunks and socks pulled up to his knees. But that wasn't the strangest thing about him: he also had a lobster pot wedged round his middle.

Mooshie let her head fall into her hands. 'Yet more madness before noon?'

Hard-Times Bob, Cinderella Bull's brother, was the last addition to the group of gypsies hiding in Little Hollows. According to him, he'd been chosen to come along because he had 'the strength of ten men' and could 'floor a Shadowmask with a single punch'. According to the others, he'd come along because Mooshie was the only one who knew how to cure his hiccups (a side effect of his dislocating various limbs to entertain other members of the camp) and keep him out of trouble.

He shot them all an embarrassed smile between rows of

broken teeth. 'I heard Siddy hurt his arm so I thought I'd dislocate some limbs and shove myself through a lobster pot to cheer him up.'

Mooshie sighed. 'If you carry on like this, Bob, I'll have to send you back to the forest to stay with the rest of the camp.' She smoothed her petticoats. 'Cinderella Bull, you'd better call upon the sea spirits for protection in the cove – and we need to make a plan once Oak is back from Inchgrundle.'

Moll and Alfie exchanged looks. Neither said anything, but they knew what the other was thinking: the Dreads from Bootleggers Bay, just up the coast from Little Hollows – a notorious smuggler gang who hauled boatloads of gin and whisky into Inchgrundle and who set upon anyone who stumbled across their path. Every journey made to Inchgrundle for supplies meant a journey past the Dreads. Oak knew how to fight – he could toss a knife blind and still hit a target – but these smugglers were lawless thugs, hungry for violence.

'Oak always comes back,' Alfie said quietly. 'The Dreads are no match for him.'

Moll nodded, but, as she slipped off towards her alcove, she felt her body tense. She stooped beneath the sheet and went inside. A clutter of sea treasures lined every ridge: starfish, shells, pebbles and washed-up glass bottles. And a storm lantern containing a single candle glowed, illuminating the strange symbols of the Oracle Bone script Moll had chalked on to the walls to try and remember them: triangles resting on prongs, eyes inside squares, circles dashed through with lines. The sandy floor below the hammock was strewn with clothes and at the far end, beside a scattering of fish bones, lay Gryff.

His yellow-green eyes flicked open, as if he'd sensed Moll's presence. '*Brrroooooo.*'

Moll loosened the ribbon that tied the sheet back from her alcove and the material hung down over the entrance, shielding them from sight. She smiled at the wildcat's greeting, then walked over and sat down beside him. 'We'll get the Shadowmasks back for hurting Sid.' She was silent for a moment, then she glanced at her catapult on a ledge and a coil of anger flexed inside her. 'And for taking Ma and Pa away and forcing us from the forest. They won't get away with it.'

Gryff curled his tail round Moll's ankle and purred.

A voice sounded from beyond her alcove – deep and soft – and Moll breathed a sigh of relief. Oak was back from Inchgrundle; he'd made it past the Dreads.

Moll listened as Mooshie told Oak what had happened. The gypsy leader said nothing, as was sometimes his way, but he was taking it all in – planning, assessing, thinking of the next steps. Moll waited quietly, then the sheet covering her alcove lifted and Oak stepped inside. Back in the forest, before Moll had learnt about the Bone Murmur, Oak would have knocked on her wagon door and asked if she wanted to go tracking for animals or climbing the biggest trees. But all that had changed over the summer . . .

Oak took off his wide-brimmed hat, set it against his

waistcoat and ran a hand through his dark hair. 'Moll, we've put it off for as long as possible so that Cinderella Bull could teach you how to read the ways of the old magic.' His eyes glinted in the candlelight, almost as black as the obsidian stone set in his ring. 'Now it's time you threw the Oracle Bones.'

Moll's heart fluttered. She was the Guardian of the Oracle Bones and this was what she had wanted, what she had been practising for every evening since they'd moved to Little Hollows. But, now the time had come to throw the bones, Moll's stomach was a knot of nerves.

Oak looked her straight in the eye. 'If we're going to destroy the Shadowmasks and their Soul Splinter, we need to know where the next amulet is.'

Chapter 3
Throwing the Bones

Outside the cave that night, a ship moved along the horizon, pushing silently through the sea below a sky pricked with stars. But, inside Little Hollows, every candle had been snuffed out and the gypsies gathered round the fire on stools.

In a large circle around them lay the good-luck charms Cinderella Bull had laid out to protect the ceremony from evil: acorns, hedgehog bristles, horseshoes bent into circles, fox teeth and thorns. Water slopped against the tunnel walls and the only other sound in the cave was the *drip drip drip* coming from the drinking-water contraption Mooshie had set up.

Cinderella Bull sat with her eyes closed, beside a battered chest she'd hauled out of her alcove with Hard-Times Bob. She bent her head low and from her cracked lips there came a murmuring. The fire flickered into the darkness and, moments later, Mooshie began to hum, her head dipped, her mouth shaping sounds that seemed to swell and soften, like the ebb and flow of a faraway tide.

Moll felt the magic of the ancient ritual stir deep inside her.

27

She was following in the footsteps of her beloved parents who had thrown the Oracle Bones ten years earlier. Something old and precious began to flow through her veins – a sense of belonging that went back far beyond her understanding, as if the presence of her ancestors was stirring in the shadows of the cave. Moll wrapped the patchwork quilt closer round her nightdress.

Oak and Hard-Times Bob let their palms drop on to the small wooden drums between their knees, their fingers rippling over the leather surface, lending an unknown rhythm to Mooshie's and Cinderella Bull's murmurs.

And then Cinderella Bull stood up, crossed the fire to where Moll was sitting and unfurled her palm. Moll knew what to do – they'd gone over it again and again – but it hadn't felt real until tonight. Her body tingling, Moll took the objects from the fortune-teller's hands: seven tiny pieces of coal, seven finger-pinches of oatmeal and seven cloves of garlic.

She glanced towards her alcove and saw Gryff watching her from the shadows – silent, still, like something carved from stone and sent to protect.

'Come,' Cinderella Bull whispered.

Moll approached the fire. A pan of water was now bubbling on a sheet of metal gauze above the flames. Cinderella Bull nodded and Moll dropped the coal, oatmeal and garlic into it, then she picked up the three-pronged stick, the one her ancestors had carved from a tree struck by lightning back in the forest, and began to stir. Mooshie's song grew louder and,

though Moll's voice was quivering with nerves, she spoke the
words Cinderella Bull had taught her:

> *'All evil that is lurking near*
> *I banish you from causing fear.*
> *I call on magic old and true*
> *To give the second amulet clue.'*

The liquid in the pan bubbled blue for a moment, then
it returned to normal as if nothing had happened. But
Moll knew the significance of that: the burning blue was
the same colour as the first amulet – the jewel they'd found
in the forest that contained her pa's soul, trapped by the
damage the Shadowmasks' Soul Splinter had done to it. In
freeing it, Moll had heard her pa's voice, she'd felt him with
her and he'd promised her the second amulet would hold
her ma's soul.

Cinderella Bull smiled. 'The old magic has heard you,
Moll.'

Moll took a deep breath as the fortune-teller hobbled
to the old chest, drew out three fragments of animal bone
and pressed them into Moll's hand. 'Just as I taught you,
remember?'

Moll sat back down between Alfie and Siddy.

'You can do it,' Siddy urged.

Alfie nodded. 'I know you can.'

Moll's insides clenched as she remembered her pa's words
to Alfie back in the forest. *'And in finding the amulets you* will

learn the truth about your past.' She gulped. Alfie needed to find this amulet as much as she did.

She looked down at the bones, smooth and white, waiting to be inscribed. Then she reached for the penknife beside her and carved a circle dashed through with a double-ended arrow into the first bone, a star enclosed inside a circle on the second, then a cross on the last bone – the symbols for the question that burned inside her:

WHERE IS THE SECOND AMULET OF TRUTH?

Mooshie stopped her song, Oak and Hard-Times Bob set the drums down by their feet and Cinderella Bull sat back down and closed her eyes. And into the silence Moll threw the bones. They clattered against the logs in the fire, then settled in the heart of the flames. Everyone watched, their breath stilled in their throats. But nobody could have predicted what happened next.

There was a bang, loud and sharp, like a gunshot – and the bones burst up into the air in tiny fragments, like flutters of puffed-up ash. Gryff shot across the cave towards Moll, was by her side in a flash, then his eyes fell on what all of the gypsies were looking at.

The fragments had fallen at Moll's feet, but they were no longer broken pieces of bone. Somehow the fragments had welded together as they fell, presenting themselves as a tablet of bone in front of Moll. Hermit retreated several steps beneath Siddy's stool and shook violently inside his shell.

Moll looked up at Cinderella Bull. 'But – but it's not like you taught me. The old magic was meant to replace my carvings with other Oracle Bone symbols – ones that spelt out a message for me to interpret. But the tablet is covered in scribbles, not proper Oracle Bone script! It's—' she bit her lip, panic rising inside her, '— *nonsense*.'

The gypsies gathered round. Letters and strange pictures had been inscribed into the bone, their grooves lined with black ash. But they weren't the symbols Moll had carved; this was something else entirely.

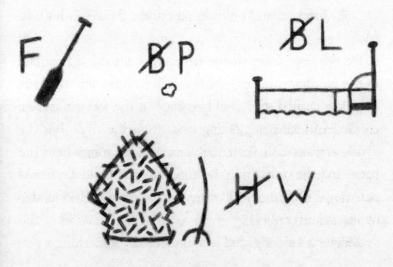

Cinderella Bull looked at Oak. 'This isn't how it's supposed to be . . . Moll's ancestors read Oracle Bone script, not letters and scribbles.'

Oak ran a hand over his stubbled jaw, then he reached for his talisman, a lump of coal kept in a leather pouch in the pocket of his waistcoat. He squeezed it hard.

Moll felt her cheeks redden. She was meant to be the Guardian of the Oracle Bones – and she knew full well that each Guardian only got one chance to throw the bones in their lifetime. She glanced at Alfie beside her; he was picking at the cuff of his nightshirt, trying not to show his disappointment. Gryff pressed his body into Moll's legs in sympathy, but it didn't change her thoughts: she'd failed when everyone had placed their hopes in her. This was the one thing that she'd wanted to do to show the camp she really fitted in. She might not have parents, but she'd had this legacy – and now it lay as a pile of nonsense in front of her.

Oak stood up and put a hand on her shoulder. 'It's OK, Moll.'

He enveloped her in his large arms and Moll breathed in the familiar smell of freshly-struck matches and tobacco. How she wished they could be back in the forest together, carving catapults or tickling trout from the river. But the Shadowmasks and their dark magic were somewhere out there and the only thing she could use to beat them would now never be found. Moll stared at the meaningless jumble of letters and scribbles.

'Maybe it's a code,' Siddy volunteered. 'Something we've

got to work out for ourselves.' He turned to Moll. 'Like you and Alfie did on the heath with the other amulet.'

Alfie blew through his lips. 'It's not like any code I've ever seen.'

Moll looked at the tablet in front of her, shame rising hard, then she got up and, without turning, made for the rocks lining the tunnel entrance. Gryff followed.

Cinderella Bull started after her, but Oak held her arm. 'Leave her be.'

From a ledge of rock, Moll lifted one of the spears she'd carved with Oak, then she stood, poised, before the tunnel. She needed a distraction – anything to get away from the thoughts crushing down on her. Through the cracks in the rock above, moonlight filtered and shimmered on the water. But it was enough to reflect off the silver eels that swam in the tunnel every full moon. Moll watched an anemone fold in its tentacles. She turned to Gryff. 'It'd help if someone could fold me up and hide me away. I'm no good for anything now.'

Gryff nuzzled her cheek, then carried on watching the eels, slivers of silver sifting through the water. Moll raised her spear and brought it down with a splash. Her aim was good and she lifted the eel, skewered on her spear, out on to the rocks. It would do for breakfast tomorrow.

But still the truth rocked in Moll's mind: she'd failed as the Guardian of the Oracle Bones, where all of her ancestors had succeeded. What would her parents have said if they could see her now? And what about her ma? Every night, since knowing the second amulet might contain her soul, Moll had dreamed about hearing her ma's voice and being in her presence, if only for a few moments.

She sat on the rocks beside Gryff, his thick banded tail curled round her lower back, and together they listened to the sea outside, moving in almost soundless murmurs against the rocks.

Chapter 4
Answers at Sunrise

Alfie couldn't sleep. He lay in his hammock, staring at the walls of his alcove. They were lined with catapults, penknives, sea creatures carved from wood and, on Siddy's insistence, shards of mirror – not for protection against evil spirits, as Mooshie assumed, but to help Hermit familiarise himself with his pincers so that he could be encouraged to move left and right as well as backwards.

Alfie glanced over at Siddy in the next-door hammock. Hermit was curled into his shell on his chest and Siddy was snoring, his flat cap pulled down over his eyes. Alfie sighed. Siddy knew who he was – knew he belonged to the camp of gypsies living in Tanglefern Forest up over the cliffs. But Alfie? Skull may have told him that he was an orphan while he'd been a prisoner of the witch doctor's gang, but Alfie hadn't believed him – that was a Shadowmask's word and it counted for nothing.

For a second, Alfie's mind wandered to the other things Skull had told him in the forest, then he pushed the thoughts back, tucking them into the darkest corner of his mind. He was happier and safer now Oak's camp had taken him in, but there were secrets behind his beginning that he had to find out and, if this second amulet was the only thing that could bring him answers, he'd hunt it down to the ends of the earth.

He swung himself out of his hammock, threw on a crumpled shirt and a pair of trousers, and tiptoed from the alcove. The embers of a fire were still glowing in the middle of the cave, bathing the cavern orange, and the bone tablet, a puzzle of letters and scribbles, was where they'd left it at the foot of Moll's stool.

Alfie scooped up the tablet. He ran a hand over the grooves filled with grey ash, then, tucking it under his arm, walked towards the tunnel. A ribbon of black lined the base of the rocks, where the tide had licked them wet, but above the sea the rocks were dry – and, through the biggest crack, sunlight poured in like liquid gold.

Balancing one foot across the tunnel, Alfie hauled himself over the water with his free hand, still gripping the tablet tightly under his other arm. Fingertips clinging to ledges, he hoisted himself up towards the crack and manoeuvred his body through the hole so that his head was poking up out of the rocks. The cool stillness of the cave vanished and a rush of salty air ruffled his hair. The sky was pink, streaked with pale clouds as the sun rose over the horizon, and spread out in the bay like a giant sheet of polished metal was the sea.

He twisted his head round to the cliffs; the gulls were perched on the highest crags again, their heads tucked under their wings. Whatever dark magic had disturbed the peace of Little Hollows the day before was not here now. But the gorse and bracken were still withered and brown: a reminder that the Shadowmasks would be back.

Alfie clambered out on to the sun-warmed rocks that jutted into the sea. They were smooth up here, broken only by rock pools filled with tiny fish and anemones, but the best thing about this place was the scalloped dish curved into the rock face where Gryff often came to rest. Behind this, the rocks climbed steeply upwards, until they met the cliff face of tangled bracken and gorse – but Gryff's spot was shielded from sight and it gave the very best views over the bay.

Sheltering from the gusting wind, Alfie settled himself inside the dish, then, rolling up his shirtsleeves, he stared at the tablet in his lap, willing it to make sense. He sighed. Moll was right – this stuff was nonsense. He twisted his earring and looked out across the bay.

Waves spilled over the sand in foaming circles, but stopped before the red rowing boat positioned halfway down the beach. Oak had promised they'd restore it, give it a new lick of paint so that they could take it out to sea, but, now the Shadowmasks knew where they were, Alfie realised the boat trip was a long way off. He leant back against the rock, and then his eyes were drawn to the oars fixed into the boat's brackets. He looked down at the tablet and his heart quickened.

The first squiggle wasn't a squiggle at all: it was a picture of an oar! Alfie couldn't believe he hadn't seen it before.

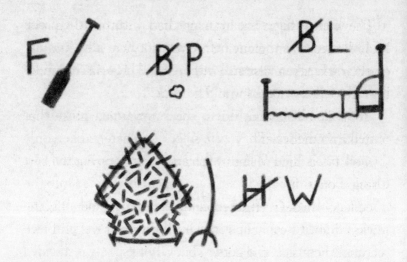

'F,' he murmured. 'Then the oar.' He was silent for several moments, chewing on his lip. 'F – OAR.' He gasped. 'It – it could be FOUR!' His eyes glittered and he blew his hair back from his face. 'This may not be Oracle Bone script, but Siddy was right, it's a code!' Alfie felt so sure of it he bent over the next set of pictures and scribbles. 'A small dot,' he said, '"B" crossed out and then a "P". The dot,' he whispered, almost to himself. 'It could be a—'

'Owww,' a voice hissed. 'Your claw's digging into my toe!'

Alfie watched as Gryff slipped silently from the crack in the cave. Moll followed, her nightdress snagging on ledges of rock, her hair bundled up on top of her head and tied with a piece of string.

'You shouldn't be out here,' Alfie said. 'It's not safe for you or Gryff. Mooshie and Oak'll go mad if they see you.'

'I'll go where I please,' Moll snapped, squeezing her body out on to the rocks behind Gryff.

The wildcat tugged at her nightdress with his teeth and Moll ducked down, glancing around. Gryff settled himself on the rocks, a safe distance from Alfie, and began cleaning his fur. Moll scampered into the dished rock.

'You take orders from Gryff, I see,' Alfie said, shifting up to make room for her.

Moll faced him. 'That's because Gryff doesn't steal my Oracle Bones.'

Alfie took a deep breath, then held out the tablet of bone towards Moll. She grabbed it, looked at it blankly for several seconds, then shoved it under her bottom.

'Pile of rubbish,' she mumbled, then, after a few seconds, 'but it's still mine so don't you go snatching it while I'm asleep.' She touched the smooth sides of the rock.

Alfie picked at his nails. 'Worth snatching if you know what it means ...'

Moll's hand paused on the rock.

'You'd get things done a lot more quickly if you let people help you once in a while,' Alfie told her.

Moll raised her chin. She hated needing people – it made being cross so much more confusing. But Alfie was like an unexplored cave, full of secrets and adventure, and somehow he always managed to find his way back to Moll.

He nodded at the tablet. 'It's a code and, before you shoved the thing under your backside, I was getting some answers.'

Moll fixed Alfie with emerald eyes, glanced briefly at her bottom, then reached down and, as if it was her idea, held the tablet out to Alfie. 'Let's get started then.'

'That "F" – followed by the picture of an oar – looks like it could mean four. Then there's a gap, like it might mean there's another word coming, and this dot. The dot could be a speck – or a bit of sand – or maybe a crumb? Only there's a "B" crossed out and a "P" instead. I suppose crumb could be crump—'

Moll's eyes widened. 'So you join the scribbles and the words . . .'

Alfie nodded. 'I think so.'

'The picture beside the crumb, if that's what it is – it's . . .' Moll squinted at the tablet. 'It looks like a bed, doesn't it?' she whispered. 'But there's a "B" crossed out before it.'

'So that leaves "ED",' Alfie replied.

Moll frowned hard at the tablet and then gasped. 'And there's an "L" instead – L.E.D . . . What if we joined that together with the last bit? You'd get crumpled!'

They looked at each other and grinned. Then Alfie pointed to the remaining inscriptions – one last word. 'A pile of scruffy lines all bunched up together in a heap – and a fork beside it.'

Neither of them said anything for several seconds and then Moll cried, 'It's hay! Like the stacks the farmer makes up in the fields above the cliff – and that fork is a pitchfork!'

'You're right! But the "H" is crossed out – and we have a "W" instead.'

'Way,' Moll said.

'Four crumpled way,' Alfie whispered, and then he huddled smaller, as if the rocks might have ears. 'It – it seems too easy.

It took us over a week to crack the code on the first amulet. This only took a few minutes.'

Moll was silent for a while. 'Let's show Oak and Cinderella Bull and ask them what they make of it.'

They climbed out of the dish and slipped down the cracks back inside the cave.

Mooshie looked up from the fire. 'Molly Pecksniff!' she roared. 'If I have to put you on a lead, I will, so help me. STAY INSIDE THE CAVE!'

But Moll wasn't listening. She charged forward, holding out the tablet. Then, in a moment of rare thoughtfulness, she glanced back at Alfie. 'You say. It was you who started it.'

Alfie looked up at Mooshie. 'We've found a message in the bones,' he said quietly. 'Three words – we made them from the pictures and the letters – only they don't make sense to us.'

Mooshie turned to Cinderella Bull who was sitting with Hard-Times Bob before the entrance to their alcove. She nodded. 'The old magic isn't straightforward, Moosh; if there's a code there, then the bones meant it.'

Alfie pointed to the tablet. 'We think it says FOUR CRUMPLED WAY.'

There was a silence in the cave; not even Mooshie spoke, though she raised her tea towel to her mouth.

Siddy ambled out of his alcove, yawning. He adjusted the bandage on his arm. 'What are we talking about?'

'The Crumpled Way,' Cinderella Bull murmured, her voice laced with dread.

Hermit leapt from Siddy's pocket and made a frantic beeline back towards the alcove.

Mooshie straightened herself up. 'Moll's not going; I won't allow it. She's only *twelve!*'

'Twelve is the perfect age for following clues,' Moll said.

Mooshie shook her head. 'Not when they lead you to The Crumpled Way, it's not.'

A voice came from inside an alcove. 'I'll take her.' Oak walked towards them, holding a boot he'd been polishing. He wiped a stain from his chin. 'I swore I'd follow those bones and find the amulets – and, if The Crumpled Way is where we're headed, that's where I'm going.' He looked at Mooshie. 'The bones don't lie, Moosh.'

Chapter 5
Four Crumpled Way

On the beach before the main entrance to the cave, rocks rose up in layers of grey and corridors of sand zigzagged between them. Mooshie had banned Moll from stepping out on to the open beach for now, but inside these hidden corridors of rock it was dry, sheltered from the wind and, above all, safe.

A few hours had passed since Alfie and Moll had unravelled the code on the bone tablet and now Moll sat cross-legged on the sand, beneath a washing line strung across the rocks. Hanging from the clothes pegs Mooshie had whittled from hazel was a row of fish Oak and Hard-Times Bob had caught – mackerel, sea bass, cod – all covered in salt so that they could be preserved for as long as they needed to be.

Moll tugged one down, slipped it across to Gryff, who was curled inside a scoop in the rock, then casually took a sip from her mug of nettle tea as if nothing had happened. She looked across at Oak who was tightening the straps on her catapult a few metres away. She smiled to herself. Oak always offered to mend anything she broke – which was most things.

He'd even built the wheels of her wagon, back in the forest, extra thick so that, no matter how much she crashed around inside, it wouldn't topple over. She jumped as Alfie and Siddy turned into the corridor of rock from the cave.

Alfie nodded to Oak. 'We've sharpened the knives like you said.'

'And we put them in sheaths outside your alcove,' Siddy added, 'because the blades were really starting to frighten Hermit – and the last thing I want right now is to knock his confidence. He's been doing so well at confronting his fears recently.'

Oak smiled. 'Well done, boys.' He looked at Siddy's bandaged arm. 'Healing OK?'

Siddy nodded. 'Much better, thanks to Mooshie's herbs.'

Oak turned the catapult over in his hands, then, satisfied, tossed it back to Moll.

'Thanks.' She budged up so that Siddy and Alfie could sit beside her. 'Why did Mooshie seem so scared of the message Alfie and me read in the tablet?' She frowned. 'Where are the Oracle Bones telling us to go?'

Oak put his hat back on and began to roll a cigarette. 'The Crumpled Way is a road,' he said quietly. 'Up in Inchgrundle.'

Alfie flinched but said nothing.

Moll shrugged. 'So we need to go up the track to the cliff tops, grab the cobs, ride into the village and snatch the amulet. Right?'

Hermit retreated nervously down Siddy's leg. 'If you're

44

going to say reckless stuff like that, please whisper,' Siddy muttered. 'Hermit's only been awake for a few hours today and he's already terrified.'

Oak shook his head. 'The Crumpled Way isn't just any old street, Moll. It's the worst road in Inchgrundle.' He lit his cigarette and sucked in the tobacco. 'The one that runs from the harbour up through the far side of the village – the one the Dreads from Bootleggers Bay use to smuggle barrels of brandy and kegs of gin up before carting them off to bigger towns to sell.'

Hermit was frantically digging a hole in the ground now, specks of sand spraying up over Siddy's toes.

Moll swallowed. Whenever Oak came back from Inchgrundle, he had tales of Barbarous Grudge and his gang of bloodthirsty smugglers. Rumour had it the Dreads had killed an entire family in their sleep because the father had leaked their names to the police. And villagers claimed the Dreads had drowned two dogs because they'd blown their cover on a raid in the harbour. And then there were the stories about Barbarous Grudge himself, tales that sent shivers rippling beneath Moll's skin: that he'd fended off eight tax officials in a smuggling raid, then stolen their money and melted the coins down to cap eight of his teeth in gold. And the bone he chewed on – the finger of another tax official who'd locked him in jail several years before . . .

'The Dreads control Inchgrundle now,' Oak said, 'and no one dares speak out against them and their smuggling. Word about town is that you'll be dead before sunset if you do.'

Siddy took his flat cap off and fiddled with it nervously. 'And the bones say the amulet is hidden *there*?'

Alfie shifted uneasily, plucking at the sand with his fingertips.

Oak nodded. 'Seems so.'

'Maybe we should look at the clues again ...' Siddy mumbled. 'Spend a bit more time working out if The Crumpled Way is *really* where the old magic wants us to go.'

Beside him, Alfie was looking more and more uncomfortable. But still he stayed quiet.

Moll drained the last of her tea, pushed down her fear and looked at Siddy. 'I'm not letting some gin-swigging smuggler stop me from righting what the Shadowmasks did to my parents.' The thought of her ma's soul trapped by their evil brought her to her feet. 'No one faces problems sitting down,' she said. 'When can we leave?'

Oak adjusted his necktie. 'Tonight; we'll need the cover of darkness to get away before the Shadowmasks come looking for you and Gryff.'

Alfie started to say something, then decided against it and fiddled with his rings.

Moll set off towards the entrance to the cave. 'I'm going to pack.'

Siddy frowned. 'Pack what? All you own is a bunch of catapults.'

Moll glanced over her shoulder at him. 'Exactly. And it sounds like I'm going to need them all.'

Oak, Siddy and Gryff followed her until it was just Alfie

left. He let his head rest back against the rock, then he shut his eyes. A journey to Inchgrundle – that would change *everything*. It would mean telling Moll and Oak what Skull had told him – things so dark and strange not even Alfie wanted to remember them. He sat alone in silence for several minutes, then he picked himself up and walked back into the cave.

After an early supper, Mooshie ushered everyone, including Hard-Times Bob, to bed. Although he wasn't going to Inchgrundle, his latest dislocation (through the handles of a wicker basket to 'lighten the mood') had left him with stomach cramps, and a lie-down in his hammock had seemed advisable.

But, only a few hours later, Cinderella Bull had woken. There were sounds in the cove again – sounds that made her throat turn dry. She was used to the sea spirits murmuring at night, lapping against the tunnel walls and crashing against the furthest point. But the sea was different tonight, full of unfamiliar whispers.

'The thresholds are opening,' she sighed to herself. 'There'll be dark magic waiting for Moll and Gryff outside the cove.'

Hard-Times Bob let out a muffled snore, then rolled over in his hammock, but Cinderella Bull crept out of bed and hastened towards the supplies Mooshie kept before the tunnel. She took a handful of ragwort from a sack and three iron nails from a jar. Then she climbed up on to the rocks lining the tunnel and dropped them into the sea. After a few minutes, she shuffled back to bed, drifted off to sleep and the night was once more still.

But, in the alcove next to Cinderella Bull's, someone else was awake. Alfie swung his rucksack over his shoulders and lifted back the sheet that hung down over the entrance to his alcove. The cave was almost completely dark, but Alfie knew it by heart now, knew every crevice and crack, every good-luck omen placed round the walls. He bent down by the last embers of the fire and, using a small stick, he traced a pattern in the sand. He bit his lip and tried not to think about what Moll would say when she read it.

Then he tiptoed from the cave and vanished into the night.

Chapter 6
Gone

Moll's sleep had been troubled, her dreams twisted into nightmares of Shadowmasks advancing towards her and Gryff, their Soul Splinter held high. So, when Oak placed a hand on her shoulder to wake her up, Moll was glad to be shaken from the darkness.

Oak bent low by her hammock, his face lit only by the candle he was holding. 'It's Alfie,' he whispered.

Gryff sat up in the furthest point of the alcove, ears twitching. Moll's heart scrunched tight. 'What's happened?'

'He's gone, Moll. Alfie's gone.'

She sat bolt upright. 'They've taken him – the Shadowmasks – somehow they've got him, haven't they?' She leapt out of her hammock, but Oak held her still.

'He left Little Hollows, Moll. Of his own accord.'

Moll heard the words, but they sounded strange, as if they were falling apart at the edges. 'No.' She shook her head. 'No.' But when Oak didn't reply her shoulders slumped and her eyes grew large and sad. 'He – he left?' she said quietly.

Oak nodded.

'But Alfie wouldn't just leave like that. We were in this together ...' Moll's voice collapsed and she felt hot tears welling behind her eyes. She shook them back. 'Alfie wouldn't leave without ... without ...'

She found herself thinking back to how they'd first met – how Alfie had kidnapped her from Oak's camp in Tanglefern Forest to hand her over to Skull. Only Alfie hadn't been what she'd expected. He hadn't wanted to be at Skull's camp any more than her ... Alfie had secrets, yes, but Moll had learnt to trust him and together they'd escaped Skull's lair and found the first amulet. He was her friend. How could he desert her now when she needed him most?

Oak tried to draw her close, but Moll stood, rooted to the ground in disbelief.

'We found his patteran, Moll – he marked it into the sand by the fire.'

Moll's ears snagged on Oak's words and she felt a hollowness grow inside her. She hadn't wanted to believe Oak, but a patteran – the sign every gypsy carves to show they've been here and settled – there was no arguing with that. She stormed past Oak, out into the cave. And there, before the embers of the fire, was Alfie's patteran, dark shadows resting in the grooves: KUSHTI BOK. The old gypsy words for 'Good Luck'.

The truth slid uncomfortably before Moll. She'd never have abandoned Alfie, no matter how bad things might have got. Never. A knot tightened inside her, half of it angry, the other half confused. She closed her eyes. Why

50

had Alfie left when he'd been so desperate to find the amulet too? Something about his disappearance just didn't make sense. She'd known he was keeping secrets from her about his past. But what secret was so big it had meant he had to leave Little Hollows without her? She forced the hurt down. Alfie had left her in the middle of their quest, after the camp had let him in and she had given him her trust. Moll pushed his face and his name and everything about him out of her mind.

'We need to get moving if we're going to make it to Inchgrundle in darkness,' she said, trying to suppress the quiver in her voice.

Oak nodded. 'I can't understand what would've made Alfie leave. I'm so sorry, Moll.'

Moll turned to him as she walked back to her alcove, her eyes hard. 'For what? He was never one of us – not really.'

She disappeared inside her alcove, drawing the sheet across it so that the entrance was covered. Then, once she was alone, the tears spilled down her cheeks.

Moll crouched inside the corridor of rocks by the entrance to the cave, her catapult and two small stones tucked into the pocket of her dress, then a cardigan and a duffle coat, the toggle fastenings buttoned up all wrong, hastily flung on top. Although not the comfiest of clothing, the coat was warm and would guard against the increasingly cold autumn nights.

Gryff waited beside her, his ears pricked to the slightest sound. Moll looked down, squinting through the dark,

51

half wondering whether she'd be able to make out Alfie's footprints pressed into the sand. She knew his and Sid's tracks by heart now, but the night was dark, giving no clues as to which way he'd gone, and Moll knew that that kind of thinking wouldn't get her anywhere. She clenched her teeth.

Siddy hung behind her, his duffle-coat hood pulled up against the night, his arm out of the bandage now – a large plaster covering what was left of the cut. Mooshie had tried to dissuade Siddy from going to Inchgrundle, but when Moll was out of earshot Siddy had pointed out: '*Alfie's left – I'm not leaving her too.*' And, after a prolonged goodbye to Hermit, Siddy had crept out into the corridor of rocks after Moll and Oak.

In front of Moll, Oak peered out at the beach. A wind rose up, stirring the surface of the sea, as if it could sense the gypsies huddled inside the rocks, and large clouds shifted across the moon. The darkness thickened.

'Now,' Oak whispered.

Moll followed Oak out on to the beach and the sea sucked back, leaving the sand a polished black beneath the glimpses of moonlight. Moll shrank deeper inside her coat. It was one thing crouching between the corridors of rocks, but out here in the open, where the owls had been just the day before, things felt very different ... Even the sand seemed to close round her feet as she ran, warning her to stay inside the cove.

Moll stuck close to Oak, darting after him as he ran past the washed-up timber to where the path up the cliffs began. Thighs burning, Moll ploughed up the incline with Gryff beside her. She glanced back at Siddy whose eyes were flitting about the path.

'Good job I didn't bring Hermit,' he panted. 'This climb would've killed him.'

Moll kept running through the bracken and gorse, sweat beading on her forehead, but she was glad of Siddy's voice, his jokes a mask for the fear she knew he felt deep down. At last, the path met the top of the cliffs and they stood on the grass, hands on knees, breathing hard. But Gryff remained alert, eyes scanning the heath that spread out before them into several miles of scrubland, heather and gorse.

Moll looked wistfully towards the dark shape of the forest beyond the heath and briefly wondered if Alfie had gone back there now Skull was gone.

The clouds withdrew for a moment and, as the moonlight shone down on to the heath, Moll gasped. It was a wasteland – giant bogs spilling out over peat, dead gorse and tree stumps. 'When we were up here last, the heath was full of heather and trees . . .' She clutched her talisman.

'The thresholds,' Oak told her. 'The Shadowmasks' magic is seeping in fast.' He straightened up and whistled through his teeth. Moments later, Patch, Oak's piebald cob, cantered through the night towards them. The cob slowed before Oak and nuzzled into his overcoat. Oak lifted the halter from his shoulder and slipped it on, then he handed another halter to Moll. 'To tie up the cobs at the other end.'

Moll clicked her tongue against her teeth twice, then whistled hard. Jinx took longer to come than Patch, but she was used to Moll's call and eventually the palomino trotted towards them through the dark. She neighed softly as she approached, but Moll put a finger to her lips, then stroked her white mane.

Oak hoisted himself on to Patch. 'Siddy, you ride up behind Moll.' He looked down at Gryff. The wildcat's striped coat was almost lost in the darkness, but his eyes glowed green. 'And Gryff,' he smiled. 'You'd outrun us all if it came to it.'

Oak turned to Moll and Siddy who were mounted on Jinx. 'We'll ride fast – along the path that lines the coast, past the fields the farmer grazes his animals on – then we'll come to Inchgrundle. It shouldn't take more than an hour to reach the harbour wall.' He nodded back down the cliff. 'If anything happens to me, ride back to the cove as fast as you can. I don't want you in The Crumpled Way without me.'

Siddy gulped and clutched Moll's waist harder.

'You can hold the rope from Jinx's halter if it'll make you feel any better, Sid,' Moll said.

Siddy gripped it hard.

'But there's not much point because Jinx only listens to my legs when we're galloping.'

Siddy groaned as Moll urged Jinx on. Then they were off, racing across the heath behind Oak and Patch, bounding over clumps of dead bracken and swerving round marshes. A nightjar shot out from a gorse bush, its cry rolling in the air around them. Jinx shied, Siddy moaned, but Moll's gaze never faltered. Straight ahead – towards the amulet, towards what she hoped was her ma's soul.

Eventually the heathland petered out and in its place fields unfolded to their left, set back from the path behind a jumbled stone wall. Sheep huddled together in the field, their heads raised as the cobs galloped by. The land here hadn't been touched by the Shadowmasks; their dark magic had been directed straight at Moll and Gryff in the cove. Moll looked down at the wildcat, bounding along between Jinx and the cliff edge some metres away. Far below them was Bootleggers Bay – the Tribe had been forbidden to enter it since the day they arrived at Little Hollows because of Barbarous Grudge and the Dreads – but the beach was veiled in shadow now and any smuggling that might be going on was drowned by the darkness.

They galloped on and on, cob hooves hammering on the path, churning the soil to dust. Moll kicked Jinx on harder, past a field of cows, and towards the ruins of an old stone cottage that lay to the left of the path.

Then Gryff stopped suddenly, whiskers twitching, tail flat to the ground. '*Urrrrrrrrrrrrrr*,' he growled.

The cobs backed up behind him.

'What is it?' Moll whispered.

Gryff was absolutely still for several minutes, watching, listening. Then, a few moments later, he grunted and broke into a run once again. The cobs followed, but Patch was shaking his head now, tossing his mane from side to side, and Moll could feel Jinx's withers tense.

She leant forward and stroked her cob's mane. "S all right, Jinx. Calm down, calm down.'

But Moll's pulse was starting to race. From somewhere inside the ruined cottage, she could hear what Gryff must have sensed a moment earlier.

Low, crooning hoots.

°° Chapter 7
Ambush on the Cliffs
°°

Before anyone could react, a wave of black creatures burst out of the roofless cottage, shaking the night with grating screeches. Patch reared up in terror and Oak clung to his mane. The owls glided towards the crumbling stone wall, towards Moll and Gryff, yellow eyes burning into the night. But, as their wings opened full stretch, there came another noise.

A slow creaking, like a very old door opening for the first time in years. Then, when the owls' wings began to beat, there came the unmistakable sound of blades sawing against each other.

Moll's skin crawled with fear. Gryff's fur tightened. But there was no time to lose. As Oak struggled to right himself on Patch, Moll drew out her catapult, placed a stone in the pouch and fired it into the throng. The stone collided with an owl and it hurtled backwards, stunned, then it regained control and circled tighter with the pack. Oak reached for his pistol and Siddy grappled for his knife.

And the wings beat on to the sound of crunching metal.

Jinx skittered backwards over the path and Gryff pounded his forelimbs, hissing. Then a cluster of owls broke free, yellow eyes unblinking, and dived down towards them. Moll dug her heels into Jinx's flanks and they leapt aside on to the grass in front of the wall.

Cracks burst out from Oak's gun and three owls dropped from the sky, slamming on to the path with a thud. One of the owls made to grip the soil with its scaled talons, but Gryff pounced and dug his claws into its throat.

The other owls screeched and spiralled higher in the sky.

Then Oak looked down at the owls by Patch's hooves and gasped. 'Blades,' he muttered. 'Their wings are grinding because they're made of *knives* not feathers!'

Moll's stomach lurched. Splayed out over the path was a wingspan of black blades, growing in size towards the tip, each edge serrated and sharp. She swallowed. The creaking sound they'd heard earlier before the wings began to beat had been hinges opening and blades slotting into place.

'But – but the owls weren't like this in the cove!' Moll cried.

Oak's face hardened. 'The Shadowmasks' dark magic has deepened since the owls were here last . . .'

Siddy clasped his knife tight. Moll pulled back on her catapult.

Again the metallic sound beat above them, slicing the air to shreds – and more owls appeared as if the night itself had breathed them into being. They wheeled above the gypsies on the path and Moll watched in horror as their blades whirred and grated like sinister fingers. Owl eyes roved about, fixing on their prey, and the birds dived together towards Gryff. He leapt back, growling, as Siddy swung his knife, Moll fired her catapult and Oak let off his gun. But Gryff was too near the cliff edge now. Soil began to crumble beneath his paws, leaving the wildcat scrabbling at tufts of grass to save him from the drop.

'Gryff!' Moll yelled, making to jump from Jinx.

Siddy held Moll fast and yanked on Jinx's tethering rope. The cob backed up against the wall, narrowly avoiding an owl's blades. Siddy struck his knife against another that came close; metal clanged and the impact of the collision was enough to send the owl swerving away. But Moll's eyes were glued to Gryff who was clinging to the cliff edge, his claws clutching at grass. Oak yanked Patch round towards the wildcat, then bent low and hauled him by the scruff of the neck back on to the path. Teeth bared in a snarl, Gryff spat and lashed at the owls with his claws. But they kept on coming.

'If we split up, we might confuse them!' Oak shouted. 'We can't beat them off like this!' Patch bucked and his hind legs shunted an owl that came close. 'Ride back to the cove and I'll stay with Gryff!'

Jinx was edging backwards now, but Gryff was leaping up into the air and thrashing his claws into the talons of an owl above him.

'I can't leave you – or Gryff!' Moll thought of Alfie suddenly. He'd have had a plan – he'd have known what to do. She drove the thought away.

'We should try and go on,' Siddy cried shakily. 'We're closer to Inchgrundle than we are to the cove.' A look of horror washed over his face as soon as he'd said the words aloud.

And high above them the owls circled and screeched.

Oak looked from Moll to Siddy, his face strained. 'There's a chance the owls won't follow you into the village,' he panted. 'They're conjured from dark magic and the Shadowmasks won't want villagers getting suspicious about stuff like that.' He ducked to miss an owl's blades and Patch whinnied in fear. 'But The Crumpled Way – I can't send you there alone!'

Moll struggled to keep Jinx steady, but her eyes were fixed on Gryff.

'Gryff'll be OK, Moll,' Sid said, courage suddenly growing where he thought he'd had none. 'And he'll come after you when he knows you're safe – he always does.'

Another owl spiralled down and Oak urged Patch forward so that he could take aim again. His shot shattered into the night and the owl fell, but as Oak turned back to them he was shaking his head. 'I can't let you go alone! It's too dangerous!'

'And this isn't?' Moll cried. She looked at Gryff and he met her eyes. 'I'll find you,' she called. The wildcat bolted towards her, ducking and shying away from the swooping blades, then he dipped his head. He'd understood – somehow.

Oak spun round on Patch as he realised what was happening. 'No, Moll! Mooshie would never forgive me if I let you and Siddy go!'

Moll kicked Jinx on. 'Tell her you didn't have a choice!'

Jinx sprang forward, grasping the chance to flee the owls, and then they were away, thundering on towards Inchgrundle.

'Follow the harbour wall all the way round the village!' Oak shouted after them. 'We'll come as soon as we can and we'll keep these beasts busy in the meantime!'

He turned back to face the owls. They wheeled high in the sky, their serrated wings outlined by the fading dark. Then they swirled together and, with renewed menace, the majority hurtled down towards Oak and Gryff and just a small group broke off to tail Moll and Siddy.

Moll leant close to Jinx, feeling her shoulders pounding at the earth, carrying them on. Behind, the owls were gaining on them, tearing through the sky like deadly bullets.

'Your coat!' Siddy hissed. 'Throw it down in case they're tracing your scent!'

Moll tensed her legs round Jinx's flanks, then tugged her coat off. She tossed it on to the path and, in seconds, the owls hurtled down and tore it to shreds. Moments later, they were up in the air again, unsatisfied, but they'd given Jinx a lead and she seized it with a second strength, surging through the wind past a field of pigs. The cob galloped on and on, further down the coast.

The night was shrinking back, but huge purple-grey clouds crowded the sky still, and the owls beat closer with a darkness all their own.

'Come on, Jinx,' Moll murmured. 'We're nearly there . . .'

Eventually the path began to wind downhill and Moll could make out the slate roofs and whitewashed walls of

Inchgrundle's houses ahead, tucked into the side of the hill. Her heart beat faster. The amulet was somewhere in that village.

The owls slowed as Inchgrundle came into view, then, moments later, they soared higher into the sky before changing direction, as Oak had said they might, and heading back along the coast. Moll breathed deeply and urged Jinx on, down the path towards the harbour wall that curved in front of the fishing village, a shelter to the sailing boats moored inside it, before stretching out on either side into the sea.

'Do you think those owls will go back for Oak and Gryff?' Moll asked quietly.

Siddy didn't answer immediately, then he said, 'If they do, Gryff'll have them.'

Jinx led them to the bottom of the path that ended at a small pebble beach just outside the harbour wall, and Moll and Siddy slipped to the ground.

Siddy inspected his arm. In the struggle on the cliffs his coat had torn, but Mooshie's plaster was still intact.

Moll held Jinx's head. 'Thank you, girl,' she whispered. The cob was panting still, her withers wet with sweat, and Moll noticed a small cut on her calf where one of the owl blades must have sliced. It wasn't deep, but Moll reached into the pocket of her dress and wiped it with her handkerchief.

'We won't be long, Jinx,' she said, tying her tethering rope to a gorse branch on the side of the path. Siddy drew out a flask from his coat pocket. Moll cupped her hands, Siddy poured the water in and Jinx drank. 'Wait here and we'll be back,' Moll said, taking a swig from the flask and offering it to Siddy.

She hugged her cardigan round her and looked up at the harbour wall in front of them. It was tall enough to withstand huge waves, but small enough for Moll to know that she and Siddy could scale it without too much bother. Moll glanced around; it felt strange not to have Gryff by her side, as if she'd forgotten something very important on the journey. Balancing their ankle boots on the jutting rocks and gripping at ledges with the tips of their fingers, Moll and Siddy hauled themselves up on to the top of it. The houses scattered up the hillside and spilling down to the harbour were still fast asleep; doors were closed and windows shuttered.

But before the houses began, where the harbour wall met the land, there was a jumbled shipyard. Boats had been jacked up on to wooden blocks to be repaired or repainted and, through the cloudy dawn, Moll could see the yard was a muddle of old buoys tangled in rope and lobster pots piled up amid crates and battered boxes.

Siddy chewed on a fingernail. 'Looks like the kind of place Barbarous Grudge and the Dreads might skulk around in . . .'

Moll considered this. 'Perhaps.' And, to Siddy's surprise, he saw that she was smiling. 'But it's going to give us plenty of places to hide from the Shadowmasks if they come after us.'

Siddy gulped. 'You think the Shadowmasks will follow now the owls have seen us riding here?'

Moll brushed her hair from her face and gritted her teeth.

'Dunno.' She began to lower herself down the other side of the wall, on to the stone walkway that led towards the shipyard. 'But it was your idea to ride on.'

Siddy took his flat cap off and punched his fist inside it. 'That's the last time I bother being brave.'

Chapter 8
Braving Inchgrundle

The paint on the hull of the boat Moll and Siddy crouched behind was weathered and chipped and all around them lay old crates and heaps of rope. Moll poked her head round the stern of the boat.

'We'll run round the length of the harbour, just like Oak said, until the wall starts peeling out to sea. Then we'll hide again before The Crumpled Way; we don't know what we might find out there.'

'Shouldn't we walk?' Siddy asked, fiddling nervously with his neckerchief. 'Might look less suspicious if we're seen strolling through the village rather than charging at it full pelt . . .'

Moll wrinkled her nose. 'Charging is more efficient.'

The sea lapped against the harbour wall and Moll took a step out from behind the boat. Siddy clutched her arm and yanked her backwards. There were footsteps clacking over the cobbles – and they were getting louder. Through a crack in the boat's stern, Moll and Siddy watched, their breath hemmed inside them.

First they saw the boots: two pairs – long, black and leather.

Moll gripped Siddy's arm. '*They're bootleggers,*' she mouthed. '*Smugglers!*'

Siddy turned a shade of green and hunkered down with Moll. Two boys, much older than Moll and Siddy, were talking in low voices on the other side of the boat. They wore long-sleeved white shirts, dark waistcoats and trousers, but, where one was tall and wiry, like a straightened-out coat hanger, the other was squat and fat, as if he'd been poured into his leather boots. Both boys had long hair though, knotted and backcombed into wild-looking dreadlocks.

'Grudge told me we can expect a big haul tonight,' the skinny boy said.

His friend smirked. 'Drinks on the Dreads in The Gloomy Tap afterwards then?'

The skinny boy nodded, then he reached into his waistcoat and turned a sheathed knife over in his hands. He slipped the blade out and held it up towards the sea, smiling as the sun surfaced from the horizon and flashed off the metal. 'We've got Inchgrundle eating out of the palms of our hands now; we'll be rich before we know it.'

The low grunt of a laugh sounded from somewhere near by.

Moll's hand slid to her catapult and Siddy's wound tightly round his knife.

'When fishing's scat, when farming's poor, there's always smuggling, boys.'

The voice was a growl and Moll and Siddy's eyes widened

as an enormous man stepped forward to join the boys, his legs as thick as the boughs of a very large tree. He held a crowbar in his hand as casually as a gentleman might hold a walking stick and hanging down all around his face were dark dreadlocks as thick and matted as sailor's rope.

'Didn't expect to see you until later, Grudge,' the lanky boy said.

Barbarous Grudge chewed on a small bone and Moll glimpsed eight gold teeth glinting in the sunlight against his black skin. She turned a pale face to Siddy who nodded. The stories Hard-Times Bob had told them about Grudge had been true: he really had melted down stolen coins to cap his teeth and he really did chew on a finger bone.

Grudge grinned. 'Thought I'd recruit a few more locals; the ship we're planning to raid tonight is big – packed high with kegs of gin, brandy and tobacco – and we'll need all the hands we can get to load the goods into the rowing boat, then haul it out to the harbour wall and away to the bigger towns to sell.'

The squat boy laughed. 'Gin, brandy, tobacco – that'll line our pockets for weeks!'

Grudge pointed his crowbar halfway round the harbour. 'I've got us a room at The Gloomy Tap; if I can count on you boys back there with me now to help plan the raid slick, I'll see you a bigger cut of the booty.'

He turned and left the yard, weaving his way between the lobster pots and boats. The boys grinned at each other, then hurried out of the shipyard.

Siddy stared after them, wide-eyed with fear, and Moll thought of Gryff and Oak suddenly, wishing that they were there beside her. Surely they'd beaten back the owls by now? Oak was quick as lightning with his pistol and Gryff was as fierce an animal as she'd come across. Why weren't they here already?

Moll shook herself; she couldn't let Siddy know how scared she was. 'He's a smuggler, that's all. We've faced much worse than him.'

Siddy looked down. 'When Gryff was with us – and Alfie.' He paused. 'I wish I'd brought Hermit.'

Moll tightened the laces on her boots. 'Well, we haven't got Gryff – or Hermit thankfully.' She glossed over Alfie's name completely, as if Siddy hadn't even mentioned him. 'We're going to have to make do with each other.'

'The Gloomy Tap sounds like an inn – or a pub,' Siddy mumbled.

'Exactly what I was thinking,' Moll said, which was a lie. She'd been thinking about boiling Hermit up in a very large pan. 'We'll creep to the edge of the shipyard, then, once we're sure Grudge and his bootlegger friends are inside The Gloomy Tap, we'll nip out and run across the harbour. Then we'll go up The Crumpled Way and look for the amulet.'

Siddy nodded. 'Do you think this amulet will be like the first one?'

Moll considered this. 'Dunno. Maybe. Though I'm not sure magic happens the same way twice.' She thought back to the sparkling blue jewel they'd found inside a hollowed tree in Tanglefern Forest and grinned. 'And the Dreads thought *they* were dealing with valuable goods on their smuggling raid! They should have seen the size of the jewel we found in the forest ...'

Moll crept out from behind the boat, glanced left and right, then tiptoed forward. Siddy followed.

Neither of them noticed the figure crouching behind a barrel a few metres away. He lay low for several minutes, thinking, then he smiled to himself and disappeared from the shipyard without a sound.

Moll and Siddy peered out from behind the last of the boats in the shipyard to see a cobbled road running between a row of houses and the harbour wall. The sky was overcast now and villagers were starting to wake. An old man opened his front door, let his dog scamper over the cobbles, then picked up some firewood from a stash beneath his porch and hobbled inside again with his dog. Moll scanned down the row of houses until she came to a weather-beaten sign hanging from a building over the street: *The Gloomy Tap*. And, to Moll's relief, there was no one outside it.

She turned to Siddy. 'If we wait any longer, the whole village will be up.'

Siddy nodded, clutched his talisman hard, a smoothed stone with a hole in the middle, then shot out from the shipyard and ran over the cobbles after Moll. They raced past the first few houses, holding their breath as they pelted by The Gloomy Tap, but when they were halfway down the street the commotion began.

'Stop, thief!' a voice screamed from somewhere behind them. 'Two children stealing firewood from old Mr Weaver!'

Siddy shot a sideways glance at Moll. 'What?'

Moll grabbed his arm. 'Just run!'

A shuttered window above them burst open. 'Thieves!' a woman shrieked. 'Down by the harbour wall!'

More shutters clattered open as men, women and children caught on and leant out of windows, hollering abuse.

'They were trying to take Mr Weaver's firewood!' a man bellowed. 'Somebody stop them!'

The village was suddenly alive with hysterical villagers screaming from their windows and, in minutes, the inhabitants had stormed downstairs and were pouring out of their front doors into the street. Moll and Siddy charged over the cobbles, tearing past the houses.

'They've got rolling pins and kitchen knives!' Siddy cried, snatching a glance behind him.

Moll kept her head down. 'Ignore it! Just keep running! If we follow the harbour round, they'll chase us on to the pier so we'll need to turn up a side road and lose them in the backstreets!'

Siddy nodded, swerving left up a narrow lane behind Moll. They took a right down an alleyway, twisted left up a flight of steps, taking them two at a time, then darted down another street lined with shops. A grocer was laying out vegetables under his shop awning and beside him a baker was arranging loaves. They looked up, startled, then, when they heard the commotion hurrying closer, they stepped forward with fists

70

raised. Moll grabbed Siddy by the arm and they dashed into a side street which climbed steeply uphill. Muscles burning, they burst out on to another road lined with houses. The shrieks of angry villagers rang louder and they dashed down the street. Moll slowed.

'It's a dead end, isn't it?' Siddy panted.

Moll nodded.

There was a shout behind them. 'Oi!'

Moll and Siddy spun round.

Standing in the middle of the street was a boy – small, scrawny and covered in dirt, like something forgotten about wrapped in rags. And yet his face was sharp: two eyes set wide apart flitting from Moll to Siddy.

Moll glanced around for a stone to lodge into her catapult, but, on seeing none, she raised her fists. Siddy drew out his knife.

The boy took a step towards them and from somewhere nearby, the shouts of the villagers loomed closer. But the boy didn't raise his fists, as Moll had expected.

'You got money?' he said. His voice was thin and watery.

Moll squinted. She could have sworn she recognised that voice. But from where?

The boy worked up a gob of phlegm, then spat it out on to the street. 'I said, have you got money? Cos if you have,' he muttered, 'I can get you out of this mess.'

Moll looked to Siddy and nodded. He fumbled for the leather pouch Mooshie had given him, then he held out a couple of coins.

The boy came closer, inspected his payment and made to snatch it.

Siddy yanked his hand back and closed his fist. 'A way out first.'

The boy sniffed, allowed the din to come closer still, then said, 'Where d'you wanna go?'

'The Crumpled Way,' Moll said firmly.

The boy raised one eyebrow, then shrugged. 'Come on then.'

He darted back along the street and slipped down a shadowy alleyway Moll and Siddy had missed before. At the end was a padlocked gate, but the boy launched himself at it, clambered up, then flipped his body over the other side.

Siddy turned to Moll. 'Scrawny little kid, but he's handy on his feet.'

Moll grunted. 'He's got eyes on the side of his head; looks like his grandmother knitted him wrong.'

They followed the boy over the gate and found themselves in a yard full of junk: ripped tyres, scraps of rusted metal and rolls of tangled wire. But the shouts of the villagers were almost muted in here – and, as they bounded over piles of discarded junk, the boy turned to them and grinned.

'Smog Sprockett,' he said. 'Street urchin most of the time – but I'm the eyes and the ears of this place. There isn't anything I don't see.'

Moll couldn't quite find it in her to smile back. Making friends with a street urchin called Smog Sprockett hadn't been part of the brief from Oak. She kept her head down, as did Siddy, and ran on.

At the far end of the yard was a stone wall. Smog was up it in a flash, chasing off the seagull perched on top. Moll and Siddy followed. They jumped down into another alleyway, dark and closed off, despite the morning light. But they were careering downhill again, which meant they were heading back towards the harbour. Towards The Crumpled Way.

Smog looked back at them as he ran and Moll could tell what he was thinking. His eyes scanned their traveller clothes – Siddy's spotted neckerchief, her colourful dress – and their dark features. 'So what are a pair of gypsies doing in Inchgrundle then? Thought your lot were up in Tanglefern Forest.'

Moll ran alongside him, remembering what Mooshie had said about keeping a low profile in the villages beyond the forest: *Don't go shouting about being a gypsy; the villagers are a suspicious bunch – they think we're all nasty curses and thieving silver.*

'Oh, we're not gypsies,' Moll panted, thinking fast. 'Sidney and me, we're – we're shepherds from the farm before Inchgrundle.'

Smog snorted. 'Pull the other leg, Bo Peep.'

Moll hung back from Smog and Siddy shot her a look. 'I got the name change,' he whispered, 'makes us less like gypsies and all that – but *shepherds?*'

Moll scowled. 'Meant to stop after "Sidney", but the words just tumbled out.'

73

Houses rose up either side of them, but lace curtains were drawn across most of the windows and the only inhabitant they could see was a stray cat slinking behind a dustbin.

Without warning, Smog screeched to a halt.

'What is it?' Moll whispered.

Three figures detached themselves from the shadows in front of them. They wore long black boots and the largest of them carried a crowbar in a clenched fist.

Moll and Siddy staggered backwards, but Smog only smiled and dipped his head at the smugglers. 'Morning, Grudge.' He jerked his thumb towards Moll and Siddy. 'As I promised – the gypsies.'

Moll's stomach dropped as she realised why she'd recognised Smog's voice. 'It was *you*!' she hissed at him. '*Stop thief* . . . You called the villagers after us even though we'd done nothing wrong!'

Smog blinked large, flickering eyes. 'Shouldn't go boasting about enormous jewels you've found in the forest then, should you?' He smiled as Grudge dropped several coins into his grubby palm.

'You were spying on us in the shipyard?' Siddy spat.

Grudge's boys smirked. 'We fancy ourselves one of those jewels, don't we, Grudge?'

Moll felt for her catapult and Barbarous Grudge stepped forward, his crowbar clanking on the cobbles. 'Aye, we do.'

Moll snatched a stone from the ground, set it to her pouch and fired. It struck the lanky smuggler in the shoulder and he doubled over, crying out.

But Grudge only smiled, eight gold teeth shining between his gums, and brushed his dreadlocks back from his face. 'Grab them,' he growled.

The children made to run, but in seconds hands clamped down on their shoulders, grinding them still. Siddy jabbed his knife at the larger smuggler, but one kick from his boot and it clattered on to the cobbles.

Moll eyed the knife desperately, writhing beneath the lanky smuggler's hold – she'd lent it to Siddy for the journey but it had belonged to her pa once and it was the one thing left that linked him to her. 'There aren't any more jewels in the forest!' she snarled, slotting a stone to her catapult.

Grudge yanked the catapult from her hand and hurled it to the ground, then he stooped low so that one dark eye loomed against Moll's. 'Ahhh, but there's this amulet, I hear.'

Moll struggled against the smuggler, then spat on to Grudge's boot. Grudge grinned as he grabbed hold of Moll and flung her down. She felt a sharp pain as her head hit the cobbles, then her vision blurred and the alleyway vanished from sight.

Chapter 9
The Gloomy Tap

I t was the sound of rain pattering against a window that finally brought Moll round. A strange numbness enveloped her body and it rested on her eyelids and weighed heavy on her limbs. But it couldn't block out the pain. Her head throbbed from where she'd hit the ground and, raising a hand to her brow, Moll felt a lump.

Forcing her eyes open, she saw that she was in a dimly-lit room, lying on floorboards riddled with woodworm and layered with dust. There was a fireplace next to her that looked as if it hadn't been used in years, and Siddy lay before it, fast asleep. Moll crawled towards him, her body slow and lumbering.

She tugged his arm. 'Sid, you OK?' Her voice was a mumbled slur.

Siddy snuffled, then rolled over and began to snore. Moll struggled against the unsettling tiredness spreading through her body; whatever the smugglers had done to her, it looked like they'd done it to Siddy too. She shook him again, hard, but he was sleeping deeply now. Moll glanced around. Plaster peeled from the walls, a single wrought-iron bed draped in musty sheets slumped in the corner of the room, and below a shuttered window was a table on which sat a pail of water and a lamp.

Moll hauled herself upright and clutched her head. The ache pounded inside her skull, but it was the strange dizziness that clouded her sight when she moved that frightened her most. She stumbled over the creaking floorboards towards the door and pulled it. Locked. Fear twisted inside her. She'd been so worried about the Shadowmasks catching them she hadn't even thought about the Dreads, not after they'd made it past Bootleggers Bay unharmed.

She summoned up her energy and staggered over to Siddy. 'Wake up,' she hissed. But, when she shook him again and again and still he slept, dark thoughts clouded in. Why couldn't she wake him?

Shivering from the cold, Moll walked over to the wooden table, cupped her hands into the water and raised it to her lips. She felt the dizziness lift a little and the tiny writing etched into the bottom of the pail became clear: *The Gloomy Tap.*

Moll bit her lip. Where was Oak? And Gryff? Had they raced into Inchgrundle after beating off the owls? A sickening feeling lodged in the pit of her stomach. What if something terrible had happened on the cliff top? Moll thought of Jinx suddenly, tied up beyond the harbour wall. Had she yanked her tethering rope free and wandered home or was she still there, waiting for Moll to come back? Moll found herself

77

wishing that Mooshie was near to heal the bruise on her head and tell her it was all going to be OK.

She pushed back the shutter from the window above the table and looked out. The cobbles were streaked with rain and it was already growing dark. Moll's insides lurched. They'd been out cold *for a whole day*; whatever the Dreads had done to them had knocked their senses completely . . . She watched a fisherman hauling a net full of fish from his boat up on to the walkway running along the harbour wall, then a shuffling noise came from behind Moll and she wheeled round.

'What – what happened?' Siddy's voice was thick with sleep, but Moll felt a surge of relief.

'You're OK,' she breathed.

Siddy rubbed his eyes and sat up against the wall. 'How long have I been asleep?'

'It's night already – we've been asleep for the whole day.' Moll shook her head. 'I remember Grudge knocking me to the ground, then – then I must have passed out cold . . .' She blinked back a wave of dizziness. 'But you must remember what happened after that?'

Siddy struggled to his feet. 'The smugglers dragged us back here, then—' He frowned. 'I remember they forced me to drink something. Something hot and soothing. Then I'm not sure what happened next.'

Moll blinked. 'I get knocked out and you sit down to a cup of tea with the Dreads?'

'It wasn't like that . . .'

Moll turned away to face the table, then she raised a hand to her mouth. 'Siddy,' she said slowly, her voice altogether different now. 'Look.'

She pointed to what appeared to be a handful of dried-out plants strewn on the table beside the pail of water: light brown stems with a circular pod at the top next to two tin cups and a pestle and mortar filled with ochre grains.

'Poppy stems and seedpods ground up to make tea!' Moll's eyes widened, but then shock gave way to outrage. 'The wretched smugglers drugged us!' she cried. 'We need to escape and find the amulet!'

At that moment, the door handle turned, the door creaked open and lamplight fell upon an enormous figure. Moll and Siddy backed up against the table as Barbarous Grudge walked into the room, the floorboards sagging and groaning beneath him. The boys they had seen in the shipyard and the alleyway swaggered in after him, locking the door behind them.

Grudge ran a tongue over his golden teeth and sat down on the bed. The springs wheezed. 'Glad to see you've had a good rest. Now it's time to get down to business. This amulet you talked about in the shipyard – where is it?'

Neither Moll nor Siddy said anything. Their silence was hard and cold as if it had been sculpted from marble.

Grudge grunted. 'Smog told us you were heading for The Crumpled Way?'

Moll willed herself to be brave, tried to make herself think as Oak – or even Alfie – would have done. 'We don't know exactly where the amulet is, but we know it's out past

Inchgrundle.' She offered Grudge two haughty eyebrows and a nostril flare even though her heart was thumping.

Siddy nodded, catching on to Moll's thoughts. 'We were heading for the first road out of here – The Crumpled Way.'

Grudge's boys whispered to each other, then the wiry lad leant close to Grudge. 'They'll be lying, boss. Pesky gypsies trying to throw us off the scent.'

Grudge said nothing. Instead, he reached into his pocket and brought out the legendary finger bone. He chewed on it as he thought, then he stood up and walked towards the children.

His eyes bored into Moll. 'You look like the kind of girl who might—'

'Bite hard?' Moll muttered. She sprang forward, a ball of furious energy, and jabbed an elbow into Grudge's stomach. When he didn't even flinch, she pummelled her fists into his ribs and began to yell. 'You've no business holding us here!'

Siddy watched in horror, thought about stepping in, then noticed the other two smugglers advancing behind Grudge and decided to stay where he was.

Grudge held Moll at arm's length by her hair. She swung with her fists and snarled, but he only laughed.

'Well, you're something, aren't you?'

Moll twisted herself free and stepped back, panting. 'Yes. No. Shut up.'

Grudge pointed a large finger at her. 'Let's get this straight. I'm in charge here so don't bother fighting me as you know who'll win.'

80

Moll glared at him. 'Moosh always says you've got to watch out for the small people; they're full of surprises.'

Grudge snorted, then drew himself up before Moll and Siddy, his dreadlocks framing his face like bundles of grimy rope. 'I'll send up some food to line your stomachs while me and the Dreads get on with the raid. It's our biggest one yet and you're not getting in the way of it.' He paused. 'But afterwards you'll lead us to this amulet – and we'll see if your stories about it are really true.'

Moll's thoughts whirred; how were they going to find the amulet before the Shadowmasks tracked them down when Grudge planned to lock them in The Gloomy Tap?

The leader of the Dreads turned towards the door, key in hand, then he looked back at Moll and Siddy. 'And don't even think about trying to break free while we're away. We Dreads own this village and you're our property now. If you so much as put a foot outside this pub, we'll string you up with sailor's rope and see you hanged before dawn.'

There didn't seem a great deal to say or do in response to this so Moll just nodded. Beside her, Siddy gulped.

Chapter 10
Midnight Raid

Hours later, after a lukewarm stew of gristly meat and watery potatoes, Moll and Siddy sat on the bed in the room at The Gloomy Tap.

'We need to escape,' Moll said quietly.

The rain pattered against the window. Siddy bit his lip.

'And we need to do it quickly,' Moll added.

'We'll be hanged before dawn if we're caught,' Siddy mumbled. 'You heard Grudge.'

Moll dug her nails into the mattress. 'Go and sit by the fireplace and practise not being frightened, then come back here when you're done and we'll make a plan.' She paused. 'Coward.'

Siddy sprang up, his face flushed. 'Don't you go treating me like I'm five, Moll! The things we've done – fighting off Shadowmasks and running from villagers with knives – it's been *terrifying*! And you feel it too, even if you're all closed up and you pretend you don't. You're scared, just like me.'

'I'm angry,' Moll muttered, scuffing her boot against the floorboard. 'With you mainly.'

Siddy threw his arms up. 'You're angry with the Shadowmasks for taking your parents away. You're angry with the smugglers for locking us up. You're angry with Alfie—'

Moll stiffened.

'—for leaving.' Siddy lowered his voice and his words came softer. 'I'm angry about all of those things too – and scared. Just like you.'

Moll felt an unexpected lump lodge in her throat. 'Don't talk about Alfie.'

Siddy sat down on the bed again. 'I didn't have to come with you to Inchgrundle for the amulet. But I did because you're my friend.'

Moll swallowed at the sudden kindness of the word 'friend'.

Siddy went on. 'There are times when you annoy me so much I wish I could . . . lock you up in a box just to stop you charging into trouble. But I don't go pointing that out every time things go wrong. We've got to work together.'

Moll fiddled with her talisman. She and Sid were so different outwardly: she was plucky and bold while Sid was cautious. But Moll knew Sid was brave too; his was a quieter sort of courage – measured where Moll's was reckless. Moll said nothing for a while, then she looked up at her friend. 'I'm sorry I called you a coward, Sid. It's not true.'

Siddy smiled. 'Good. Because I think there's a difference between being scared and being a coward.'

Moll nodded. 'Yeah, but I'm afraid Hermit's both.'

They grinned at each other as the rain drummed against the windowpane.

'So what are we going to do?' Moll asked.

'We need something to pick the lock.'

They glanced around and Moll thought back to the time Alfie had used a rabbit bone to pick the lock on the cage Skull had trapped them in in Tanglefern Forest.

'There's nothing in here we could use,' she sighed. 'Nothing.'

Siddy sat still for a few minutes, then he looked at Moll. 'Maybe . . .' He leapt up, ripped back the dusty bed sheet and tore at the mattress with his nails.

Moll frowned. 'What are you doing?'

Siddy's hand wriggled through the mattress and he yanked hard, then drew out a metal bedspring. 'Looks like there's something left in here to pick the lock with after all.'

Moll beamed. 'Nice one, Sid.'

They huddled by the door as Siddy twisted the spring this way and that. At first, nothing happened, then there was a familiar click and the door creaked open. The corridor was dimly lit and empty – the Dreads would be out on the raid now – so Moll and Siddy crept along it, towards the staircase at the far end. But, just as they were about to turn down it, footsteps and voices clattered up. Moll yanked Siddy into the shadows as two drunken guests stumbled up the stairs and passed by the children. When the coast was clear again, Moll and Siddy tiptoed down.

'Left at the bottom,' Moll whispered. 'Should lead us back towards the door out on to the harbour.'

Eyes darting this way and that, Moll and Siddy stepped off the last stair and scampered down the passageway. It was dark save for the tiny lamps positioned on the walls above paintings of stormy seas and ships docked in the harbour, and, behind a half-open door, Moll and Siddy could hear rowdy voices and chinking glasses – a bar perhaps. Holding their breath, they raced past, on towards the wooden door at the end of the passageway.

'Nearly there,' Siddy breathed.

They hauled the door open, felt the rain splatter against their skin, then they darted out into the night – and charged straight into Barbarous Grudge. Siddy screamed. Moll staggered backwards. But in seconds Grudge had collared them both.

'You!' he spat. Moll and Siddy twisted against Grudge's hold, but he only tightened his grip. 'You little tykes *dared* disobey me?' He shoved Siddy towards the squat smuggler boy, then he raised his crowbar above Moll.

'No!' Siddy yelled.

Moll closed her eyes, bracing herself for the blow.

'Boss, we could use them,' the smuggler holding Siddy muttered. Grudge's crowbar halted in mid-air. 'We're short of hands and we can't afford to mess this one up. I've got a couple of spare capes over by the wall.'

Only then did Moll and Siddy notice the dozen or so smugglers huddled into the shadows before the harbour wall. They were a jumble of different heights and builds, but they all wore the same black capes buttoned at the neck, long boots in which to stash stolen bottles and, as a mark of allegiance to their boss, each one of them had grown a knot of dreadlocked hair. But there was one boy who stood out from the others. Smaller than the rest by far, he flitted between the smugglers excitedly, like a beetle in need of squashing: Smog Sprockett. Moll glowered at him.

Grudge grunted and lowered his crowbar. He yanked a piece of rope from his pocket and bound Moll's wrists then Siddy's before dragging them up to his nose. 'You're gonna be sorry you were even born after this raid's done and the amulet's ours,' he snarled. 'Now get a move on.'

Heads down to fend off the rain, Moll and Siddy followed the Dreads round the harbour wall. The houses behind them were shuttered up against the night, as if they knew all too well what was going on outside their front doors. A street light cast a hazy glow on to the cobbles and Moll glimpsed a child crouched before a window, watching wide-eyed. Seconds later, a woman appeared and bolted the window fast.

The group hurried on, following the harbour wall round to the far side of the village. The sea below them moved like a phantom, gathering and swelling before crashing against the stones and mingling with the rain. They were nearing the walkway that ran along the inside of the harbour wall now and, just where it started, Moll noticed the stone steps leading down to the water's edge. There, two smugglers battled against the waves to keep a large rowing boat steady. Moll looked out to sea; in the distance, a light was edging slowly through the gloom. Just as Grudge had said, a ship was sailing right past Inchgrundle.

With no choice but to keep moving, Moll hastened on

with the smugglers, watching the sea heave and churn below them. She thought of the Shadowmasks plotting to find her still – of their dark magic seeping in through thresholds after her and Gryff. Would the witch doctors stay outside Inchgrundle, as Oak had hoped, or did they not mind being seen by smugglers so wrapped up in dark deeds of their own that their evil might go unnoticed?

Closing her eyes for a moment, Moll listened to the wind and tried to read its spirit, as Cinderella Bull had taught her. It surged in wild gusts, whipping rain into her face, and with a shudder Moll remembered the words of the Bone Murmur. *And storms will rise; trees will die, if they free their dark magic into the sky.* Perhaps this storm was a sign that the Shadowmasks' evil was lurking close by. A cold sweat crawled over her skin. She and Siddy needed to get away and find the amulet fast.

As if he'd been thinking the same thing, Siddy turned to her and, in words softer than a whisper, he said, *'Don't get on the boat. We need to make a run for it, whatever Grudge threatens.'*

Moll could have hugged Siddy then. She could sense his fear – her own heart was trembling – but hearing those words beneath the storm and Grudge's threats made her feel bigger, bolder. Somehow they'd get out of this mess together. She nudged Siddy with her elbow as they passed a track wide enough for a cart to pass through, leading away from the harbour and out of Inchgrundle. Siddy followed Moll's gaze to the wooden signpost fixed at its entrance which had **THE CRUMPLED WAY** stamped in crooked, worn-out lettering on it.

The smugglers crept down the stone steps towards the rowing boat, a snake of moving black. The first few clambered into the vessel, cloaks wrapped tight against the driving rain. Moll queued up on the walkway behind Siddy, racking her brain for something that would distract Grudge so that they could get away – but it was hard to think straight when she could feel Grudge's breath hot on the back of her neck.

Then one of the smugglers holding an oar in the boat suddenly roared in pain. 'Argh!' He turned to the smuggler next to him. 'If you go smacking your oar at my head again, I'll see you drowned tonight!'

The other man shook his head. 'Wasn't me! The wind whipped it up and I lost control!'

Moll blinked into the rain. She could have sworn she'd seen a figure wrapped in a tattered brown cloak reach out and jerk the oar into the smuggler's head. But, when she strained her eyes again, she could only make out the black-caped Dreads.

The smugglers began to bicker with one another and, as Grudge stepped forward, peering closer to see what was going on, Moll and Siddy took a tiny pace backwards, away from the steps.

Grudge whirled towards them. 'One move and you're goners,' he growled. 'I'll drown you in seconds.'

As the leader of the Dreads loomed before her, Moll noticed her knife tucked into his belt. She eyed Barbarous Grudge with disgust; he had no right to something her pa had given her. But, before she could make a swipe for it, another smuggler yelled out.

'Ahhh!' he cried, slipping from the steps and lunging forward, into the man in front.

Moll frowned. There it was again – unmistakable this time. A figure nipping between the Dreads. But the strangest thing about it was that none of the smugglers seemed able to see it. Moll's heart quickened. There was magic involved here – she was sure of it – and she wondered if Siddy could feel it too.

'What's wrong with you all?' Grudge hissed. 'We gotta job to do!'

It was at that point that Smog Sprockett screamed. He had been standing on the final step, waiting his turn to board the boat, but now his arms were flailing, whirling in circles, trying to keep him steady. A second later, he toppled backwards into the sea with a loud splash.

And once again Moll glimpsed the strange, cloaked figure dart back into the shadows.

'Someone pushed me!' Smog gasped, choking up seawater. 'I can't swim!' The smugglers on the steps bickered and whispered, all of them denying having laid a finger on Smog. The street urchin thrashed in the sea, grappling for an oar one of the others held out to him from the boat, and the smugglers glanced at each other uneasily.

'Something's not right,' one murmured as he made his way down the steps and climbed into the boat.

Moll flinched. First the oarsman, then the smuggler on the step, now Smog Sprockett. What was happening? Who *was* this strange figure? And was it trying to help Moll and Siddy break free or ... Moll chewed her lip. Was it fending off the Dreads for a more sinister reason of its own?

Grudge looked at Moll and Siddy as the last of his smugglers climbed into the boat. 'Is this your gypsy magic then? Muttering curses to muck the whole raid up?'

Siddy's eyes widened. 'No! We didn't do a thing!'

Grudge's hands tightened on his crowbar. 'I'm not having you mess up our biggest raid yet.' He shot a glance at the fat smuggler. 'Guard them here until I get back. Any trouble – drown the boy and we'll make the girl show us where the amulet is.'

But Grudge couldn't see the figure behind him. Though the person was obscured by a cloak and half masked by shadows, Moll glimpsed a hand moving slowly towards Grudge's crowbar. Quick as lightning, the figure yanked the metal rod back and swung it into Grudge's shin.

The smuggler roared in pain and stumbled backwards, but it was clear he couldn't see the figure who had dealt the blow and who was now crouched low by the harbour wall. The smugglers shifted in the boat; Moll could almost smell their fear. But she and Siddy had a window of opportunity now, and they seized it for all they were worth. Hands still bound, they turned and ran.

'Grab them!' Grudge bawled, lumbering forward.

But his legs buckled beneath him, as if someone had wound rope round his ankles, then yanked it hard. He thumped on to the stone and brandished angry fists at the Dreads. 'After them!' he roared. 'Don't let them escape!'

Moll threw a glance behind her. Had the cloaked figure been responsible for knocking Grudge over? The smugglers were clambering out of the boat and up the steps now, the light-footed Smog at their head. But, as the street urchin reached the top step, his whole body juddered to a standstill, then he tumbled backwards into the other boys. The line of smugglers crumpled to the left and right, some losing their footing and toppling into the waves, others gripping the stone steps to stop themselves falling.

'It's gypsy magic!' they muttered, refusing to climb back up. 'A curse because we kidnapped them! Let's leave them behind and get on with the raid!'

Grudge glanced up at the ship's light moving past the harbour, then back to Moll and Siddy, his face racked with indecision.

Moll shot the smugglers a deranged look, hoping it was enough to convince them that she and Siddy were up to their necks in gypsy curses. Then, because she couldn't resist, she yelled, 'Told you to watch out for the small people, Grudge!' Siddy grabbed Moll by the shoulders in a bid to shut her up, but stopping Moll now would be like trying to hold back an avalanche with bare hands. 'We're ten times as fierce!' Moll shouted before disappearing down The Crumpled Way.

Smog, still dripping wet, looked up at the leader of the Dreads. 'I'll go after them – once we've done the raid. And, if they're gone from Inchgrundle, I'll track them. They won't get away.'

Grudge nodded, then he stormed down the steps behind his boys. 'Let's get this raid started!'

Moll and Siddy hurtled down The Crumpled Way. Unlike the cobbled streets of the village, this was a sandy track with tufts of grass and weeds running down the middle and a stone wall on both sides, shielding gardens and houses behind. There was one street lamp at the start of the track, but after that the road sank into darkness, a perfect passageway for the Dreads to smuggle goods out of the village. Moll and Siddy pelted down it, their bound hands jiggling awkwardly in front of them.

'There!' Siddy panted.

Moll squinted into the night until she saw it too. Propped up against the wall was an abandoned anchor, partly overgrown with weeds.

'Good spot,' Moll puffed, setting the rope around her wrists against the rusted metal and sawing it back and forth.

'Did you see it too?' Siddy asked, sliding a glance to Moll. 'Back by the harbour steps?'

Moll nodded. 'A figure – all cloaked up – messing with Grudge's plans . . .'

Siddy let the rope fall away from his wrists. 'Phew. For a moment, I thought I was having visions – that I might have fortune-telling powers like Cinderella Bull or something.'

Moll looked at him. 'Sid, you're the last person on earth that I can think of who'd end up a fortune-teller. You'd be a shepherd before a fortune-teller.' She looked back towards the harbour. 'It was as if something was watching out for us back there – something giving us a way out. Wasn't it?'

Siddy wrapped his cape tighter round his shoulders. 'Or something trying to get us away for itself.' He shuddered. 'Whatever it was, it worked – and the figure hasn't followed us out here.' He looked down the track. 'There are numbers on the gates in the walls. We're at number ten – number four must be further on.'

They kept running, dodging the rabbit holes and keeping to the shadows, until they stood before a wooden gate. It swayed back and forth, nudged by the wind and rain, and nailed to a slat was a hand-painted sign. The words on it would have been lost in the darkness had it not been for the light coming from inside the house. All of the other houses on the road were merely dark shapes, but this one sent a hazy glow out into the night from a ground-floor window. And, though the lace curtains blocked the interior from sight, the light spread across the garden and fell upon the wooden sign: 4 CRUMPLED WAY.

Moll's heart drummed inside her cloak; the amulet was only moments away.

Chapter 11
Inside Number Four

°°

'Who do you think lives here?' Moll whispered.

Siddy shrugged. 'I dunno. I just hope it's none of Barbarous Grudge's relatives.'

He pushed the gate open and stepped inside the garden. Moll followed. The house had whitewashed stone walls, a perfectly arranged slate roof, four large windows surrounded by ivy and a freshly-painted red door.

'It all looks so – so ordinary,' Moll said.

Siddy glanced around. 'What did you expect?'

Moll didn't reply. But, ever since they'd found the first amulet and discovered its powers, she'd been expecting the second one to involve magic, to be hidden away somewhere secret, somewhere unusual, not a simple cottage like this.

Siddy pointed to the chimney. 'Smoke. Whoever lives here is still awake.'

'And what, we just ask them if they've seen an amulet recently?'

Siddy blinked hard against the clattering rain, then

gripped his stone talisman in his pocket. 'One thing at a time. Let's just get inside first.'

They tiptoed over the flagstones that led to the house. There were flower beds either side of them, but they were shrouded by darkness and all around them shadows seemed to shift and stir.

Moll stood before the door, huddled beneath the porch with Siddy. Could the amulet, her ma's soul, really be inside this house? She glanced down at her cape. 'We should take these off. We don't want whoever's inside thinking we're smugglers.'

'Don't go blathering about shepherds or gypsies either,' Siddy said, wriggling out of his cape. 'We've been in enough bother as it is. Try to act normal when you're inside.' He shook the rain from his flat cap and brushed his curls back from his face. 'And be polite.'

Moll thought about kicking Siddy in the shin for being bossy, then she remembered their conversation in The Gloomy Tap: they had to work together. Tucking her hair behind her ears, she stretched out a hand and knocked three times on the door.

Almost immediately footsteps sounded, clacking over floorboards towards them. Then the door opened a crack and a man's face appeared: two bespectacled eyes, set amid a face of absolutely flawless skin. There were no freckles, no wrinkles round the eyes or colour in the cheeks; he might almost have looked young had he not been entirely bald, wearing corduroy trousers that were a little too short and a tie tucked under his jumper.

He looked Moll and Siddy up and down. 'Who are you?' His words were scuffed with a lisp.

Moll's mind reeled with gypsies and shepherds, but she said nothing.

'We're from Tanglefern Forest,' Siddy replied. 'We're – we're looking for something and we,' he stopped, suddenly unsure, 'think you might have it.'

The man was silent for a moment, then he nodded, opening the door further. 'My name's Jones. I used to be the headmaster of the village school, but more recently other,' he paused, '*interests* occupy my time.' He adjusted the glasses on his nose. 'I've been expecting you both. You'd better come in.'

Neither Moll nor Siddy moved; something about the man's manner made them cautious.

Jones watched the rain falling about the porch, then he smiled. 'You can trust me; we have friends in common.' He leant against the door frame. 'I've journeyed to the heath before Tanglefern Forest many times in my life – it was there I met Mellantha.'

Moll frowned. 'You knew Mellantha?' She felt a sudden sadness as she remembered the witch doctor who'd died trying to help Moll and Alfie escape from Skull. But how had Jones known her?

The man nodded again. 'My parents – and my grandparents before them – swore by Mellantha's herbal remedies. Bilberries to fight eye infections and cramps, dandelions to cure kidney disease, hawthorn for the heart.' He paused, his lisp more noticeable now. 'It was Mellantha who told me about a deeper magic lying hidden in the forest. It was she who told me about the Bone Murmur.'

Moll glanced at Siddy.

Jones added. 'She said I'd have a part to play in it all, that sooner or later a girl from the forest would come looking for an amulet.' He went on. 'I heard the smugglers talk in the village about two gypsy children running loose – and I wondered whether that might be you.' Jones blinked at Moll and Siddy through his spectacles. 'If you want the amulet, I suggest you come inside.'

Moll and Siddy looked at one another. This was their only lead on the amulet – they'd got this far and they had to follow it through – and so, gripping Siddy's hand, Moll stepped over the threshold and followed Jones down a lamplit corridor.

She leant in close to Siddy. 'I don't trust him. There's something strange about his skin, how it's all perfect and unlined. It's creepy.'

'That's just his face,' Siddy whispered. 'Do *not* bring it up, Moll.'

'In here,' said Jones, ushering them into the sitting room. 'It's the warmest place in the house on a night like this.'

Moll and Siddy followed him in. A fire crackled in the hearth and a dog lay curled before it, sleeping peacefully. Two well-worn armchairs had been positioned either side of the fireplace, next to side tables scattered with old books; paintings hung from the walls, their gilt frames glowing in the lamplight. It all looked so cosy, but for some reason a sense of unease tugged inside Moll.

Jones fetched two blankets from a trunk and passed them to Moll and Siddy. 'Wrap yourselves up and take a seat. You look as if you've had quite a night.'

They took the blankets, then perched together on an armchair by the fire. Moll let the warmth from the fire spread right through her and tried not to think about how Jones's skin barely moved when he spoke. She watched in silence as he lifted a log from a wicker basket and placed it on the fire, then sat in the armchair opposite them.

'You're the child from the Bone Murmur, aren't you?' Jones said.

Moll shifted her weight uncomfortably and a loneliness swelled inside her. Gryff was the beast from the Bone Murmur – but where was he? And Oak? She'd have bet her life on them both coming after her as soon as they could. And yet . . .

She looked at Jones for a while, then nodded.

Siddy fiddled with the hem of the blanket. 'Do you have the amulet? Moll threw the Oracle Bones and they led us to you.'

'Yes, yes!' Jones lisped excitedly. 'Mellantha told me to guard it with my life should any witch doctors come hunting it out.' He took a sip of brandy from a glass on the table, then he shook his head and his glasses wobbled. 'Where are my manners? You'll both need a drink to warm yourselves up.'

'We just need the am—' Moll began.

But Jones was already hurrying from the room and, as he passed the mirror above the fireplace, Moll frowned. For a moment, there seemed to be a movement flickering within the glass, something not cast by Jones's reflection. Then it was gone.

She turned to Siddy. 'We need to get the amulet and head back to the cove – fast.'

Siddy motioned towards the door. 'I don't think Jones gets much company up here.' He rolled his eyes. 'It sounds like he wants to talk.'

Moll tapped her boot against the rug impatiently, then she glanced down at the dog before the fire. She squinted at it more closely and gasped.

'It's stuffed!' she hissed.

Siddy peered at it. 'So it is.' He shivered and fumbled for his talisman; there was something slightly unpleasant about the dog, as if the homeliness of the room had wilted just a little.

Then Moll grabbed Siddy's arm. 'Look!'

Siddy raised a hand to his mouth and a shaky moan escaped from his lips. 'The mirror – what's happening to the mirror?'

Chapter 12
Trapped!

The glass in the mirror seemed to ripple under the lamplight. Then a shadowy blur slid and slipped within the frame before stilling and hardening into an image.

A face. And Moll's blood curdled as she took it in.

A mask of snakeskin stared back at her, diamonds of brown and green scales split by a smile that held a flickering forked tongue, and two milky eyes. Moll made to leap up, but her limbs wouldn't move; they were frozen like Siddy's seemed to be beside her – stiffened by fear or by something darker. The mouth in the mirror pursed and Moll didn't need to hear its voice to know the single word that it was shaping: *Molly*.

Her pulse raced; she knew all too well that witch doctors could control people once they knew their name. And was this a Shadowmask buried somewhere deep inside the mirror? Or ... She gulped. Was the Shadowmask here in the room already? She glanced back, just her neck free from the sinister hold she appeared to be trapped under. But only Jones was there, staring in silence at the hideous face within his mirror.

Moll tried to speak, but her words were snared inside her. Whatever dark magic had crept into the room had seized her voice as well. She blinked terrified, wide eyes at Jones, but all he could do was stare straight ahead at the mirror. There was a snakeskin mask glinting back at him where his reflection should have been and, powerless to help, Moll could only watch.

And then Jones reached a hand behind him and clasped at something at the nape of his neck. Unhooking some sort of catch, he pulled a fist of skin up over his head.

Moll's stomach heaved. Siddy's eyes swelled with horror.

Jones was *peeling* his face away. His spectacles tumbled to the ground and, glinting in the lamplight as he pulled the skin back, was what the mirror had shown all along: a face of snakeskin, as if the markings themselves had been tattooed on to his skin.

Moll's blood ran cold. Jones was a Shadowmask. She tried to spring up and Siddy thrashed his head, but the curse they were under held their bodies still.

Jones let a handful of skin slither to the floor and laughed, his forked tongue darting between his teeth, his milky eyes settling on Moll. Then he tore off his jumper to reveal a dark green cloak that draped down to his ankles.

'I suppose the mirror was bound to un-hex itself sometime.' He smirked, his voice dry and lisping, like a snake's hiss. 'And you thought you were following an Oracle Bone clue sent to you by the old magic ...'

Moll's heart plunged.

'Darkebite may be a Shadow Keeper who called in the owls to track you down,' Jones sneered, 'but it was I who intercepted your bone reading, twisting the old magic and turning it bad. It was all part of my plan to lead you to me.'

Moll's thoughts crashed in on her. They'd walked right into the Shadowmasks' trap.

Jones dipped his snakeskin head and Moll glimpsed the markings running over his scalp like a path of scales.

'As you'll have guessed, I was never a headmaster.' He sucked in the last syllable as if to savour it. 'My name's Ashtongue. I am the fourth Shadowmask and I can communicate with the dark spirits of the Underworld, calling on them to turn your magic against you.' He smirked. 'You had no idea you were dealing with a Spirit Talker when you knocked on my door, did you?' He looked around casually. 'A shame your wildcat's not here, Molly.'

Moll shuddered at her name.

Ashtongue went on. 'But we'll make do without him and I think I can have some fun with your little friend here.'

Moll made to move, her heart drumming inside her ribcage, her muscles straining against the curse. But it held her fast. She thought of the pattern Mellantha had explained to her and Alfie within the word *Shadowmask* – each letter in the word *shadow* standing in for a witch doctor's name: Skull, Hemlock, Ashtongue, Darkebite ... Panic bubbled inside Moll's throat. Skull had come with his Dream Snatch, Hemlock had brought poison, Darkebite was a Shadow Keeper, but this distortion of the old magic was even worse somehow – and she and Siddy couldn't even move against it. Cinderella Bull had been right: the thresholds were opening fast now and the dark magic was all around them.

Ashtongue made to move closer, but, instead of walking, he dropped to all fours and scampered to the middle of the room, his hands and feet turned inwards like some sort of sinister lizard.

Moll turned to Siddy and saw her fear mirrored on his face. And, as Ashtongue dipped his head, Moll could only listen, every muscle inside her quaking with dread. The words came in a mutter, the Shadowmask's forked tongue hissing at the end of sounds:

'Here is the girl who walks with the beast.
She is trapped and afraid; on her fear I do feast.
Her name I have used to make her hold still,
Until Darkebite comes, bearing all kinds of ill.
Molly Pecksniff you are, I've claimed you as mine.
Now you'll wait with me here for the Shadowmasks' sign.'

A scratching inside the chimney started, slow at first and then louder, faster, like a frantic animal scrabbling to break free. The flames in the grate shrank and dimmed until they fizzled away completely, leaving the logs black and still. The noise was now a scraping sound, like nails on a blackboard, and then a small brown creature tumbled into the grate – a bat with a furred body tucked beneath two leathery wings.

The bat crawled out of the grate into the hearth and as

103

it moved it began to grow. A putrid smell, like burnt skin, clogged Moll's nose and the bat continued to swell. Where its body had been there was now a human torso draped in black robes; from its back two giant wings arched up into peaks, all leather and veins, and between them was a mask of charcoaled wood, surrounded by a shock of wild black hair. The Shadow Keeper had emerged in all its menace.

Moll's muscles seized up, clamped by Ashtongue's curse, and her eyes glazed with fear.

'Welcome, Darkebite, Master of the Soul Splinter,' Ashtongue hissed, drawing his body up to full height.

Darkebite took a step closer to Moll and Siddy, jet-black eyes sunken inside the mask. 'Molly Pecksniff.'

The words were neither a question nor a fact. They were a claim. And the voice that spoke them was unmistakably female.

Moll flinched. The other Shadowmasks had been men and Moll had presumed Darkebite would be no different. But the Shadow Keeper was a *woman* – a woman so riddled with evil it made Moll's mouth turn dry. And for some reason, this made Darkebite feel even more sinister than before.

Darkebite reached a hand inside her cloak and pulled out a shard of glimmering black ice. Moll's breath choked inside her. The Soul Splinter. The weapon that had killed her parents and that had to be destroyed to save the old magic. Darkebite's long, thin fingers clasped it tight and her wings seemed to tremble with anticipation.

Moll tried again to work her way free of the curse, but her

104

limbs were like stone. She thought fast. Back in the forest Alfie had told her that the Shadowmasks could only break the Bone Murmur if they killed the child and the beast at the same time.

Darkebite's mask tilted to one side. 'Think I won't use it on you because your wildcat's not here?' Her voice was scratchy, like a bat screech, and behind slits in the mask red lips curled back and two dark eyes gleamed. 'Now the thresholds are opening the dark magic is growing stronger, and we're going to destroy your precious Bone Murmur piece by piece.'

Darkebite raised the Soul Splinter high and her wings twitched with pleasure.

Moll thought of Oak and Mooshie – of all her friends back in the cave and in the forest willing her on. She thought of Gryff who could build courage inside her just by being at her side. And she found herself thinking of Alfie, of the horrors they'd faced in the forest and how they'd fought past every single one together. Beside her, Siddy's eyes were wide, his nails digging hard into the armchair. But Moll could sense his stubborn strength, his refusal to give in.

Darkebite drew closer still, then lowered the Soul Splinter so that it was pointing right at Moll. The girl shut her eyes and let the fear beat louder inside her while Ashtongue, sloping down on to all fours, crawled up and seized Moll by the hair. Siddy threw back his head from side to side, trying to break the curse, but Darkebite brought the Soul Splinter up to Moll's face.

'Yes,' hissed Ashtongue. 'At last . . .'

Moll pressed her lips together tight; every muscle in her throat clenched. She wouldn't let them drip the darkness in.

'Open her mouth, Ashtongue,' Darkebite crooned. 'And—'

Her words were cut short by an enormous crash. The front window Moll and Siddy had seen lit up from the track exploded into the room. Shards of glass smashed down on to the floorboards, broken pieces skittering across the wood. And standing among them, panting but alive, was a boy with a jay feather earring and a wildcat.

Chapter 13
Alfie's Amulet

A familiar boldness surged inside Moll and her legs grew fierce as she fought her way out of the Shadowmasks' curse.

'Gryff!' she cried, twisting from Ashtongue's clutch and dragging Siddy behind the armchair. And then in a quieter voice, one less sure of itself, 'Alfie.'

Gryff rushed towards Moll and as she knelt down he threw himself against her, burying his head in her cardigan. Moll cradled him tight as if a missing part of her had been returned, and as she drew back she noticed the blood on his fur where the glass had nicked him. But there was no time to do anything about it. Alfie tossed aside the branch he'd used to break the window and eyed the Shadowmasks with loathing.

'It – it's *him*,' Ashtongue whispered, recoiling.

Darkebite shifted, quickly tucking the Soul Splinter beneath her cloak.

Moll glanced towards Alfie, her chest full of unlearnt things.

'You – you came back,' Siddy said.

Alfie nodded. Then he held up a small, rounded piece of rock for the Shadowmasks to see. Half of it seemed to be made of crystal and it glinted a deep orange under the lamplight. Ashtongue and Darkebite took a step backwards.

'I found the second amulet,' Alfie said, glaring at the Shadowmasks. His voice was hard and loud. 'And it's filled with a power that can break you both, just like the first amulet destroyed Skull and Hemlock.'

The orange seemed to glitter brighter, but, as Alfie thrust it higher, Moll frowned. Was that *really* the second amulet inside Alfie's palm? She'd been waiting for this moment – waiting to have her ma back, even if only fleetingly – but something didn't feel right.

Darkebite slid a look at Ashtongue. 'They're both here. The child and the beast. Now the Soul Splinter will be even more powerful; just one step and we can splinter their souls.' Her wings unfurled and the room seemed to darken.

Ashtongue's forked tongue slipped between his teeth. 'But the boy, he could—'

Darkebite raised a hand and Ashtongue's words were cut short. 'He could – but *would* he?' She watched Alfie intently, a column of shadows searching him out.

Gryff leapt on to the back of the armchair, snarling and ripping the fabric with his claws. He swiped his paw at a vase that stood on the table beside it and it crashed to the ground, a sprawl of broken china. Moll and Siddy huddled behind him.

Ashtongue slithered to the floor, creeping towards the fire on all fours. He raised a snakeskin face to Darkebite. 'It needs to be without the boy.'

Gryff lowered his body into a crouch and Moll could tell that he was getting ready to pounce, to smash the Soul Splinter to pieces.

Darkebite nodded at Ashtongue, then she glanced at Alfie's amulet. 'And with more power from the Underworld on our side.'

Alfie lunged towards them, clasping his knife tight, and Gryff leapt into the air. But the Shadowmasks were fading, their bodies breaking apart like grains of sand, and, seconds later, they had vanished from the room completely. Moll stared at the floor; all that was left was a snakeskin recently shed – and the smell of burnt wood lingering in the air.

For a few seconds, no one said anything, then Moll turned to face Alfie, her jaw set hard. 'You left.' The hurt and anger beat inside her. 'You didn't tell anyone. You just left.'

'You could've told me,' Siddy said. 'But you snuck out of the alcove without saying a word.'

Alfie looked at the ground. 'You don't understand, Sid. Neither of you do.'

Moll took a step forward. 'You didn't give us a chance!' Her cheeks were hot and red. 'Then you – you just come back and—'

Siddy stepped in. 'We're grateful you helped us against the Shadowmasks, Alfie, we really are – but how do we know you're not just going to run off again?'

'I'll explain, I promise I will,' Alfie said. 'But we've got to get out of here, back to Little Hollows before the Shadowmasks summon the owls again.'

Moll raised her eyebrows. 'You're staying around to help us?'

Alfie nodded. 'If you'll have me.'

Moll threw him a defiant look.

'We'll have you,' Siddy said after a pause. 'So long as you explain things when we're back in the cove.'

Moll whirled round, seized by the urge to pinch Siddy. 'How can you let this go so quickly?' she spat. 'Alfie left us to face The Crumpled Way when he knew the Shadowmasks were out there!' She breathed deeply, barely able to rein in her emotions.

'Because we need to work together, Moll. Remember?' Siddy glanced at the window. 'That way we'll stand a chance of getting back to Little Hollows unharmed.'

Moll kicked the floorboards. Siddy was right, she knew that, but her pride still stormed inside her. She glowered at Alfie. 'Fine. We'll discuss it back in Little Hollows, but don't expect me to be polite or nice to you until then.' She waited, her mind racing on to other things. 'Oak – have you seen him? Is he OK?'

Gryff nuzzled against Moll's legs, but Alfie avoided her eyes. 'I found Oak, Patch and Gryff on the cliff top when I realised running away wasn't the answer, and I turned back for the cove. The owls had gone, but they'd cut Oak's leg pretty badly. I could tell Gryff had wanted to run off and find you, but he wouldn't leave Oak when he was injured. I helped Oak up on to Raven and led him and Patch back to the cave with Gryff.'

'And Jinx? Did you find her?' Siddy asked.

'When I realised you two weren't in Little Hollows, I rode Raven hard to Inchgrundle. I heard Jinx whinnying for Moll down by the harbour wall. Gryff and I walked her to the cliff top and watered her, then I tied her up again; we're going to need her to get back to the cave.' Alfie glanced from Gryff to Moll. 'Your wildcat and I got off to a bit of a shaky start – lots of hissing and snarling – but I think, when he realised I just wanted to find you too, he trusted me a little more and we got along OK – so long as I didn't get too close to him.'

Gryff held his head high, twitched his whiskers, then stalked round Moll's legs.

'That's not really the amulet, is it?' Moll asked, looking at the stone in Alfie's palm.

'No, it's an old charm of Cinderella Bull's. She trapped a sunbeam inside the rock and told me it would shine in times of danger.' Alfie shoved it into the pocket of his shorts. 'Did the trick though.'

But Moll couldn't help feeling cheated. She'd been so sure that her ma's soul was waiting for her in Inchgrundle. And now what? They didn't even have a bone reading to guide them …

Siddy was looking at Alfie closely. 'It was more than that. Those Shadowmasks were *scared* of you – not just the amulet. Something about you made them leave.'

Alfie shifted his weight from one foot to the other. 'I think I might have an idea why, but I'm not sure … Let's talk back in the cave; we need to get moving in case we run into Grudge and the Dreads with their loot.'

Moll looked Alfie up and down. 'You've got a lot of explaining to do later,' she muttered. 'That kind of running-off behaviour could get you expelled from the Tribe.'

Siddy nodded. 'And it really offended Hermit.'

'Come on,' Moll said, sizing up the window now fringed with jagged glass. 'Urgh. It's going to be a right pain climbing out of that.'

'We could always leave through the door,' Alfie said.

Siddy slapped him on the back. 'There's a reason we need you around, Alfie. That kind of clear thinking just doesn't happen with me and Moll.'

Moll charged out of the house with Gryff. Siddy might be fine with letting Alfie back into the Tribe and joking around with him, but with Moll it was more complicated. There was still a mountain of hurt inside her.

Outside, the rain had stopped and the night was wearing thin. A clear sky stretched above them, dark blue before the sun came up, but full of promise for a bright day ahead. Moll shuddered as she took in the garden now the night had faded. It was a charred mess of dead grass, weeds and withered flowers while further up the road another garden was a burst of shining rhododendron bushes. The Shadowmasks' magic had been all around them, but they hadn't even noticed it.

'We'll go on up The Crumpled Way,' Alfie said, 'then skirt

behind the village before heading across the cliffs and back to Little Hollows. Less chance of us being seen that way.'

They found Alfie's cob, Raven, tethered to the gate, and he whinnied as they approached. Alfie hoisted Moll and Siddy up on to his back, then, undoing the buckle on the leather satchel tucked behind the gate, he passed Moll and Siddy two hunks of bread and a flask of water.

'You not riding too?' Siddy asked, his mouth full of bread.

Alfie shook his head. 'I'll walk with Gryff; Raven's got enough on his back with you two.'

The cob's hooves clopped softly on the track as they made their way down The Crumpled Way. Moll willed herself to stay awake – the Dreads could come back at any moment and who knew where the Shadowmasks were lurking? After a while, Alfie turned Raven left off the track, down a narrow country lane. At the end of it was a gate leading into a field and Alfie unhooked it to lead them through. Cows were grazing on grasses untouched by the Shadowmasks' magic and, some metres away, a farmer was filling a trough with water.

He glanced up and looked at the children. 'A couple of gypsies, a cob and a—' he looked at Gryff, whose eyes were now yellowed slits, and shook his head in disbelief, '—a *wildcat*. I'd be picking up speed and heading home if I were you – that village lot don't look kindly on outsiders.'

After smugglers and Shadowmasks, Moll's patience was wearing thin. 'We're going as fast as we can, but we can't fit three of us on the cob's back, can we?'

The farmer nodded at Gryff. 'With legs like his, he won't need a ride.'

Moll frowned. 'Not the wildcat – *him*!' She pointed to Alfie, then noticed that he'd dropped Raven's tethering rope and was hastening ahead.

The farmer looked at where Moll was pointing, his eyes scouring the grass, but never fixing on Alfie, then he shook his head again. 'You gypsies are a strange old bunch. Now hop it off my land or I'll set the bull on you.'

Moll kicked Raven into a trot after Alfie. He was running now and, when he reached the far side of the field, he clambered over a stile before jumping down into longer grass strewn with poppies. Moll squeezed Raven's flanks with her legs and he broke into a canter, leaping over the stile into the field beyond. Gryff followed.

Alfie was standing in front of them, the wind ruffling his shirt, grass swaying about his shins. And his eyes were filled with tears.

Moll slid from Raven so that she was standing before him. 'The farmer – he – he couldn't *see* you!'

Alfie's lip quivered, but he said nothing. He wouldn't cry; nothing would change by crying.

Siddy gasped. 'It was *you*! Down by the harbour wall. You were the cloaked figure messing up Grudge's plans so that we could escape. But, just like that farmer, the smugglers couldn't see you either!'

Moll gasped. 'That was *you*?'

Alfie nodded. 'Found an old rag in the shipyard and I wore

114

it to disguise myself from you two. I knew if you realised it was me there'd be too many questions and you wouldn't run away.' He reached into his satchel and drew out a dagger, its handle tipped with bone. He handed it to Moll. 'Stole your pa's knife back from Grudge.'

Moll looked at it in disbelief. 'But – but,' she stammered. The mountain inside her shrank a little. 'Why can't some people see you? I see you, Siddy and Gryff see you, all of the gypsies in Little Hollows and Tanglefern Forest see you. So why . . .' Her voice faltered into silence.

Alfie looked at the sea beyond Inchgrundle, spread out below them like a giant bruise, then he turned to face her. 'I'm not real, Moll.'

His words hung in the air.

'Not – not real?' Moll's voice was close to nothing.

Raven stepped forward and nudged Alfie's shoulder with his nose, but Alfie didn't respond, and the only sound to break the silence was the farmer in the field behind, herding up the cows.

Chapter 14
Charmed Pebbles

Alfie led Raven through the poppies, on towards the gate at the far end of the field. No one spoke. But his words were still ringing in Moll's head, turning over and over in tangled shapes. Not real? How could Alfie not be *real*? She watched him lift the latch on the gate, pushing his fair hair from his eyes as it flopped across his face, and pull Raven through.

He looked so different from the dark-haired gypsies in Oak's camp that Moll had almost expected him to fit in with the villagers in Inchgrundle. But they couldn't even *see* him. Who *was* Alfie? Moll noticed Gryff quicken his stride down the sandy path that led towards the cliffs so that he was walking abreast with Alfie. Back in the forest the wildcat would never have done that; he had snarled and spat when Alfie came too close. But Gryff had learnt to trust the boy – obviously even more so since their time together on the cliff tops.

Moll watched, caught between anger and doubt. Alfie had abandoned her on their quest – he'd left her to face the

Shadowmasks without him – and yet something about his words just now suggested maybe he was even more alone in this world than she was.

She felt Siddy lean in closer behind her. 'Do you think Alfie's a – a ghost?'

Moll observed Alfie closely: his old brown boots leaving prints on the sand, his shirt flapping in the wind. She could see him, clear as day, and yet the farmer and the Dreads hadn't – they hadn't even seen Alfie's clothes or the rag he'd been huddling under. 'No,' Moll said firmly. 'Ghosts are white and wobbly and they only come out at night.'

But, as she turned to face forward again, a coldness slid beneath her skin. She could throw Siddy off with a line like that, but what Moll had seen of spirits and ghouls in the forest made her quite sure ghosts weren't white and wobbly. She kept her distance from Alfie and shook the thought away; it wouldn't help matters thinking about him like that. And, besides, there must be more to it; Alfie needed to tell them what he meant.

The path unfolded towards the cliffs and below them was the sea, waves pinched into glistening points. Moll smiled as she glimpsed Jinx grazing on the grass near the cliff edge. She clicked her tongue and whistled. The cob looked up and, on seeing Moll, strained against her tethering rope and neighed. Moll slipped from Raven's back and hurried over, wrapping her arms round Jinx's neck.

'I'm sorry for leaving you,' she whispered.

'We'll need to ride fast,' Alfie said, glancing down the

117

path that ran along the cliff tops. 'The Shadowmasks won't be far away.'

Spraying sand up behind them, and with Gryff moving so fast his limbs were just a ripple of black and grey, they galloped past the fields of pigs, cows and sheep and sped by the tumbled stone cottage the owls had ambushed them from.

Eventually they came to the heath and Moll felt a sense of calm when she saw Little Hollows down below them. She dismounted from Jinx's back, then frowned at the pebbles, each one marked with a chalked star, set out in a line at the cliff edge across the length of the cove.

Alfie followed Moll's gaze. 'Protection charms – the ones Cinderella Bull has been working on since we left the forest.'

Siddy nodded. 'I remember her saying she was conjuring more and more magic inside them so that eventually they'd be strong enough to keep the Shadowmasks from the cove.' He dismounted Jinx and patted the cob's neck. 'Suppose that means we're safe so long as we stay inside Little Hollows.'

'Only there's no amulet in the cove,' Moll muttered. 'We'll have to leave again soon . . .'

'Let's get the cobs down too,' Alfie said. 'I don't want Raven up there with the Shadowmasks' magic around.'

Alfie led his cob carefully over the pebbles and down the winding path. Siddy followed, then Moll with Jinx and Gryff. A rabbit shot out of the bracken that lined the path and Jinx shied, but Moll coaxed her on with Siddy's help, and, in their haste to get back into the cove, neither of them noticed that Jinx's hoof had nudged aside one of Cinderella Bull's pebbles.

As they edged down the cliff, it was Hard-Times Bob they spotted first. He was sprawled on the sand like a starfish, wearing orange braces over his wrinkled chest to hold up a pair of tattered shorts. Beside him was an open-topped barrel.

Siddy whistled. 'Oi! Hard-Times Bob!'

The old man sat bolt upright, jerking his neck this way and that, then his eyes rested on Siddy and the others making their way down the path.

'You made it!' he cried, leaping up and dancing excitedly on the spot. He pointed to the barrel beside him. 'I've been beside myself with worry. Dislocating's gone to pot – couldn't even wriggle my limbs inside this old whisky barrel that washed up this morning!'

Moll thought of Grudge and the Dreads. Perhaps the barrel had floated away from their raid ... She shivered at the thought of the smugglers and stepped down on to the beach. The sand curved over her feet and, for the first time in days, she felt safe again. Taking the halters off the cobs so that they could roam the cove, the children hurried over to Hard-Times Bob.

He gave Siddy and Moll a hug. 'So Alfie found you both in Inchgrundle, did he? What happened over there? Mooshie's been worried sick.'

Moll scuffed her foot in the sand and took a deep breath. 'We got tricked by an annoying street kid, kidnapped by the Dreads, then trapped by Darkebite and another Shadowmask

called Ashtongue, who pretended to have the amulet, and—'
She looked at Alfie, then back to Hard-Times Bob. The old
man's face was aghast and Moll realised that telling him
about Alfie might send him over the edge – or bring on a
fresh bout of hiccups.

'Did you find the amulet?' Hard-Times Bob ventured.

Moll blew through her lips. 'No. It wasn't even *in*
Inchgrundle. Ashtongue distorted the bone reading; it was
a trap all along.'

The old man shook a crinkled fist. 'When I get my hands
on those Shadowmasks – and the wretched Dreads – I'll show
them.' He hiccuped, a side effect of the morning's attempted
dislocation. 'These fists have wrestled sharks and whales in
their time.'

There was a snort from the corridor of rocks by the cave
as Cinderella Bull hobbled towards them. 'You're safe in
the cove at last.' She looked up at Alfie. 'Well done for
bringing them back. The sunbeam charm worked against
the Shadowmasks?'

Alfie nodded and Cinderella Bull's gaze fell on Gryff. She
glanced at the dried blood crusting his coat. 'Come inside –
all of you. You'll need washed up and fed, I've no doubt.' She
paused and laid a hand on Moll's shoulder. 'Oak's not in a
good way, Moll. It's best you're prepared.'

Moll stiffened at her words. 'Alfie said it was just a cut from
the owls. I thought—' Her words dissolved. She sprinted
forward, darting between the corridors of rock, her heart
thudding in her throat. *Please let Oak be OK,* she told herself,

over and over again. Twisting round a boulder of rock, Moll ducked down low and entered Little Hollows.

Candles flickered on every ledge, the only movement inside the cave. The fire was out, just a pile of charred ash, which sent panic shooting through Moll's veins. Mooshie never let the fire go out . . . Her eyes scanned the lobster pots, washing line and crates of supplies. Nobody there. All was quiet, save for the gentle slopping of water inside the tunnel.

Moll ran towards Oak and Mooshie's alcove, flinging the curtain aside. On ledges, Mooshie's best china had been neatly arranged, and in the middle of the alcove, in their hammock, lay Oak. His leg was bandaged from the ankle to the knee and his eyes were closed.

Mooshie sat on a stool beside him, holding his hand and occasionally wiping the sweat from his forehead with a damp cloth. She looked up at Moll.

'Oh, Moll, you're all right.' She stood up and clasped her tight. Alfie and Siddy hung back by the entrance. 'Thank goodness you're all OK.'

While locked in The Gloomy Tap, Moll had craved Mooshie's arms around her, but now she wriggled free.

'Oak – is he . . . ?' She crept nearer to the hammock, stretched out a hand and squeezed Oak's arm. 'It's me,' she whispered. 'Moll.'

Oak said nothing and Moll leant closer until she could feel his breath on her cheek. It was colder somehow, and weaker.

Moll swallowed. Oak was their leader. He built wagons from scratch and found secret coves. But the Oak lying there, pale and cold – this was a man Moll didn't know. She breathed in and out. 'He'll be OK,' she whispered. She'd meant it as fact, but even to her it sounded like a question.

Mooshie sat back down on the stool. 'The owls' blades must have been coated in a curse. When he came back to the cove with Alfie, it looked like a clean wound, but it was deep enough for a curse to slip in, and within hours the fever had started.' She took a deep breath. 'He's been quieter since I dressed the wound with woundwort and elder blossom. All we can do now is wait.' She squeezed Moll's shoulder, then her face brightened for a moment. 'The amulet. Did you—'

Cinderella Bull saved Moll the answer. 'There was no amulet in Inchgrundle,' she said from the entrance to the alcove. 'We should get a fire going to warm up these children and talk about a new plan.'

Moll shook her head. 'We can't talk it through without Oak. He – he—' Her voice trembled. 'He always makes the plans. Without him, we—'

Cinderella Bull came into the alcove and laid a hand on Moll's back. 'We don't have time, Moll. The Shadowmasks have opened the thresholds and it won't be long before their dark magic eats its way into everything, not just the places where you and Gryff are.'

Moll looked over at Mooshie and noticed that her eyes had filled with tears. Mooshie tried to turn away to stop Moll from seeing, but, when the woman's shoulders started to shake, Moll realised she was crying. Something deep inside Moll rocked with pain and the sand beneath her seemed to sway.

'Mind yourselves,' Hard-Times Bob said as he hobbled past Cinderella Bull, Siddy and Alfie at the entrance of the alcove. He opened his old, wrinkled arms and tucked Moll inside them. 'There are few things worse than seeing your parents weep – and Oak and Mooshie are as good as parents to you, Moll.' He stroked her hair. 'But it's going to be all right. I won't let anything happen to you or Moosh. I'll look after you both until Oak is back on his feet.'

'Will – will he be OK?' Moll whispered.

Hard-Times Bob hugged her tighter. 'Yes,' he said quietly, as if one word might be enough to convince the world that Oak wasn't allowed to leave it.

Mooshie wiped her eyes with her pinafore. 'Thank you, Bob,' she said. 'There's firewood by the tunnel. And Moll, Gryff's coat will need to be wiped down with the dried rosemary and water.'

Cinderella Bull nodded, then, as she turned towards the cave, she looked at Alfie. 'And it's time you told us about your past, young man.'

Chapter 15
Alfie's Story

I t took Moll most of the day to wash Gryff's coat. She had coaxed him into the hammock easily enough, but, when she advanced with a bowl of water sprinkled with rosemary, Gryff had kicked the whole thing over and skulked off to the far corner of the alcove before burying himself in Moll's patchwork quilt. A while later, Moll had lain next to him, counting her heartbeats against his as they drifted in and out of sleep. But only when she offered up a sea trout Hard-Times Bob had caught did Gryff let her tend to his cuts.

When they emerged from their alcove, Alfie and Siddy were already eating around the fire with the grown-ups. No daylight seeped through the cracks above the tunnel now; it was night and, outside in the bay, the sea would be dark and cold. Moll watched the flames from the fire flicker over the words of the Bone Murmur on the cave wall.

'We've fed and watered the cobs,' Siddy said as Moll approached. 'And I managed to get Hermit to look at his pincers in the mirror without charging off backwards.'

Moll glanced at the crab perched on Siddy's knee – every

leg, pincer and claw tucked out of sight beneath its shell. 'You go through pets very quickly, Sid.'

Siddy scowled. 'It's not my fault Porridge the Second didn't fancy the change of scene. Personally I think the sea air would have done wonders for his melancholy. But he was having none of it.'

Moll shrugged. 'You should get a decent animal, like a fox or – or a badger.'

Mooshie rolled her eyes. 'Siddy is *not* adopting a badger.'

Moll sat on a stool between the boys, then shuffled it closer to Siddy – a sign to Alfie that things weren't as they had been – and took the bowl of mussels Mooshie held out for her. She ate hungrily. The garlicky taste of the peppered dulse tingled on her tongue and, when she had finished eating, she wrapped a blanket round her shoulders. Gryff slunk beneath it, out of sight.

Cinderella Bull sat forward, licking the last of the sauce from her fingers. 'Siddy told us all about Ashtongue distorting the Oracle Bone reading. What with the Soul Splinter and the Dreads, it looks like you had a lucky escape.'

'Mmmmmn.' For a while, Moll said nothing more, then she turned to face Alfie. 'Somehow we've got to find this amulet without a bone reading – but I can't even think about where to start when I don't know who you really are.' She looked towards Mooshie's alcove. 'Oak always says trust is what comes first in a friendship – everything else follows. So, if that's anything to go by, you'd better tell us who you are, Alfie.' Her face was stern. 'Why did you run away?'

125

Alfie twisted his earring between his fingers and looked at Moll. 'I left because I didn't want you finding out the truth, not after you all took me in and treated me like I was one of you,' he said slowly. 'I couldn't face telling you that ...' His voice unravelled and he looked down.

Moll stared at him, unblinking. 'Couldn't face telling us what?'

There was pride and hurt in that voice; Alfie knew Moll well enough to hear it. He met her eyes and took a deep breath. 'That I can only be seen by animals and by those who knew me in the forest. Skull's camp first – then yours.'

'And the Shadowmasks,' Siddy added.

Alfie nodded, his face grim. 'And by them, it seems.'

Moll shook her head. 'I don't understand ... The Shadowmasks were *scared* of you.'

'I can't think why,' Alfie muttered. 'Skull told me that he took me in as an orphaned baby from a farm – to look after the cobs when I was old enough.' Alfie sighed. 'But it was for another reason – I'm sure of it. I may have ended up looking after his cobs, but I don't think that's what Skull wanted me for at the start. Otherwise his boys wouldn't have treated me like they did. They wouldn't have said all those things.'

Mooshie leant forward on her stool, folding her cardigan over her chest. 'What did they say, Alfie?'

He didn't look up, but his words came stiff and cold. 'They used to taunt me. Saying I was different from them, that I was *broken* inside.' Alfie reached for the knot of Raven's hair hanging round his neck and clutched it so tight his knuckles

126

turned white. 'Skull told me I was cursed, but he'd made a promise to keep me close – so he couldn't abandon me, however much he wanted to.'

Cinderella Bull pulled her stool closer in. 'Maybe Skull did make a promise to keep you close, but if he did I'll bet it wasn't to the farmer, more likely to the other Shadowmasks. For some reason, Darkebite and Ashtongue don't want you near them.'

'They were afraid as soon as they saw Alfie,' Siddy said.

Moll crossed her arms. 'Couldn't you have run away from Skull? I've seen you pick locks and dig escape tunnels.'

Alfie shrugged. 'Tried to but it never worked. I was eight the first time I ran away – Skull's boys had just started the beatings. They said that if I was cracked inside anyway a few more punches and kicks wouldn't hurt me.' He looked away.

'That first time, Skull found me on the outskirts of the forest and I'll never forget what he said: *"You've been raised with a sickness inside you, a hole where most people's 'real' is, and, if you leave the forest, you'll cease to exist."* I didn't believe Skull, and a few weeks later I tried to run away again. Got as far as Tipplebury village, but – but—' His voice faltered. 'Skull was right. No one could *see* me outside the forest – not even the clothes I was wearing or the rucksack I carried. Anything that touched me, apart from people and animals, seemed to disappear. It was as if I didn't exist, as if I wasn't even real. But Skull could see me all right and he dragged me back to his camp.'

Hard-Times Bob's face was dark. 'My guess is that the

Shadowmasks performed a curse on you when you were a baby. What I can't work out is *why*. And why would it mean they're afraid of you now?'

Alfie turned to Moll. 'When I heard you and Skull talking about the amulets back when he kidnapped you, I thought maybe they could cure me – make me real. That's why I really wanted to help you at first ... But we don't have a bone reading to go on now and I'm not even sure finding the amulet will help; I just hoped it might after hearing what your pa said to us when we found the first one.'

He looked at the gypsies sitting round the fire. 'I'm sorry I left; I knew if I went to Inchgrundle you'd realise people can't see me and I couldn't face you all knowing the truth.'

Mooshie stood up and walked round the fire towards Alfie, then she knelt by his stool and put a hand on his knee. 'It doesn't matter whether passers-by and farmers in the fields can see you or not. What matters is that *we* see you – people who have grown to trust you and care for you. That's what truly makes you real.'

Siddy nodded. 'You're real to me, Alfie.'

Hard-Times Bob smiled and patted Cinderella Bull's back. 'And us.'

Moll caught Alfie's eye. This was her opportunity, her chance to let Alfie back in. She thought again of how she'd felt seeing his patteran in the sand the morning he'd run away – of the hurt and the anger that had stabbed inside her because Alfie hadn't trusted her enough to tell her the truth. But she'd missed him, up on the cliff tops with the owls and locked in the room at The Gloomy Tap with Siddy. The three of them were a Tribe now and it hadn't felt right without Alfie there. Moll thought of their friendship – scratched and broken as it was – but something about Alfie was worth fighting for and she summoned up the words she needed to patch things back together and forced them out over the pain.

'You're real to me too,' she said softly, her head bent low so that she didn't have to meet Alfie's eyes. 'And Gryff – and he *really* didn't like you at first.' She plucked at her blanket, then looked up at Alfie. 'Whatever the Shadowmasks may have done to you, I'm going to make it right again.'

Siddy smiled. 'We're in this together.'

Alfie dug his toes into the sand. 'Thank you.'

They stacked up the dirty bowls, then Moll wandered towards the Bone Murmur chalked on to the wall. She traced a finger along the words that were so familiar to her now that it felt as if they'd been breathed inside her since the day she was born. She thought of the last two amulets lying hidden beyond her grasp, one holding her ma's soul, the other belonging to an unknown soul, and felt a sudden yearning for her parents and for Oak. She needed their guidance as to what to do next now that their plans had come to nothing and they didn't even have a bone reading to go on.

She slumped against the cave wall. The old magic seemed to be crumbling all around her. Her heart heavy, she looked at the bone tablet lying on a ledge of rock.

Throwing a quick glance behind her to check Mooshie wasn't watching, Moll shoved the tablet to the ground and gave it a hard kick.

'That's for tricking us, Ashtongue,' she muttered, 'and for leaving us with no clue to find the next amulet.' Her palms were hot with anger now, but Moll was surprised to find herself feeling a tiny bit better. She gave the tablet another thump, then another and another, and the fury rushed through her. 'And that's for Oak's leg and Alfie's past.' She stopped, panting hard, then propped the bone tablet back on the ledge and turned round.

Siddy and Alfie were standing in front of her.

'What are you *doing*?' Siddy asked.

Moll flared her nostrils. 'Kicking the bone tablet.' She paused. 'Want a go?'

Siddy reached into his pocket. 'Hermit might.'

'Wait.' Alfie's eyes were growing big. 'Look! Look at the bone tablet now!'

Moll took her time turning round; even though she wanted things to be normal again, she was still guarded with Alfie, more wary after everything that had happened. Then curiosity got the better of her and she peered closer with Siddy.

Beneath the candlelight, the pictures that had seemed so clear were blurring before their eyes. Edges that had been clear-cut were now smudges of black, and, moments later, the whole tablet was just a surface of ash.

Moll picked it up. 'The message – it's – it's *gone*!' she

gasped. Alfie and Siddy leant in either side of her as she blew the ash away. Then she blinked in disbelief.

Symbols had been etched into the surface of the bone tablet:

'What is it?' Alfie asked.

Moll ran a finger over the grooves, then she grinned. 'Ashtongue's dark magic has gone!'

Siddy shifted. 'How do you know?'

Moll looked up at them both, her face glowing. 'Because I can read these symbols; this is Oracle Bone script.'

Chapter 16
Moll's Bone Reading

Moll whirled round the fire. 'Mooshie! It's my bone reading. My real reading!' Mooshie looked up from the pan she was cleaning and Moll held out the tablet. 'I kicked it. Twice. And then Ashtongue's code faded into nothing.'

'You *kicked* the bone tablet?' Mooshie cried shrilly.

Hard-Times Bob shuffled over to Moll. He peered at the tablet and clapped his hands. 'Well, I never! It's Oracle Bone script, sure enough!'

Cinderella Bull's eyes glittered. 'It's the old magic fighting back.'

Moll beamed. 'I kicked some sense into it.'

Cinderella Bull's smile vanished. 'Please don't talk about the old magic like that, Moll.'

But Moll was no longer listening. 'I need a few minutes on my own to work out what it means. I can't concentrate out here.' She hurried towards her alcove, Gryff pacing after her.

'Can me and Alfie come?' Siddy asked, grabbing Hermit from his stool.

Moll shook her head. 'I need to think hard for this. I have to be alone.' She dipped beneath the sheet pulled back from the entrance to her alcove and slipped inside. Fumbling for the matches she kept in a hollow in the rock, she lit the tea-light candles lining the walls just as Cinderella Bull had told her to do when they'd practised the ritual a few days before.

'*Magic works best under candlelight*,' the fortune-teller had said.

Moll dug her hand into the hollow again and drew out a leather pouch. She emptied the contents into her palm: curls of dried lemon peel and twelve acorns, one for each year she'd been alive. Then she arranged the protection charms in a circle round her hammock and looked at Gryff sitting beside her, his eyes wide and green.

'You can stay,' Moll smiled, stroking the soft white fur on his throat.

Gryff purred and slunk to the far corner of the alcove while Moll clambered into the hammock, crossed her legs and rested the bone tablet on her knees. She listened to the silence inside her alcove. This was her chance to prove to everyone that she was the Guardian of the Oracle Bones, that even though she had no family alive she was part of something ancient.

Minutes passed and Moll sat in silence, tracing the symbols with her finger, searching for the answers deep inside her. She tried not to think of all that rested on it, but when she closed her eyes she saw Alfie's desperate face and Oak lying in his hammock. Could the amulets really help them both?

She thought harder, willing the code to make sense. The candles flickered around her, the silence swelled and then her breathing quickened. She looked at Gryff. 'I've – I've done it, Gryff. I've translated the bone reading! I've actually done it!'

The wildcat made a noise, soft and wild, as if disclosing a precious secret. *Noine, noine, noine.* Moll smiled. It was the sound Gryff made when he was happy.

There were excited whispers coming from behind Moll's hanging sheet, then a mop of brown, curly hair poked itself inside. 'Well?' asked Siddy.

Moll watched as they all clustered by the entrance, her thoughts skittering inside her. She looked at Cinderella Bull. 'I've translated it, just how you taught me.'

'I *knew* you'd do it, Moll!' Hard-Times Bob cried. 'Oak would be proud of you right now.'

Cinderella Bull stepped forward. 'And? What did the bones say?'

Moll took a deep breath.

'They said: **FOLLOW THE SILENCE TO THE BLINKING EYE.**'

Chapter 17
Broken Charms

They rose early the next morning, everyone except Oak, who lay inside his hammock, his forehead gleaming with sweat. From the bags under Mooshie's eyes, it was obvious she hadn't slept, but still she mixed another dressing by the tunnel to draw the curse from her husband's wound.

Moll peeped round the sheet hanging over her alcove and watched curiously as Alfie helped Siddy fill a water bucket for the cobs. She hadn't expected Alfie to run away in the night – she felt sure he'd stay with them now – but she was still cautious and, although she knew deep down she'd do anything to make him real, a little part of Moll wanted Alfie to show her he'd never let her down like that again. She crept out of her alcove and walked across the cave towards the boys.

'Did you two come up with any ideas about the bone reading?' she asked.

'No,' Alfie said. 'Follow the silence . . . It just doesn't make sense. How can you *follow* nothing?'

Siddy nodded. 'And the blinking eye? What on earth are the bones harping on about?'

Moll chewed her lip. 'Maybe there's a message hidden inside the words. Like the last time?' She sighed. 'If only Mellantha was here to help us.'

'We're on our own with this one,' Alfie said flatly.

'Then we need to figure out a plan.' Moll lowered her voice. 'Last night, after I cracked the bone reading, Cinderella Bull told me she heard the sea spirits murmuring. She said they seemed afraid.'

'I'm not surprised with the Shadowmasks opening up thresholds left, right and centre and letting all kinds of dark magic in.' Siddy stood up. 'Come on; let's get some fresh air. We're safe in the cove with Cinderella Bull's protection pebbles on the cliff top. We can make a plan while we're watering the cobs.'

Outside the cave, Moll drank in the fresh, salty air. Fleecy clouds drifted across the sky and the morning sun cast a dazzle of light on to the sea. Gryff leapt up on to the rocks to prey on fish in the rock pools, but Moll walked towards the shore with Siddy and Alfie. She let the tide wash over her feet, pushing and pulling as the waves rolled.

Beyond the jutting rocks at the far side of the bay, a pod of dolphins arched out of the sea before spiralling down into their underwater world. Moll walked on. Any other day she would have raced across the beach, scampered over the rocks and leapt into the sea with them. But the bone reading was pressing in on her thoughts, the answer to it whirring just out of her reach.

They walked over the beach towards the cobs by the gorse, but, when Alfie laid his bucket at Raven's hooves, he tossed his head from side to side then whinnied. Alfie reached out a hand to still him, but the cob backed up and flicked his tail.

'What is it, boy?' Alfie whispered. He raised his hand and this time Raven let him stroke his mane, but his eyes were wide and wild.

Moll flinched. 'Something doesn't feel right; Raven's never jumpy like this.'

'Maybe he heard the sea spirits moaning, like Cinderella Bull,' Siddy said.

Jinx was further down the beach, but when Moll whistled she trotted over. Once more Raven backed up, away from the children, then he blew hard through his nostrils.

'Easy, boy, easy,' Alfie soothed.

Jinx took several loud slurps from the bucket in Moll's hand and Moll frowned as she stroked her neck. 'I could've sworn I took Jinx's halter off yesterday.' She shook her head, then, when Jinx had finished the water, she turned to Alfie and Siddy. 'I can't think straight in the cave; I'm going to ride out across the beach and see if the bone reading becomes any clearer.'

She swung herself up on to Jinx's back, dug her heels into the cob's flanks and, before Alfie or Siddy could reply, she was off. Moll let the wind course through her long dark hair and pummel inside her dress. But, as the sand sped past beneath them, she realised something was different about the way Jinx was moving. Moll knew her cob's movements by heart, but her strides seemed unfamiliar today and, however hard she tried, Moll couldn't settle into them. She leant forward and rubbed the white hair between Jinx's ears, the place where sensitive cobs keep their souls. And, as she did so, a coldness fastened round her chest. This cob looked like Jinx, but she knew the rhythms of Jinx's soul. And this cob wasn't Jinx.

She yanked at the halter, but the cob twisted its head free and galloped on. Moll made to leap from its back, but her body seemed welded to the cob's and she couldn't fling herself off. And then slowly the cob's appearance began to change. Its palomino coat dimmed to a dull grey, like dirty steel, and its glossy white mane stiffened into strands of rotted seaweed. The cob's nostrils flared, foam began to drip from its mouth and its coal-black eyes fixed on the sea at the far side of the cove, where the current was at its strongest. Moll's stomach lurched. This was the Shadowmasks' magic and she could feel their darkness closing in around her.

She struggled to free herself, but her body was still locked in place, just as it had been by Ashtongue in Inchgrundle. Her gut twisted as she remembered Cinderella Bull's words – about water spirits called kelpies who claimed the bodies of well-loved cobs to lure their riders into the sea and drown them. There was a way to stop kelpies – Cinderella Bull had told her – but, as the sea loomed closer, Moll's mind was a terrified blank. She snapped her head back, the only part of her free to move, and yelled to Siddy and Alfie back over the other side of the bay.

'Help me! It's not Jinx!'

Within seconds, Alfie was up on Raven, speeding across the sand, and behind him Gryff leapt down from the rocks.

But Moll could feel the kelpie's power growing. It thrashed through the shallows, driving Moll on to meet her fate, and as the water grew deeper it rampaged through the waves and plunged downwards, nosing its ghastly head beneath the surface and dragging Moll deeper towards the churning current.

She scrabbled with her arms, clawing at the surface with ragged breaths, but the kelpie pulled her under. Water gushed up Moll's nose and beat at her lips, but the more she struggled, the deeper the kelpie sank. Its seaweed hair moved in ghostly wisps and all the while its black eyes searched for darker waters.

Moll jabbed with her legs and bucked with her body, but the kelpie's hold was fast. Her eyes widened, blinking with panic. There was no breath left in her lungs; she was going to drown . . .

It was then that she glimpsed the dark shapes moving in a blur above her: four black cob legs shredding through the water towards them. Raven. And were those Alfie's legs dangling down, his head just above the water? Moll's heart leapt. In the next second, Alfie ducked beneath the surface and stretched out frantic arms towards Moll. She reached out with the last of her strength and their hands met, clasping tight. Moll felt the kelpie's hold weaken as Alfie hauled her upwards, then she broke through the surface, gasping in shuddering lungfuls of air.

'Grab my waist!' Alfie yelled.

Moll reached out, but the kelpie's strength swelled again and it smashed its weight against her, sending her spinning down into the sea. For a moment, the kelpie was gone from sight, then it rose from the depths beneath her, sliding under her body so that she was fixed once again on its back, and Moll understood: no amount of hauling would free her. She had to remember Cinderella Bull's secret to escape the kelpie.

Paws powered through the sea behind her, then Gryff was beside her, shunting his weight against hers, trying to shove her free. But the kelpie sank lower and the sea grew colder; the current was closing in. Gryff's claws beat faster towards Moll, then Alfie dived deep behind her. But, as the blood roared in her ears, Moll knew the kelpie was heading to a place the others could not follow.

The sea below her was dark and cold and still and Moll's eyes grew heavy. The others had vanished and Moll felt herself sinking with the kelpie as she gave in to its pull.

And then, out of the corner of her vision, there was a flash of colour: something red moving through the sea towards her. Moll's eyelids slid closed, then they flickered open for a second, long enough to see someone – something – reaching for the kelpie's halter.

A memory stirred inside Moll, and Cinderella Bull's words floated back to her: *You can only master a kelpie if you take off its bridle.*

There was a terrible moan, then the kelpie's whole body shuddered. Its mane flaked away, floating round Moll as dead seaweed, then its body shrivelled like haggard skin before dissolving completely into the sea. Moll felt herself hang for a second in the cool dark waters, then hands plucked at her, lifting her up, up, up . . .

Chapter 18
A Stranger in Little Hollows

○ ○

Moll felt the sand beneath her body – tiny, dry grains under her legs and back. Her head was raised, on someone's lap perhaps, but before she could open her eyes her breath was forced into spasms and she choked up mouthful after mouthful of stinging salt water.

A pair of ringed hands pushed her hair back from her face and pulled a blanket up round her shoulders. Moll's eyes fluttered open and rested on Mooshie's face, then she groaned as she spewed another mouthful of seawater on to the sand.

'It's all right, Moll,' Mooshie said. 'It's all right.'

'I – I thought it was Jinx and—'

'Shhhhh now.'

Moll's eyes flickered open again to see Gryff, Alfie and Siddy standing over her in front of the rocks at the far side of the bay. Gryff bent low and nosed her cheek.

'What happened?' Moll croaked.

Mooshie drew the blanket tighter round Moll. 'One of the cobs must have nudged Cinderella Bull's pebbles aside. The protection charm was broken when she went to inspect it a moment ago. My guess is that Darkebite conjured a kelpie from the Underworld which slipped inside.' She paused. 'The Shadowmasks must know you're back in the cove; they'll have hoped their kelpie could drag you to a place so deep only they could follow. But the kelpie failed and, although Cinderella Bull has renewed the protection pebbles, sooner or later the Shadowmasks will break in.'

'Is Jinx OK?' Moll asked.

Alfie nodded. 'We'll need to leave as soon as we can and work out the bone reading as we travel.'

'But how did I escape? Even you and Gryff couldn't haul me off that beast.'

Siddy and Alfie looked at one another, then they stepped aside to reveal a small child sitting with her arms crossed on a rock behind them. Moll blinked several times and struggled up so that she was leaning against Mooshie.

The girl was dark-skinned, no older than six or seven, but she was unlike any child Moll had ever seen. She wore a scrap of old red sail with a hole cut through it for her head, and a piece of matted blue sailor's top twisted up round her waist as a belt. Slung over her shoulder was a deflated lifebuoy and on one foot she wore an oversized leather boot. She looked more like washed-up flotsam than a girl, but what irked Moll most was her hair – a nest of dreadlocks dyed red with henna, tied back from her face with a piece of rope.

This was a smuggler's child. One of the Dreads.

'Her?' Moll whispered in disbelief. '*She* saved me?'

Mooshie nodded. 'Apparently so.'

The girl reached for a battered oar by her feet. She clasped it like a weapon, but her face was full of fear.

Moll dipped her head. 'Thank you.'

The girl backed up further, then jabbed the end of her oar into a rock pool and bared her teeth.

'It's OK,' Siddy whispered to the girl. 'We're not going to hurt you.'

Alfie turned to Moll. 'Don't make any sudden movements. She scares easily. Hasn't said a word since she brought you ashore.'

The girl jabbed her oar in Alfie's direction, then her eyes slid nervously from Moll to Siddy to Mooshie.

Siddy looked at Moll. 'She can't see Alfie, but she knows there's something strange going on. I think she can hear his voice. It's got her spooked.'

The girl edged down from the rocks and crept closer to them, brandishing her oar in front of her. She took a step towards where she thought Alfie should be, then stopped and shook her head.

'What's your name?' Moll asked her.

The girl opened her mouth, then tucked her head down and turned her back on them all.

Mooshie clutched Moll's arm. 'She's not afraid,' she explained. 'The poor child's mute; she hasn't got a tongue!'

'Hasn't got a tongue?' Moll shuddered. 'Do . . . do you think someone cut it out?'

Mooshie held a hand over her mouth. 'Who knows what happened. Poor lamb.'

The girl turned to face them again, her lips pursed tight, her oar beside her like a trusted friend. She jabbed a dirty thumb at her chest, then grabbed her sail tunic and shook it.

'She's trying to tell us who she is, I think,' Moll said slowly. 'Red, sail . . .'

The girl shook her head.

'Cotton?' Mooshie said.

'Sack?' Siddy suggested.

The girl rolled her eyes.

'Scrap?' Alfie said.

The girl stiffened suddenly, looked towards Alfie, but, not seeing him, kept searching. After a few seconds, she nodded.

'Scrap,' Moll repeated.

And, finally, the girl smiled.

Moll looked at the oar. 'Did you come here by boat from Bootleggers Bay?'

Scrap shook her head and mimed several swimming strokes.

'You swam all that way?'

Scrap nodded.

Moll looked the small girl up and down. 'And you carry the oar—'

Scrap shrugged.

'—just in case?'

Scrap nodded.

Moll smiled. 'I carry a catapult just in case too. And my pa's knife when things get really rough.'

Scrap looked at Gryff, then she tilted her head and smiled.

Gryff stared back, unsure what to make of her, then Scrap made a funny face and her smile broadened. Gryff's whiskers twitched and he narrowed his eyes.

Siddy crouched down in front of Scrap, his elbows resting on his knees. 'So you heard trouble in the water when you were swimming near our cove and came to help?'

Again Scrap nodded.

'Good job you did,' Moll said.

Siddy gasped suddenly and, when he spoke, his voice came in a rush of breath. 'Moll, the bone reading!' He gazed at Scrap. 'It said *follow the silence!*'

Everyone looked at Scrap and then, one by one, their eyes widened.

'Scrap – she's the silence?' Moll whispered.

Mooshie raised a hand to her mouth. 'This child looks like she's one of the Dreads. You think a smuggler like her can lead us to the amulet?'

Moll glanced up at Mooshie. 'There's only one way to find out.' She looked hard at the small girl. 'Scrap, do you know where something called the Blinking Eye is?'

For a while, Scrap said nothing, as if thinking, then she nodded twice.

Gryff stood up and slunk towards Scrap, his ears low to his head. But Scrap didn't move; she just watched as the wildcat stalked his circle round her. After a while, Gryff grunted and padded away – and Moll knew what that meant because the wildcat could read people like no one else.

'Scrap's telling the truth,' Moll said slowly. 'I know it

146

sounds crazy – I don't even understand it myself – but if Gryff believes Scrap then so do I. And, since we've got no other leads, I reckon she's our best bet at finding the Blinking Eye.'

Siddy looked at the little girl. 'Can you write the directions down for us?'

Scrap wrinkled up her nose.

Moll held on to Mooshie's arm and raised herself upright. 'Can you lead us there?'

Scrap nodded.

'But what about the Dreads? What about Grudge?' There was a tremor in Siddy's voice. 'He'll come after you, won't he?'

Scrap's jaw stiffened and only then did Moll notice the dark bruise stamped across her shin. 'I don't think Scrap was just swimming around. I reckon she was running away from Grudge and his gang.'

Scrap looked down as if she was afraid to agree.

Mooshie shook her head. 'But we can't promise her safety, not with the Shadowmasks out there waiting. And she's so young!'

Alfie shrugged. 'Maybe we can't promise Scrap safety and maybe she is too young.' He paused. 'But we can promise her friendship – just like you all did me – and maybe that's what she needs now she's come this far.' He looked at her. 'You've got to be pretty tough to escape Grudge.'

Scrap took a step closer to where Alfie's voice seemed to come from, not afraid this time. Just curious. Then she reached out her hand, feeling for something she couldn't quite understand.

Alfie watched as the little hand sought him out, just centimetres away. His cheeks reddened, suddenly aware of everyone watching, then he raised a tentative palm to Scrap's. She jumped as her fingers touched his.

Alfie gasped. 'You can *feel* me?' he whispered.

Scrap wrapped her hand round Alfie's fingers and nodded. And, for the first time since they'd returned to the cove, Moll saw that Alfie was smiling.

Chapter 19
Cinderella Bull's Spell

Scrap had entered the cave cautiously, but, after accepting that Mooshie wasn't trying to poison her, she had put down her oar and eaten some sugar kelp: crisped-up pieces of seaweed that Mooshie had coated in honey. Moments later, the gypsies had got to work: sharpening weapons, preparing food and packing blankets so that they could set off from the cave as soon as possible. From what they could gather from Scrap, the Blinking Eye was a two-day journey from Little Hollows.

Scrap sat beside Alfie on the slabs of rock lining the tunnel. And, while he tried his best to focus on sharpening the knives, Scrap kept poking and prodding and squeezing him, just to be sure that he was there. Alfie glanced behind him at the fire, embarrassed at the attention, but, seeing the others talking among themselves about the journey ahead, he told Scrap his story, as he knew it. Scrap didn't flinch at the mention of Shadowmasks and their dark magic – she didn't need to after seeing the kelpie; she just sat and listened, dangling her little legs in the cool waters of the tunnel and swinging them back and forth.

Alfie looked at her. 'We're not so different, you and me.'

Scrap scratched her dreadlocks and looked at her reflection in the water.

'People look right through both of us; they can't see me and they can't hear you.'

Scrap thought about it for several seconds, then nodded.

Alfie let his hand sift through the water. 'What happened? To your tongue?'

The child hunched her legs up to her chin and chewed on her red sail tunic. Alfie was silent for several minutes, then Scrap jabbed a finger towards the knives he'd been sharpening.

Alfie stiffened. 'Someone cut it out?'

Scrap bared her teeth for a second, then her shoulders sank and she nodded.

Alfie shook his head. 'There are bad people out there, Scrap.' He glanced at the little girl and noticed a tear trickling down her cheek. He looked away, uneasy for a moment, then he turned back to her. 'It's going to be OK; we won't make you go back to the smugglers if you don't want to. You can be one of us.'

Scrap shuffled closer towards Alfie's voice until she could feel his body next to hers. They sat like that for several minutes, watching the water lapping against the tunnel, and then Alfie turned back to sharpening his knives.

'I'll protect you, Scrap,' he said quietly.

At the other side of the cave, Moll and Hard-Times Bob

emerged from Oak's alcove; it was clear from their faces that Oak was no better. On seeing them, Scrap fiddled with her deflated lifebuoy, then blew gently on the whistle.

Alfie smiled. 'You could use that to communicate with us.'

Scrap stood up on the rocks and blew the whistle again, hard, so that her cheeks swelled like balloons.

Alfie tugged it from her mouth. 'Not so loud, Scrap!'

Mooshie covered her ears with her hands. 'We may as well dance a jig on the top of the cave and invite the Shadowmasks to tea!'

Scrap picked up her oar and advanced to the fire, shrill bursts sounding from her whistle every few seconds. Hermit scuttled over the cave floor in panic, knocked into a lobster pot, then froze in absolute terror. But, when Cinderella Bull put a finger to her lips, Scrap lowered the whistle and watched.

The aged fortune-teller walked silently over to the collection of glass bottles on the cave wall. She picked one up and hobbled towards the tunnel. The others followed her movements because they knew that whenever Cinderella Bull went to the tunnel, she meant magic.

'We need to get going,' Moll hissed. 'We don't have time for spells.'

Hard-Times Bob put a hand on Moll's arm. 'If you and the others are going to leave this cove unharmed, you'll need every ounce of magic that Cinderella Bull's got left inside her to keep you all safe. She's been working on this spell for some time now to prepare for this moment.'

They watched as Cinderella Bull knelt down on the

rocks. She pulled the gold-penny shawl over her head and whispered into the stillness, soft, swishing sounds that seemed to flitter over her tongue and slip into the cave. A moment later, she lowered the bottle into the sea. Moll heard the water glug inside it and watched as the fortune-teller set it on the rocks, then reached inside her pinafore pocket for several small items.

Mooshie leant close to Moll. 'A dolphin tooth to conjure speed, a fragment of rock to call protection close and a crab claw to summon strength.'

Siddy's face filled with dread and he shoved a hand beneath his stool. Breathing a sigh of relief, he brought Hermit up on to his lap; all of his useless claws were intact.

Cinderella Bull tipped each of the objects into the glass bottle, then turned a wrinkled face back to the fire. 'Moll, I'll need you for this.'

Mooshie got up suddenly and hugged Moll tight, then she drew back and sat by the fire. Moll was used to Mooshie's embraces, but something about that one made her feel uneasy; what exactly would Cinderella Bull's spell involve?

Moll made her way towards the tunnel and Gryff stalked after her from their alcove.

'Come close, child,' Cinderella Bull instructed.

Moll sat cross-legged beside the fortune-teller and Gryff tucked himself into the shadows a few metres away. Moll eyed the bottle of seawater nervously. The stone had sunk to the bottom, but the crab claw and dolphin tooth floated on the surface. 'Do I have to drink it?' She fiddled with her jumper cuff. 'It's just I'd rather not if that's OK by you; I swallowed a fair bit of water this morning when the kelpie came after me.'

Cinderella Bull smiled. 'Not drink it, no. We'll use it in another way – to help you pass freely from the cove.' She said, 'Let your legs dangle in the water.'

Moll did as she was told and the cool water folded round her shins.

Cinderella Bull picked up the bottle and handed it to Moll, then she placed a wrinkled hand on her shoulder. 'When the next sunbeam shines into the cracks in the cave roof, hold the bottle up high.'

Moll waited and waited and then, just when she thought it would never come, a sunbeam shone down, its light so gold it was almost white. It showered on to the bottle like rain and, as it did so, Cinderella Bull began to speak, her voice low and gusting, like a gathering wind.

'Spirits of the sea, I call you near.
Your magic I seek for this gypsy child here.
She has a journey ahead, full of danger and peril.
And I ask for your help—'

She paused and peered at Moll out of the corner of her eye.

'—though the girl is feral.
Lend her the gift that will help her to pass
Safe from this cove. Lend her soles of glass.'

153

Moll turned an appalled face to Cinderella Bull. 'Soles of glass?'

But Cinderella Bull had closed her eyes and was sitting very, very still. Moll watched with her arm stretched out, and then a strange thing started to happen. Instead of glistening against the bottle, the sunbeam was swirling round the lip of it. Gryff raised his head and Moll gasped, feeling a gush of cold air rippling over her fingers, then she watched, open-mouthed, as the sunbeam slipped inside the bottle, mixing with the seawater. Moll blinked. The tooth, claw and stone had vanished.

'Bring the bottle down,' Cinderella Bull said quietly.

The water stilled inside it, now a glittering gold. Gryff moved closer until he was just a metre from Moll.

'Keep your feet in the water and pour the liquid over them until just a small amount remains in the bottle.'

Moll leant forward and did as Cinderella Bull said. The liquid hit the water, but, instead of sinking or dissolving, it hung round her feet like flecks of floating gold. And out of the corner of her eye, where the tunnel wound out to sea, Moll glimpsed something else – something scaled and shimmering beneath the surface. She peered closer, her heart thumping, as a purple tail swished like silk through the shadowy waters.

'What – what is it?' Moll's voice was little more than a whisper and she felt a sudden urge to yank her feet out of the water, but Cinderella Bull placed a hand on her shoulder.

'Keep still, child. A sea spirit has heard my call.'

Moll watched, hardly breathing, as a creature covered in

purple scales swam slowly beneath the water towards her. It stilled, as if suspended below her feet, and Moll saw that its entire body was scaled, even the hands and face. Thick black eyelashes curled round its eyes, its lips were emerald green and long strands of black hair swayed with the current. Moll's eyes widened as the sea spirit reached out two scaled hands and began swishing its fingers through the gold flecks around Moll's feet. The gold seemed to bend and move, as if it was firmer than liquid, and a moment later Moll noticed the sea spirit was holding two gold shapes – long, transparent and thin – and they were moving slightly, as if they had a life of their own.

'What are they?' Moll asked.

But Cinderella Bull said nothing. She simply watched as the sea spirit slipped the shapes beneath Moll's feet. Moll jumped as they touched her skin; they tickled her toes and sent tremors up and down her arches. But the sea spirit held them there and, after a while, the shapes settled beneath Moll's feet. And then the creature sank deeper into the water and, with one flick of its satin tail, it disappeared down the tunnel and the water fell dark and still once more.

Moll breathed again. It was hard to believe that what she'd seen had been real.

Cinderella Bull smiled. 'Our world is full of magic, Moll.' She nodded towards the bottle in her hands. 'Gryff needs to drink the rest of the liquid. It'll keep him safe from the Shadowmasks too.'

Moll moved closer to the wildcat and looked at his

yellow-green eyes glowing in the darkness. Tipping the last few drops from the bottle into her palm, she held it out to him. Gryff twitched his nose above the gold water, then his whiskers bristled and for a while he just stood there, not moving, not trusting. But, when Cinderella Bull looked away, Gryff dipped his head and slowly licked the mysterious liquid from Moll's palm.

'Now bring your feet up,' Cinderella Bull said.

As Moll did so, she gasped. 'The soles of my feet! They're – they're gold!'

One by one, the others left the fire and gathered round the tunnel.

'What did you see?' Siddy whispered. 'There was magic in the tunnel, wasn't there? We could all feel it!'

Moll's eyes sparkled. 'I saw a sea spirit – right here in our cove.' Siddy's jaw dropped, Alfie raised a hand to his mouth and Scrap shrank further inside her sail tunic. Moll rolled her ankles over and stared at her soles; they were so gold they looked as if they'd been painted with sunlight.

Mooshie helped Cinderella Bull to her feet. 'You did it,' she said.

Cinderella Bull smiled weakly, as if performing the spell had drained not only her magic but a little part of her life too. She leant against Mooshie for support. 'I did. Though it won't be nice for Moll . . .' She tightened the shawl round her shoulders. 'When you leave this cove, Moll, your soles will protect you – provided you go barefoot. They will enable you to pass from here unseen by the Shadowmasks, and the same magic that surrounds you will keep Gryff safe too. The Shadowmasks might see Siddy, Alfie and Scrap, but without you and Gryff they won't bother coming close – it's not them they're after. It'll be slower progress than on cobs – but until the moon comes up you'll be safe, so you'll need to get as far away from here as you can in that time.'

Moll looked from Cinderella Bull to Mooshie who were both avoiding her eyes. 'There's something else – a catch, isn't there? What are you not telling me?'

Cinderella Bull twisted her rings. 'The soles will provide safety, but their magic comes at a cost. When you set foot outside my protection charms in the cove, it will feel as if you're stepping on glass.' She fiddled with her shawl. 'I called upon the sea spirits for the only safe passage spell I knew – but it called for soles not paws – and it will mean that you have to carry the pain, Moll.' The fortune-teller looked away. 'It was the only way I knew to get you and Gryff safely from Little Hollows. I'm sorry.'

Moll turned her foot over and bit her lip. 'Like running *on glass*?'

Cinderella Bull nodded. 'I wish there was another way.'

Gryff blinked at Moll, then he nudged her feet over and licked her soles.

Alfie tried to object. 'We can't do this. It'll be agony for Moll!'

Moll took a deep breath, then, holding Gryff close to her, she looked Alfie in the eye. 'Maybe. But it'll get us closer to

157

the amulet and helping Oak.' She paused. 'And to the truth behind your past.'

Alfie's face twisted. 'But—'

Moll shook her head. Since Alfie had ridden Raven into the sea after her, she had felt the distance between them shrink a little. 'You helped me with the kelpie earlier. And I said I'd make you real – so that's what I'm going to do.'

Chapter 20
Soles of Glass

Fingers wrapped tight round the catapult Hard-Times Bob had carved for her, Moll crouched inside the hollow dish of rock above the cave with Gryff, Alfie, Siddy and Scrap. Further along the coastline, beyond Little Hollows, the sea swirled inside inlets and broke against rocks and the afternoon sun lay hidden behind clouds. There was no sign of Ashtongue or Darkebite and her owls, but, as Moll glanced down at the smuggler child beside her, almost swamped by the duffle coat she had borrowed, her heart filled with doubt. Could she really lead them to the Blinking Eye?

'You're sure we should follow the rocks round the coast rather than taking the cliff path?' Moll whispered.

Scrap nodded.

'And you're absolutely certain the Dreads won't be in Bootleggers Bay?' Alfie asked. 'They'll still be selling their goods inland?'

Scrap sighed impatiently and nodded again.

For a second, Moll craned her neck back to where Mooshie, Cinderella Bull and Hard-Times Bob were huddled down on the beach. She knew they couldn't follow – Mooshie needed to look after Oak, and the fortune-teller and her brother were too old for a journey like this – but, despite all that, Moll couldn't help wishing they were all up on the rocks together.

Siddy lifted Hermit from his pocket and cradled the crab close.

Moll took a deep breath. 'I suppose however scared we feel we'll know Hermit's probably feeling a hundred times worse.'

Scrap crept out of the dish first, stepping carefully over the line of pebbles Cinderella Bull had arranged to keep them safe. Alfie followed, then, hardly daring to breathe, Moll, Gryff and Siddy did the same.

Almost at once the air stirred. A wind seemed to come from nowhere, curling round the group, whipping bigger, darker clouds over the sun, and Moll stood absolutely still, transfixed by fear. Gryff growled. But the sea spirit's spell held the darkness at bay, and moments later the clouds slid back and the wind grew quieter.

Moll squeezed up her toes and shuddered. Soles of glass, and she'd have to endure them until the moon rose. A seagull called above them and Moll jumped and felt for Gryff, then she set off over the rocks after the others. She winced, waiting for the pain to sear through her feet – but it never came. Her soles felt tender, as if she might be walking over newly-cut gravel instead of smooth rocks, but this was a pain Moll could bear. Darting catlike from rock to rock, she leapt over crevices and scrambled up crags.

She slid a glance to Gryff and, to her surprise, he shied

away from her, leaping towards the cliff face. He carried on running and Moll frowned. Ever since the Shadowmasks had started coming for her, Gryff had run by her side, always alert for danger. But today something was different. He had deliberately moved away.

Alfie paused on a rock to tighten the straps of the rucksack that held the blankets and extra food. He looked back at Moll. 'Are your feet all right?'

Moll nodded. 'They're nothing like as bad as Mooshie and Cinderella Bull said they'd be.'

Siddy hoisted himself up on to a boulder. 'Maybe they were just being overprotective.'

The coastline was getting wilder now and the rocks fell away sharply to their right, dropping down to waves that sucked and smashed far below. The children edged closer to the cliff face and Moll felt the barnacles and limpets digging into her soles. But they were speeding away from Little Hollows now – every step bringing them closer to the Blinking Eye.

Only Gryff seemed to linger, his pace slower suddenly, his strides jerky and unnatural. Siddy raised an eyebrow at Moll – he could tell something was up – but they were rounding the headland now and there was Bootleggers Bay, the beach strewn with junk and barrels and lined with driftwood shacks below the cliffs. Scrap stopped, biting down on her sail tunic, and they hunkered down together before passing a flask of water around. The sun was lower in the sky now, half masked by a haze of cloud, and, although

161

there was no activity in the bay, the gorse spreading down the cliff was dead, an unsettling sign that the Shadowmasks had been here too.

Gryff hung back from the group still and, though Moll called out to him, he refused to come any closer. Moll glanced from Scrap to Alfie and Siddy. No one said anything, but it was obvious what the Tribe were thinking. Was Scrap someone they could trust? Was she leading them to the Blinking Eye or straight into the hands of the Dreads? And then, to their surprise, Scrap began lowering herself over the edge of the rocks. The sea swelled and crashed some ten metres below.

'Scrap, be careful!' Moll hissed.

They peered over the edge of the rocks to see the smuggler child perched on a ledge overhanging the sea.

'What are you doing?' Siddy moaned. 'Hermit and I are *not* following you out there.'

But Scrap was pointing at something below, her eyes wide and pleading.

Moll moved closer so that she could see more clearly and there, knocking against the rocks, were two double-seated kayaks. They had been tied to a rock with rope and inside were four paddles.

'They're kayaks,' Alfie said. 'They must belong to the Dreads.'

Siddy clutched at his hair. 'No. Absolutely no. We are *not* going in kayaks. We don't even know if they're watertight.'

Alfie looked at Moll. 'It'll be easier on your feet and it's the only way on, isn't it? These cliffs are too steep to scale now.'

Moll nodded. 'We need to keep moving, Sid; we've only got until the moon rises before I lose the gold soles.'

Siddy screwed up his face. 'How are we even going to get down to the kayaks?'

A whistle sounded from the ledge and they peered over to see Scrap edging towards the lip.

'Get back, Scrap!' Siddy yelled.

The smuggler child grinned, then, without warning, she hurled herself off the rock. The others gasped. Seconds later, a mop of dreadlocked hair popped up from the sea and Scrap hauled herself and her drenched clothes on to the rocks beside the kayaks.

'Come on,' Alfie said, and before Siddy could stop him he reached out a hand, shot it inside Siddy's pocket, yanked Hermit out and lowered himself on to the ledge.

'You've – you've kidnapped Hermit!' Siddy spluttered.

Alfie nodded, creeping further across the platform of rock. 'Because that's the only way I'm going to get you off this ledge, Sid!' He leapt from the rock into the sea and Siddy found himself scrambling down on to the platform, legging it across the ledge and charging head first after his beloved crab.

He bobbed up, red-faced, and dragged himself up on to the rocks. Hermit lay upturned in Alfie's palm and Siddy snatched him back. 'You made him faint,' he muttered. 'And you soaked our rucksack.'

Scrap giggled as she wrung out her coat and Moll climbed back over the rocks towards Gryff. She bent down opposite him and the wildcat did something he had never done to her before. He bared his teeth and hissed before lashing out with his paw. Moll jerked away, just missing the blow, then she watched, stunned, as Gryff turned his back on her. Moll's skin prickled with unease. Although the others were cautious around Gryff, she'd never felt afraid. Until now . . . Why was he acting so oddly? Did he sense that this was a trap? That Scrap wasn't someone they could trust? But what other option did they have?

Moll edged away from the wildcat, back towards the cliff edge. Clutching her catapult so that she didn't lose it on jumping, she lowered herself on to the ledge and peered down. The waves loomed beneath her and Moll felt her body sway, then she thought of the amulet and of Oak lying wounded in the cave and she scrunched up her fists and leapt. Her stomach swung into her mouth as she tumbled through the air before crashing down into the sea. She surfaced, breathless and cold, then swam towards the rocks and pulled herself up.

They untied the kayaks and Moll tucked herself into the smaller one behind Scrap while Siddy begrudgingly manoeuvred himself and Hermit into the larger kayak with Alfie. They pushed out from the rocks, wobbling and yelping as they adjusted their balance to the rhythm of the boats. But Gryff remained ashore, his back turned, his head hung low.

Moll called out to him. 'Come on, Gryff! You've got to follow us!' He growled and stayed where he was and Moll glanced at the boys. 'I'm worried. Gryff just lashed out at me and he's never done that before. What if he's acting strange because he's suspicious.' She paused, not daring to catch Scrap's eye – but the others knew what she was thinking. And so did Scrap.

The smuggler child twisted round to face Moll and smacked her paddle against the water, her eyes filling with tears.

'Gryff seemed OK with Scrap back in the cove, didn't he?' Alfie said.

Scrap nodded, blinking back her tears.

Alfie dug his paddle into the sea and moved his kayak closer to Scrap's. 'We don't think you're spying for the Dreads, Scrap. It's OK.' She reached out a hand to find him and Alfie held up his palm until their fingers met. 'We trust you to get us to the Blinking Eye.' He looked up at the wildcat on the rocks. 'Gryff's never liked the sea, Moll – perhaps it's that. He'll follow if we keep moving.'

But Moll knew it was more than that and, as the group got into a rhythm with their kayaks, she kept casting anxious looks behind her.

They were halfway across Bootleggers Bay when Moll started shouting. 'Yes, Gryff! Keep going!'

The others turned to see Gryff out on the ledge, ducked low in a crouch. He sprang into the sea and they all cheered as the wildcat swam towards them, on and on through the rolling waves. After a while, he heaved his weight up on to the end of Moll's kayak, but to her dismay he didn't face the girls. He curled up into a ball, his head turned out to sea, and watched the waves ripple in the early evening light.

They paddled on – past Bootleggers Bay and the fields

stretching over the cliff tops. Moll swallowed. The day before, the pastures had been bursting with life, but, even at a distance, she could see that now the grass was charred and the stubble fields blackened. It seemed the Shadowmasks had trailed her and Gryff from Inchgrundle the night before, leaving a path of darkness in their wake. The villagers would notice, surely, and it would be the gypsies who took the blame for cursing their land.

They kept paddling, leaving Inchgrundle and the trickle of cottages dotted along the coast beyond the village well behind them, until their stomach muscles ached and their palms grew blistered from the paddles. But they were making quicker work of the journey than they would have been up on the cliff path, and they'd stayed clear of the village and the Dreads.

A seal head popped up beyond their kayaks, then slunk away, leaving froth rocking on the surface, and in the distance a boat passed them, its sail fluttering in the wind. Siddy and Alfie chatted between strokes about what the Blinking Eye could be and, as Moll and Scrap eased their kayak on, Moll tried her best not to think about Gryff's strange behaviour or the setting sun and how soon they'd be on their own against the Shadowmasks.

Eventually the land ahead veered into the sea, a giant headland jutting out for miles.

'It's going to take ages to round that,' Siddy groaned.

Scrap lifted her paddle and pointed inland to a small cove with a pebble beach. A fisherman was hauling up a net nearby, but he seemed uninterested by the kayaks and the cove looked deserted. They paddled towards it, letting the kayaks grind ashore over the rocks, and clambered out. Moll turned to Gryff, but he had already slipped from the kayak and was waiting, half hidden in the dunes beyond the pebbles.

A dull ache throbbed in Moll's soles as she followed Scrap and the others up over the rocks and into the dunes. The gorse here was lush and full of flowers and Moll felt a surge of relief to be somewhere the Shadowmasks hadn't been. They picked up speed, following Scrap on to a sandy track that cut through the headland they'd have spent hours rounding in the kayaks. The path ran through stubble fields full of bales, and before long hedgerows brimming with blackberries, cow parsley and rosehips shielded them on either side. Moll let her feet sink into the softer grass in the middle of the path and, some way behind them all, Gryff followed. They ran on and on and then Scrap stopped suddenly before a large elm bursting out of the hedgerow. She was red in the face and panting hard, just like the others.

Alfie wiped the sweat from his brow. 'You're right, Scrap. We need to rest for a while. But somewhere out of sight – we can't risk being seen.'

Scrap ducked down and began twisting her way into the knotted hedgerow. Then her whistle sounded, muffled somewhat, and Alfie edged beneath a prickled branch before he too disappeared from sight.

Siddy groaned. 'Gobbled by Shadowmasks before sunset . . . Just our luck.'

Moll waited for Gryff to catch them up, but he hung his

head low, deliberately avoiding her eyes. Did he feel guilty for having struck out at her earlier? Moll wondered. And then she felt suddenly cross. It was *her* feet that were aching, not Gryff's. Surely she was the one with the right to be irritable. What was wrong with him?

Moll gave up thinking about it and bent down beneath the brambles. They snagged on her coat, but she pushed them back, weaving further inside. And then she saw what Scrap must have known was there: a gap in the bark of the elm tree, almost a metre high and just wide enough to slip through. She and Siddy squeezed themselves inside.

The elm was hollow and its bark stretched upwards in gnarled scoops and curves. A sliver of light spilled in through the crack, but otherwise it was dark. Moll sat back against the bark and smiled.

'Well done, Scrap,' Siddy whispered. 'We'll be all right resting in here. You did good with those kayaks – even Hermit will admit that.'

'How did you know about this place?' Alfie asked. Scrap dipped her head and pretended she hadn't heard. 'Did you run away here once?' he said quietly.

Scrap nodded but still she didn't look up.

Alfie shuffled nearer to her. 'Did ... did Grudge cut out your tongue? For running away?'

Scrap looked at her feet and twisted her old sail tunic beneath her coat.

'Here, Scrap, have this.' Siddy handed her a sea-kelp muffin, the least damp item of food from their rucksack.

168

Scrap took it and nibbled the corner.

Moll turned her feet over in her hands. They were still gold from Cinderella Bull's spell, her skin only etched with a few scrapes and scratches – nothing like she'd been expecting.

A twig snapped. Gryff was somewhere close by.

Moll craned her head out of the crack in the elm. 'Gryff? Come inside,' she urged. 'It's safer in here.'

She listened for his near-silent steps. They padded closer, then the wildcat came into view. Gryff stood before the entrance, his ears sunk low to his head, his eyes half closed and glassy. He lifted a paw, tried to take one more step inside the tree, then slumped to the ground.

Moll was out of the elm like a shot, kneeling in the brambles beside him. Gryff hadn't been irritable before; he had been *in pain*. She could tell that now. She ran a hand over his body, but it was only when she turned over his paws that she understood.

The skin between his white-grey fur had been sliced to shreds and blood was oozing through the cuts.

Moll felt suddenly sick inside. 'You . . .' She gasped as she thought of the strange way Gryff had been running. 'When you licked my feet back in the cove, somehow you – you took the pain I was meant to bear. You've been carrying it all the way here, walking on soles of glass!'

Chapter 21
Marsh Spirits

Moll hauled Gryff inside the elm and this time he didn't have the strength to hiss her away. He lay on his side, his eyes closed, whimpering.

Moll swallowed back the tears. 'All that time I was telling him to keep going and getting annoyed at him for acting strangely ...' She ran a hand down the wildcat's back; his breathing was slow and shallow. 'But he was running on glass!'

Moll used some water from the flask to wet a handkerchief, then she dabbed Gryff's paws, carefully cleaning the blood from his wounds. She sat back and bit her lip. 'We need to help him! It's not enough just cleaning his paws!'

Suddenly remembering, Alfie rummaged in his rucksack and drew out the small tub of ointment Mooshie had made for them in case of emergencies: hedgehog fat which the gypsies believed contained a precious healing oil, melted with ribwort leaves to draw out infection. He handed it to Moll and she smeared it over Gryff's paws. But still the blood oozed and he lay, whining.

Siddy clutched Moll's arm. 'That plant Mooshie used to pick from the hedgerows beyond the forest – the one she said could stop bleeding and heal even the deepest cut – what was it?'

Moll thought fast. 'Woundwort. But she used the last on Oak's leg; we don't have any in our supplies.'

'There are hedgerows here,' Siddy said. 'If we find some of the right leaves, we can press them into the ointment and, together with the hedgehog oil, it might just work.' He looked at Moll. 'I'll need your help though; you've always been better at spotting herbs than me.'

Moll held Gryff's paw inside her handkerchief. 'I can't leave him, Sid. Not like this.'

'If you don't go, Gryff will get worse,' Alfie said. 'I'd go with Sid if I knew what I was looking for. You *have* to go, Moll. Scrap and I will stay here with Gryff.'

Moll nuzzled her head against the wildcat, then pulled herself away. She swallowed. 'He won't let you touch him – no matter how much pain he's in – but he'll know you're here. Tell him it's going to be OK.'

She crept out of the elm after Siddy and they pushed their way through the undergrowth until they emerged on the path. Moll's eyes darted frantically up and down the hedgerow. The sun was setting and the darkness huddled closer – it wouldn't be long before the moon was up.

'Where do we look?' Moll spluttered. 'It might not even be here!'

Siddy stood in front of her. 'You've got to stay calm, Moll.

Describe woundwort to me so I'm sure I'm looking for the right thing.'

Moll tried to force the image of Gryff's paws from her mind and summon a clear picture. 'Tall green stalks and at the top of the plant there are purple flowers with white-flecked centres.'

'And dark green leaves – the ones that are toothed, right?'

Moll nodded. 'Like nettle leaves only they don't sting.'

'Right. You take the left hedgerow, I'll take the right.'

Moll began slowly, scouring every bit of greenery: cow parsley, brome, blackthorn, brambles, dock leaves, nettles, chickweed.

'There's none here!' she cried after a few minutes. 'It's hopeless.'

'Keep looking,' Siddy said. 'Gryff wouldn't ever give up on us. We've got to help him now.'

Moll picked up speed, her eyes scanning the plants, grasses, bushes and flowers with eagle-eyed precision. The back of her neck tingled with sweat and a sense of helplessness worked its way up her fingers and into her body. What if woundwort didn't grow in this part of the country? What if they had to go back to Gryff empty-handed? Then her eyes caught on a single stem at the foot of the hedge – and her heart leapt.

'There!' she gasped, rushing forward and snapping up the plant. 'Woundwort!'

Seconds later, they were racing back to the elm together, charging through the hedgerow and spilling into the hollow tree. Gryff was where they'd left him and Alfie and Scrap looked on with anxious eyes.

'Moll found it,' Siddy panted. 'I knew she would.'

But Moll could barely hear the others talking. She ripped the leaves from the stem and pressed them into Mooshie's ointment. Then she smeared some on to her finger and smoothed it on to one of Gryff's front paws. She did so tenderly, as if she was holding his hand, and his eyes flickered open then closed again.

Alfie leant closer. 'I think it's helping. Keep going, Moll.'

As carefully as she could, Moll rubbed the ointment on to Gryff's paws. When she reached the last paw, she held it gently and curled up opposite the wildcat, blinking large, frightened eyes.

Then they waited.

Minutes passed. Nobody spoke. And still the wildcat lay with his eyes closed.

'It's not working,' Moll whispered, her voice breaking.

'Look,' Alfie cried.

Gryff's chest began to rise and fall in deeper, stronger breaths and each one filled Moll's heart with hope. Then the wildcat's eyes struggled open. But it was Scrap who noticed his paws. In a flurry of excitement, she sat bolt upright, blew on her whistle, tugged Moll's arm, then, finally, pointed to them.

Moll raised a hand to her mouth. The cuts on Gryff's paws were shrinking to slits and the blood had completely disappeared. A second later, the wounds were nothing more than a few scratches and then they vanished completely.

Moll's heart felt ready to burst. 'Oh, Gryff!'

The wildcat picked himself up so that he was sitting, then he looked Moll straight in the eye and dipped his head.

Moll wrapped her arms round him. 'Sometimes I don't think I really deserve a friend like you.' She closed her eyes and felt her thoughts weave in and out of his. 'You've never let me down, Gryff. Thank you.' She looked up after a while and turned to Siddy. 'I couldn't have found the woundwort without you, Sid. You kept a cool head when I was panicking.'

Siddy grinned. 'When you're friends with dangerous people, you learn to keep a cool head.'

'I'm not dangerous,' Moll retorted.

Alfie squinted at her. 'Yes, you are. Spending time with you is like hanging out with a volcano.'

Scrap snorted.

'Don't worry, Moll,' Siddy said. 'It was actually quite nice to be telling someone other than Hermit to calm down – makes a change.'

They shared out the sea-kelp crisps and dandelion-and-burdock cordial Mooshie had packed for them and then, after a bit, Alfie said quietly, 'We'll need to get going again. If Gryff's able to.'

Moll buried her head in Gryff's fur. 'You don't have to carry my pain any more. I can do it; I can run on soles of glass.' But Moll knew deep down that they didn't have a choice. Magic wasn't something you could bend and twist to suit yourself.

Gryff growled into the elm, then he stalked towards the

174

crack opening up into the undergrowth. And everyone knew what that meant: Gryff was ready to run.

They crouched inside the hedgerow and listened to the wind whistling through the branches of the elm. Moll shuddered beneath the dusk light as she remembered Cinderella Bull's words: . . . *until the moon comes up you'll be safe, so you'll need to get as far away from here as you can in that time.*

Scrap pushed through the hedgerow, out on to the path, and set off at a run. The others followed and Moll winced – not at the aching in her own feet, but because of the pain she knew Gryff must be suffering. She paused several times, bending down and trying to scoop the wildcat up to carry him. But he was too large and he always shook her off with a determined growl and the only thing Moll had to comfort her thoughts was the knowledge that they still had some of the ointment for him.

The path wound on, further down the coast, past a beech tree riddled with rook nests. The birds tore off into the sky as the children approached, then all was still again. But, as they ran on, Moll's blood quickened. The moon would be riding high soon and then the spell would wear off and the Shadowmasks would be on to them.

Eventually the hedgerows petered out altogether and in their place was a small copse of trees. Gryff limped level with Moll and she pulled the ointment from the rucksack and smoothed it over his paws. He breathed deeply as once again the balm of the oil and the strength of the herbs entered his skin. Scrap blew her whistle gently and Moll and Gryff hastened on towards the others. They had paused by the edge of the trees because, spread out before them, was a sprawl of reeds, rushes and bogs.

'Looks like a marsh,' Alfie whispered.

Siddy exhaled. 'Oh, great. Hermit and I can't wait to cross it.'

Scrap pointed out over the boggy land. A mile or so away there was a large dark shape: a forest.

Moll felt a familiar yearning for the cover of old, knotted trees. She nodded. 'We need to get to the forest before the moon's up – at least it'll give us somewhere to hide.'

Alfie set off first, feeling a way into the reeds, then the others followed. After only a few steps, the reeds grew taller, pinging against their waists as they trod a path through. The ground beneath their feet was soggy, the marsh full of unfamiliar noises, and Moll stiffened as the weeds oozed through the gaps between her toes and folded over her ankles. But the water was cool, soothing her feet; she only hoped it was doing the same for Gryff.

Alfie stopped before a patch of water. The wind skirted across its surface, shaking the sedge and bog-myrtle bushes around it, and Moll could just make out the weeds stretching up from the bottom of the bog, swaying slowly. She took a deep breath and slipped a foot into the water after Alfie.

She hadn't gone more than a few strides before she felt it: a cold, bony hand closing round her ankle.

Chapter 22
Snatched

Moll shrieked, her eyes filling with horror.

Alfie whirled round. 'What is it?'

'In the water!' Siddy cried, leaping backwards.

Beneath the surface was the unmistakable image of a face. But it didn't belong to a person; it was more like the ghost of one. The skin was pale, an almost translucent green, the cheeks sunken hollows. It stared up at them with wild, veiny eyes, its mouth open in a silent scream.

Alfie was by Moll's side in a second. 'Run!' he screamed, yanking her arm.

He pulled her free and they charged on through the marsh, water splashing up and drenching their faces, reeds snagging at their pounding feet. But whatever had seized Moll's ankle wasn't giving up. From behind them came a moan, threading through the reeds, and then a pattering, like footsteps skimming the surface of water.

'Faster!' Siddy roared, clutching Scrap's hands and dragging her on behind Moll and Alfie.

But the creature was drawing closer and Siddy could feel

177

its rotted breath drumming at the back of his neck. Scrap's body was rigid with fear, but the creature, a hunched wisp of bones and sagging green flesh, sped right past them. It reached out long, gaunt fingers towards Moll and Gryff.

Alfie seized his knife and turned to face it. But, when he jabbed at the ghost-like shape, his blade passed right through it. The creature raced on, its feet flicking the surface of the water, then it lunged for Moll, wrapping skeletal arms round her ankles.

Moll crashed to the ground and, as her stomach smacked the water, air punched from her lungs and mud spattered over her coat. Gryff launched himself against the creature, but it made no difference. It was hungry for something and, though Alfie, Siddy and Scrap were hurtling towards it, the glint in the creature's eye made Moll feel almost certain it was going to get what it came for.

Sharp nails plucked at her feet.

'My soles!' Moll gasped, grabbing at reeds with frantic arms. 'It's – it's after my soles!'

She twisted her feet against the creature's pull, but it only smiled darkly, its mouth a cavern of jagged teeth. Then it lowered its jaw to Moll's feet and tugged at the gold soles Cinderella Bull had worked so hard to conjure. A ripping sound tore through the marsh and Moll's head jerked in pain.

Then the creature drew back, cradling the soles in its bony hands. 'Shadowmasks' dark magic grows stronger.' The words came in a gurgled spew, as if the creature's throat was choked by mud and water. 'Creatures like me claw through thresholds to find you; protection spells won't hold darkness back . . .'

Moll scrambled backwards, grasping at the reeds to help her, but, as Alfie, Siddy, Scrap and Gryff gathered close, the creature dropped to its knees, melted into the water and was gone.

Moll was breathing fast, her heart fluttering inside her. For a while, she said nothing at all, then she wiped the mud from her face and turned her feet over; her soles were pink and ordinary again. 'I don't know *what* that was but it took my soles. We're on our own now; there's nothing left to protect us.' Shaking the water from her coat, she glanced at Gryff who was stamping on the reeds and snarling at the place where the creature had disappeared. Moll sighed. 'At least Gryff's not in pain any more.'

Alfie rummaged in his rucksack for Moll's boots, then he gazed around the marshland. 'The Shadowmasks could be anywhere; that creature might tell them where we are.' A snipe cried overhead, startled by the commotion on the marsh. 'We need to take cover in the forest.'

Cautious now, they hastened towards the trees behind Scrap. The wind rose, hauling dark clouds across the sky, blocking out any chance of stars or moonlight. And when, finally, they approached the forest, it was almost completely shrouded in darkness. Tall trunks closed in around them and Moll shivered inside her damp coat and stretched out a hand for the bark: rough, thick and cracked. Pine trees. They would be tightly packed together; hard to steer through, but good for getting lost in. Without Cinderella Bull's soles to protect them, perhaps that was exactly what they needed.

They edged further into the forest, feeling a way between the trees. The wind whistled through the trunks and Moll tried to listen to its spirit, as Mooshie had taught her in Tanglefern Forest. But it was whining in a way Moll hadn't learnt, as if its breath was full of dread.

Now and again the children's clothes snagged on branches and, although none of them said anything, each one could tell that this forest had been brushed by the Shadowmasks' magic. The branches of the pine trees had lost their needles and were now just stumps and, as Moll breathed in, she noticed that their sharp scent had changed to something stale and rotted. Moll stooped, picked up a stone and slotted it inside the pouch of her catapult. Just in case.

Gryff prowled in front of her, his whiskers twitching. Then he stopped suddenly.

'What is it?' Moll whispered.

Gryff's ears cocked towards the sound, a scratching in the undergrowth, then he grunted, and Moll glimpsed a deer bounding further into the trees.

They walked on and the deeper into the forest they went, the faster Moll's heart began to beat. She knew the smells, barks and leaves of all the trees in Tanglefern Forest, but this woodland made her skin crawl. After a while, the trees thinned and they walked into a small clearing. But the hush that had fallen around them seemed unnatural; not a single woodland animal stirred.

Then they heard a noise that made their stomachs twist.

A creaking sound, like an unoiled door opening. And the sound of knives sharpening.

'The owls!' Siddy gasped.

The children clung to one another, hardly daring to breathe. Only Gryff moved, prowling round them, hissing.

The sound of the blades slicing came closer, but in the darkness no one could see where they were coming from.

'Which way do we run?' Moll cried. 'If we split up, we'll never find each other!'

But there wasn't time for anyone to answer. Dozens of yellow eyes gleamed in the distant darkness around them and the sound of blades grinding filled their ears from all directions.

Moll raised her catapult and fired into the forest, fear searing through her. But without an obvious place to aim it was useless, and the owls screeched and loomed closer. Beside her, Alfie and Siddy clutched their knives and Scrap shoved her whistle into her mouth. She blew it as hard as she could and, as the sound blared into the darkness, the owls shrieked and wheeled backwards. Scrap blew again and again, but in moments the owls saw through the threat and advanced, their wings beating to the sound of grating metal, their yellow eyes slits in the darkness.

The children cowered together, waiting for the inevitable, for the whirring blades to slice down on them.

But then a silvery glow, not unlike moonlight, sifted through the pine trees and settled on those surrounding the children. A second later, as the owl wings beat just metres from the clearing, the shimmering trunks of the pines began to swell. With a loud crunch, huge, gnarled branches burst from the bark, groaning and creaking as they plaited together before arching over the group, enclosing them in a shining woodland cage.

The owls clawed the trunks with desperate screeches, but the gaps were too narrow and their blades couldn't penetrate the mysterious barrier.

Chapter 23
The Woodland Cage

They all crouched together, sheltered beneath the glowing trees. The sound of serrated wings and talons thrashing against the bark rang through the forest as the birds desperately tried to prise a way in. But the trees stayed firm.

'The forest!' Moll whispered. 'It's ... it's helping us.'

A yellow eye filled a crack between the branches and blinked at them slowly.

Alfie shifted closer to Moll, then he pointed to the gnarled trunks around them. 'Look at the bark!'

Carved into each trunk was a symbol, lit up by the silvery glow. On one, a star inside a circle; on another, a dash surrounded by dots; on another, a triangle balanced on an arrow.

'It's Oracle Bone script,' Moll murmured.

'Does that mean it's the old magic fighting back?' Siddy asked.

Scrap stood up and walked towards a crack in the trees. She craned her neck against the bark, then blew hard into her whistle.

Moll scrambled to her feet and pulled her back. 'Careful, Scrap. Those owls are dangerous; we can't take any chances.'

Scrap stuck out her bottom lip and pointed towards the crack in the branches. Moll took a step closer, then screwed up her eyes and peered through the gap. She gasped, squeezed her eyes tight, then opened them again, just to be sure that what she was seeing was real.

Something silvery white was gliding between the trees. It was moving too fast for Moll to understand what it was, but, as it swooped and soared, they could see its glow swell round the owls, snatching them from the air and thrashing them to the ground. Siddy and Alfie huddled behind Moll, stretching their necks to see more. The owls that had been hurled to the floor were croaking and shuddering and then, one by one, their bodies crumpled until all that was left were scattered heaps of feathers and blades.

They all watched, open-mouthed, until just one owl remained. It dived towards the crack the children had gathered at and they leapt backwards. But once again the glow intervened, blocking the owl's path. Moll blinked at its brightness. The bird crashed to the ground and the light faded to a wisp and was gone. The forest was dark once more; only the trees around the children were left glowing.

Suddenly the owl on the ground hauled itself upright and screeched with such bite the sound juddered inside Moll's bones. It wasn't dead, but it seemed weakened by the fight and, dragging its bladed wings behind it, the bird hobbled away, lost in the darkness of the forest.

There was silence once again and the children looked at one another.

'What on *earth* was that light?' Siddy asked. 'Was it part of the old magic?'

Moll shook her head. 'I've no idea.' She peeked out of the crack in the trees. 'Do you think that last owl will be back?'

Alfie fiddled with his earring. 'It's hurt so it's not going anywhere fast. But if it manages to leave the forest it won't be long before—'

'—the Shadowmasks are back,' Moll finished.

She looked at the enormous trunks around them, their branches knotted tight. The bark had ridges so knobbly and rough they could have been centuries old and yet these trees had grown up in front of their eyes. Moll's gaze followed the trunks upwards to where the branches swept over their heads.

'Leaves!' she cried.

The green foliage covered the roof of the woodland cage, shining with life in the silvery glow.

'These are the only trees living in the forest,' Siddy said. 'They're untouched by the Shadowmasks' magic.'

Alfie squinted upwards. 'Dark green leaves with blunt lobes. These are oak trees.'

'Just like the Sacred Oaks in Tanglefern Forest.' A smile spread across Moll's face; it felt like someone had sent them a message telling them not to give up. She looked at the others in turn. 'We can rest a while in here, but with that owl out there we'll need to set off for the Blinking Eye soon.'

'If we can get out,' Siddy said quietly.

No one said anything. The thought hadn't even crossed Moll's mind. Leaves above them rustled and a pigeon appeared. Swift as light, Gryff darted up the tree and leapt into the canopy. The pigeon didn't reappear, but they could hear the wildcat's jaws working amid the leaves. He leapt down and hung back by the trunks, watching through the cracks for danger.

Siddy shuffled away from Gryff, then looked at Moll. 'If he eats Hermit, I'm expelling you both from the Tribe.'

Before anyone could reply, the glowing trees around them seemed to dim and the darkness grew.

Moll moved closer to the trunks and felt for Gryff.

And then, one by one, tiny lights appeared in the canopy above them and dozens of fireflies lit up the night like candles.

'It looks like whatever helped us out with those owls is still watching out for us,' Alfie said.

Moll nodded and somehow she didn't feel afraid.

They talked together long into the night – discussing ways to escape from the trees and reach the Blinking Eye before the Shadowmasks found them – but eventually their eyes couldn't fight the tiredness and they lifted the blankets from the rucksack and lay down to sleep.

Chapter 24
A Way Out of the Forest

When Moll woke, the fireflies were no longer visible. Instead, sunshine seeped through the gaps in the oak trees, falling in rays of sparkling dust. From somewhere nearby a woodlark called and in the canopy above them Moll spotted a squirrel scavenging for acorns.

She sat up. Her muscles were stiff from a night on hard ground, but there was something familiar and right about waking in a forest; she'd missed the comfort of branches and bark. She blinked. It had to be mid-morning at least; they should have been up, working on a way to get out of the trees. Gryff opened one eye beside her, then, realising how close he was to the rest of the children, crept off to the far side of the cage. Moll shook the others awake.

Almost immediately, Scrap shoved her whistle into her mouth and blew hard.

'Shhhhh!' Moll hissed.

Then she looked to where Scrap was pointing. Half a

dozen scoops of bark were laid out on the ground before the trunks opposite them, and each piece was laden with foods from the forest: blackberries, chanterelle mushrooms, garlic leaves, elderflower, chestnuts, hazelnuts, walnuts. There were deeper scoops holding crystal-clear water too.

Alfie had been right: someone – or something – really *was* watching over them.

Gryff crept over towards the food and narrowed his eyes.

'Might be poisonous,' Alfie whispered.

Gryff sniffed the items, one by one, then his ears pricked and he grunted. Taking this as a good sign, Siddy scrambled forward and picked up a blackberry, then he turned it over in his fingers and popped it into his mouth. The others watched.

'Well?' Moll said.

He helped himself to some hazelnuts, then grabbed a mushroom and some garlic leaves. 'Hard to tell,' he mumbled. 'I should try some more.'

Alfie grinned. 'Liar!'

They snatched at the food ravenously.

'Who do you think left it all?' Siddy asked, chewing on a mushroom.

Moll shrugged. 'I don't know, but it tastes good. Enjoy it while it lasts, Sid; the Shadowmasks can't be far away, not if that owl found them . . .'

There was a rustling from the canopy above them. The children froze. Something white was emerging through the

188

leaves. They all edged backwards until they were pressed up against the tree trunks. Then their jaws dropped open as a woman leapt from the branches, her white dress billowing around her as she fell. Moll gasped. The woman was unlike anyone she had ever seen.

Her skin was pale and sparkling, like freshly-fallen snow beneath sunlight, and her hair was so silver it looked as if it might have been spun from moonbeams. It stretched down to her feet in a shining plait, but the strangest thing about the woman was her face: it told of magic, of a creature not born of this world. Blue swishes of colour arched from her cheekbones right up over her brow, and pale green dots curved beneath her eyes.

'My name is Willow.' The woman's voice was rich and strong, like notes played on a cello.

Moll fumbled for her catapult, but, when it was in her palm, she felt suddenly small and silly. She held it by her side, cautious still, untrusting.

Scrap stepped forward and blew her whistle.

'*Shhhhhh*, Scrap!' Alfie hissed.

The woman looked at Alfie, not through him, not around him, but *at* him. Whoever she was, she could see Alfie all right.

'Thank you, child,' she said to him.

'You can *see* me?' he gasped.

Willow nodded.

'But – but . . .' He took a small step backwards and Moll fumbled in her pocket for a pebble, then raised her catapult to her chin.

189

'Only the Shadowmasks can see me outside Tanglefern Forest,' Alfie said quietly.

'I'm not a Shadowmask, Alfie.'

The boy flinched at his name. How had this strange woman known it?

'You can trust me,' she said.

Moll pulled back on her catapult. 'We don't trust anyone outside of Tanglefern Forest and Little Hollows. Who are you?'

The woman smiled, making the blue and green markings curve round her eyes. Then she took a step towards them. 'I'm the old magic, Moll.'

Moll stiffened. Willow had called her by her name – as if she knew her – and the recognition stirred something deep within Moll's soul.

'And I know all about each one of you. Your friend Siddy from Tanglefern Forest, little Scrap who ran away from the Dreads.'

Moll's eyes darted about the cage. 'You – you don't know *him*,' she muttered, nodding towards Gryff.

Then, to her surprise, the wildcat slunk forward, stopped before Willow and dipped his head. Willow bent down and ran a hand over Gryff's back. Moll wanted to leap forward, to pull Gryff away, but something about their connection made Moll still and watchful.

Siddy shook his head in disbelief. 'It was *you* last night, wasn't it? You helped protect us from the owls. But . . . where did you come from?'

Willow smiled and Moll realised that she knew, even without being told. 'Are you from the Otherworld? The one Cinderella Bull told me about?' Moll blinked at the strangeness of it all.

Willow nodded. 'I am. There are many like me there. But when the Shadowmasks began tearing open the thresholds I was sent to help you.' She looked from Moll to Gryff. 'We would do more, but the Bone Murmur has foretold that it will be the gypsy girl and the beast who force the Shadowmasks back. If too many of us break through thresholds from the Otherworld, the power of the Bone Murmur will be weakened and there's no telling whether the old magic will triumph.' She paused. 'But we're all behind you. And, if you listen very carefully on a still, quiet day, you can hear the Otherworld breathing.'

'How can you see me when so many other people can't?' Alfie asked.

'Because you're real, Alfie,' Willow said softly. The dots beneath her eyes sparkled.

'No, I'm not. At least, not according to anyone outside of Oak's camp – and the Shadowmasks.'

An idea was taking shape inside Moll's head and she looked Willow straight in the eye. 'Can you make Alfie real? Properly real, so that *everyone* can see him?'

Willow sighed and a sadness seemed to settle in her eyes. For a while, she said nothing, but Moll could feel untold truths whirring just out of her reach. 'Alfie *is* real,' Willow said to them eventually. 'What the Shadowmasks may have done to him doesn't change that.'

Alfie leant forward. 'So it *was* the Shadowmasks? What did they do to me?'

'I'm sorry, Alfie. But it would go against the old magic to reveal things to you before you're ready to find out for yourself.' She paused. 'Know that you are more real than you realise, child. And you'll understand more soon.'

Siddy nodded towards the oak boughs twisting up around them. 'Can you let us out of here?' he asked. 'One of the owls survived the attack last night and we're worried it'll call the Shadowmasks.'

Willow nodded. 'I can guide you through the forest unharmed, but the rest – finding the amulet and destroying the Soul Splinter – that must be done by you.' She looked at Moll. 'There are things I need to show you before we leave here, though.'

Willow blew through her lips – gently at first, then stronger, like the first breath of a faraway wind. And, as she did so, the great oak boughs surrounding them creaked and groaned before slowly untangling themselves and opening up a way back into the forest.

Some distance away, beyond the dead pine trees and the woodland cage, still further along the coast, Ashtongue and Darkebite stood before a cauldron, on a beach scattered with bones. Candles flickered green on ledges of rock inside the Crooked Cave, but everything else was still.

'One of the owls I sent to the forest beyond the marsh returned,' Darkebite muttered, her charcoaled mask dipped low. 'The children and the wildcat are alive, protected by a spirit from the Otherworld.'

Ashtongue put a snakeskin hand on the lip of the cauldron; the green liquid inside was still like glass. 'We can't approach while the Otherworld guards them. But we are close now; we know *exactly* where they are.' His mask glistened. 'It's time to conjure wilder beasts.'

Darkebite's wings bristled, then stretched out either side of her. She stalked over to the far side of the cave, bent down to a ledge of rock and took a dead rat from a cage. She paused for a moment, thinking, then she smiled and lifted a glass bottle from the rock beside the cage and walked back over to the cauldron.

'Behold the Shadow Keeper's curses,' she gloated.

The scales on Ashtongue's mask quivered with delight as Darkebite let the rat slip into the liquid. Green bubbles belched inside the cauldron, then the Shadow Keeper tipped the contents of the glass bottle in: dozens of fanged teeth. They bobbed on the surface and the liquid hissed and spat before sucking the teeth down.

The liquid stilled for a moment, then an entire jaw-full of perfectly arranged teeth burst from the surface. They were bigger now – and even sharper than before – and they gnashed together, sending liquid spurting over the edge of the cauldron. Then they sank lower, out of sight.

But as the teeth disappeared something large and black and scaled pushed through the water beyond the beach. A ridge of fins arched then disappeared and the grate closing in the cave juddered and clanged. Darkebite had awoken something and it brooded beneath the surface of the sea, waiting to be unleashed …

Chapter 25
Willow's Gift

Willow led the children further into the forest, winding in and out of the withered pines, and, wherever she went, the glow shimmering on her fingertips seemed to fall like drops of rain on to the forest around them: bark toughened, branches bore shimmering autumn leaves again and bracken that had wilted shone green.

Siddy and Alfie walked alongside Willow, asking questions about the Otherworld, while Scrap listened intently: were there really mer kingdoms at the bottom of the sea, as Hard-Times Bob had suggested? Was it true goblins lived in the clouds and unicorns came out under full moons? But Moll hung back from them all with Gryff. She had already trusted Ashtongue's bone reading and look where that had landed them. Moll's trust was hard to earn and Willow wasn't just going to sweep in and steal it. She may have helped them against Darkebite's owls, but Moll wasn't letting her guard down too soon.

They came to a murky river that wove a sluggish course

through the trees, but, when Willow stooped from the bank and swished her hand through the shallows, the water rippled brighter and quickened through the forest.

'This river comes in from the marshland,' Willow said, 'then flows right through the forest out across the countryside to the sea.'

Scrap blew her whistle enthusiastically.

Alfie looked at her. 'I think that means we're following it to the Blinking Eye . . .'

Scrap beamed proudly and nodded.

Siddy looked at Hermit in his palm and smiled fondly. 'Hermit's extremely excited about the prospect of seeing the sea again, aren't you?' The crab waved one pincer feebly.

Scrap stripped down to her vest and pants and jumped from the bank into the river. Alfie and Siddy followed, glad to be shaking off the mud that had clung to their clothes since their encounter with the marsh spirit, even if the water was cold. But Moll sat on the bank with Gryff, her arms folded across her knees.

'You don't trust me, do you?' Willow said quietly, sitting down beside Moll. She let her plait trail down the bank.

Moll watched as Alfie and Siddy swung Scrap by her legs and arms, then flung her into the water. She felt for Gryff's paw and ran her hand over it.

'Trusting gets me into scrapes. I followed what I thought was an Oracle Bone reading, but it turned out to be one of the Shadowmasks trying to trap me. And now Oak is injured and Alfie . . .' She looked away. 'Alfie isn't even properly real,

196

no matter what we all say.' Her eyes stung with the truth of it, as though she was betraying her friend by saying it out loud. She blinked back the tears and plucked at the reeds. 'Everything's so – so—' she struggled for the right word, missed it and ended up with '—knotty.'

Willow nodded. 'Life is rarely clear-cut and simple. You've got to search through the knots to find out what you believe in, even if others doubt you.' She looked out over the river and Moll glanced at the blue-green markings curling over Willow's cheekbones; they glittered in the sun. 'Your wildcat, Gryff, he trusts me,' Willow said after a while.

Moll looked at Gryff as he licked his fur clean. It was true; Gryff wouldn't be so comfortable with a stranger if there was anything to fear.

'I knew your name before I met you, Moll. I've known you since the day Gryff found you in Tanglefern Forest – when you were only two years old and the Shadowmasks killed your parents.' Willow leant closer to Moll. 'Only the old magic could know you like this – even the Shadowmasks had no idea who you were at first. But you're part of the Bone Murmur, part of the old magic. Just like me.'

Moll bit her lip, wanting to trust but doubting too hard.

'What if I told you something about Gryff only you know?' Willow said. 'Would you trust me then?'

Moll stared at the river for a very long time, then she looked up. 'Yes, I would. Because no one knows Gryff like I do. It would have to be a great old magic to know the things I know.'

'Gryff is strong,' Willow said. 'No matter whether his soles are cut or his skin is nicked by owl blades, he always fights back. He's always there to protect you.'

Moll nodded and the pride she felt for the wildcat almost brought her to her feet. It made her fierce and ready, willing to risk everything there and then.

'But Gryff has a weakness,' Willow said, 'a vulnerability that only you know. You've no idea why you know, but deep down you do. Because the bond between you and Gryff goes deeper than understanding and reason.'

Moll's body stiffened and Willow leant in so close her voice was barely more than a whisper in her ear. But Moll heard the words and she listened to their truth.

And, when Willow pulled away, Moll said, 'I trust you.'

Willow smiled, then she and Moll watched Alfie, Siddy and Scrap splashing in the rapids. Dragonflies pinged together above the shallows and, further upstream, in a calm pool of water, a fish jumped. Moll looked on. This was a world where promises got broken and darkness lurked, but it was also a world of sparkling rivers, hidden pools and friends who stuck by you – it was a sort of broken beauty that Moll was only just beginning to understand. She turned to Willow. 'Can I ask you something?'

Willow nodded.

'When the Shadowmasks killed my parents with their Soul Splinter, they shaved their heads.' Moll picked at the cuff of her coat. 'Oak and the other Elders don't know why. But if you're the old magic then I reckon you might.'

Willow shifted beside her and said nothing for several seconds, then she took a deep breath. 'The Shadowmasks needed your parents' hair for thread.' Her cheekbones tightened and she shook her head. 'I can't say any more; there's too much at stake. You and Gryff have to find out the rest for yourselves – like Alfie, I can't reveal more than you're ready to know.'

Moll's mind reeled with thoughts. Thread? What kind of thread needed hair? A weight settled in her stomach. Thread meant stitching, making. Were the Shadowmasks *creating* something? The thought of that turned Moll's insides to ice. She shook herself; that kind of thinking wouldn't help them find the amulet. She needed to focus on that for now and concentrate on getting to the Blinking Eye.

Moll looked up and listened to the wood pigeons cooing. 'I know you're probably extremely busy with—' she paused, 'magic, but I wondered if you could do something for me?'

'Go on,' Willow said.

'I wondered if you could check that Oak is OK back in Little Hollows.' She glanced at Willow quickly. 'If you have time.'

Willow beamed. 'Of course. Oak has done so much to protect you and to restore the old magic. I'll visit him before I return to the Otherworld.'

The coldness that had fastened round Moll's heart every time she thought of Oak thawed a little. Wriggling out of her mud-crusted coat and jumper until she was just in her dress, Moll hurried along the bank towards the others and leapt into the river.

She sank beneath the surface to where it was cold and quiet and where her thoughts belonged just to her. And, when she popped up, she swam over to Siddy and dunked him down hard. Alfie grinned, then swiped at her, but she kicked away to where Scrap was splashing and for a while, as they dived and wrestled and kicked, it was just them and the river. Nothing else seemed to matter. Moll threw her head back and laughed at the thrill of it. The Tribe had needed this, she realised – she and Alfie had needed this – and there in the river it felt as if nothing had happened to pull them apart.

Hours later, Willow led them on through the trees and by twilight they had reached the edge of the forest where the river widened, gurgling over large rocks and cutting a channel through the countryside. There were trees here and there along its banks – ash, alder and poplar – but mostly the countryside was wild with long grasses and flowers lining an almost forgotten path beside the river. There was no sign of dark magic having passed this way at all.

Moll glanced to her left beyond the forest and took in the dark shapes of the hills in the distance. She'd heard Oak talking of the snow-capped mountains in the northern parts of the country and the Bone Murmur spoke of the 'beast . . . from lands full wild' – an old expression for the northern wilderness. Perhaps that really was where Gryff had come from; perhaps that was his home. But as she looked down at him now, his eyes trained on the river, she felt thankful he'd left to be with her. Moll gripped her boxing gloves talisman; if they could get to the Blinking Eye before the Shadowmasks returned for them, *everything* would be all right, and she would be in with a chance of freeing her ma's soul.

Willow turned to them. 'I can't go any further with you, but I can give you something that may help against the Shadowmasks.'

Siddy breathed a sigh of relief. 'Thank goodness. I wasn't looking forward to facing Darkebite with just a catapult.' He rubbed his hands together. 'So what have you got for us? Giant knives? Pistols? Shotguns?'

Willow smiled, then she lifted both her hands and began twisting and turning them through the air, as if drawing in the dusk with invisible paints. A silvery glow slipped from her fingertips, swirling into unrecognisable shapes. Then the glow floated down before her feet, a web of silver shapes, and hardened into something real, into objects begging to be touched. Willow reached down and handed three shining bows to Alfie, Moll and Siddy.

Moll noticed Scrap's face fall so she whispered to her to come close, held out her catapult and placed it in Scrap's hands. Scrap grinned, pulled back on the rubber pouch and scurried into a rhododendron bush to collect ammunition.

The wood of the bow was smooth, silvery and strong; Moll recognised it immediately. 'Silver birch,' she murmured. 'A tree that grants protection.'

'The string,' Alfie gasped. 'It's so fine it's almost not there at all! Surely that'll snap in seconds?'

Siddy groaned. 'We were better off with our catapults.'

Willow placed her palm on to the string of Alfie's bow. 'Feel it again,' she said.

Alfie frowned. 'It's cold!'

'It's a moonbeam spun across each of your bows – as strong as iron but as thin as gossamer,' Willow explained. 'It'll never snap. This is what I used to fight the owls.' She twisted more silver shapes in the air before them and a moment later three leather quivers filled with arrows lay at their feet. The arrows themselves seemed to have been carved from silver birch, fletched with white owl feathers, but each tip was sharpened metal, inscribed with an Oracle Bone symbol.

Moll traced hers with her finger, a small dash inside a circle. 'It means *Hope*,' she said, turning the arrow over in her hand. Then she looked at Siddy's, a square cut through with a line: '*Courage*.' She turned one of Alfie's arrows over: two interlinked circles. 'Yours means *Friendship*.'

Willow nodded. 'Though sometimes you might feel alone – that things are hopeless, your courage is faltering and friendships aren't as straightforward as you'd thought,' Moll glanced at Alfie, 'know that together you can do anything. You can beat the darkness that stalks this world. Those arrows will snare anything fighting against the Bone Murmur.' Willow pointed upwards. 'Like these trees poisoned by the Shadowmasks' evil. But they won't work against those who know nothing of such magic.'

Alfie blew his hair away from his eyes, fitted the moonbeam with an arrow and pulled back. He closed one eye against his target – a crow's nest hanging in a withered tree – then fired. The arrow thrummed from the bow, spiralled through the air, then, just as it hit the nest, a billowing cape shot out from the tip, curled round the twigs and yanked them down. The nest crunched as it split apart inside the cape, then it thumped to the ground, a tangle of broken sticks. The cape hung above it, like smoke from a recently snuffed candle, then it was gone. A flicker of disbelief crossed Alfie's face.

'What *was* that white cape that came out of the arrowhead?' Moll asked.

'A spirit,' Willow answered. 'And, though it seems to disappear, it is bound to the arrow tip and, so long as you can find your arrow, you can use the spirit again.' She smiled. 'The spirits you learnt about when you were younger – wind spirits, earth spirits, river spirits, sea spirits – they all came from the old magic in the Otherworld when Time first dawned. But what you have inside your arrow tips is Oracle Spirit, the most powerful one of all. And somehow Alfie knew how to unleash it.'

Alfie blushed. 'I'm not sure I did. I was just thinking about something when I fired. Everything around me sort of slipped away, then, when I fired, somehow I knew I wouldn't miss.'

'An impossible dream,' Willow said quietly. 'To unlock the Oracle Spirit you have to believe in an impossible dream – something you want more than anything in the world, something that you hope for even when you're not thinking about it.'

Moll looked at the Oracle Bone script engraved on the

tip of an arrow and thought of her parents, of Oak lying ill in his hammock, of the lurking Shadowmasks. So many impossibilities.

'You must never tell anyone else what your impossible dream is,' Willow said. And then she added, in an even quieter voice, 'Unless you feel they really need to know.'

Moll slid a glance at Alfie. She didn't need to ask what he'd been thinking about.

Chapter 26
Beyond the Forest

Willow gathered the group beside the river, a dark ribbon snaking away from the forest through the countryside. Above it, clouds hung in the sky, opening now and again to reveal the moon, strung up like a silver coin.

'This is where I must leave you,' Willow said. 'But I'll be watching from afar – we all will. Keep heart and have faith, however bleak things seem.'

Moll shuddered. Willow had stayed with them for several hours, helping them practise with their bows and arrows, and while she had been beside them the threat of the Shadowmasks had dimmed; they'd even made a campfire and eaten a rabbit Gryff had killed for them. But as they got ready to leave, a sense of menace brooded in the air.

Willow nodded towards Moll's quiver. 'May I?'

Moll shook it from her back and Willow set an arrow to the moonbeam, took aim at a low-hanging branch leaning over the river and fired. The Oracle Spirit billowed out, but, instead of snatching round the branch and hauling it down, it held fast, pinned to the bough where the arrow had jammed, and, like a hammock made from moonlight, the rest of the cape hung down in front of them, swaying slowly in the breeze. They clustered before it on the riverbank, their eyes wide.

Willow handed the bow back to Moll, then stretched out a hand and slipped it inside the cape. 'Go on, touch it,' she whispered.

They held out their hands and let their fingers brush against the Oracle Spirit; it was softer than satin, smoother than silk, and yet it felt strong too, as if it would never break.

Willow slipped her body inside a gap in the folds and sat there, her legs dangling out. 'If you need protection – if you can't fight any more – think of the Otherworld instead of your impossible dream and the Oracle Spirit will form a cocoon and keep you safe.' She paused and looked at each one of them in turn. 'When you're inside, nothing can harm you, but you can only use your arrows in this way once, so use them wisely.' She drew her legs in and wrapped the Oracle Spirit round her so that all the children could see was a pale cocoon of silk hanging from the branch.

'That's brilliant!' Siddy cried. 'We can hide inside them and the Shadowmasks won't be able to touch us!'

Moll stretched out a hand and pulled the fold of material back.

Willow was gone, as Moll had almost expected, and they were alone again in the forest. Taking a deep breath, Moll scrambled up the tree, using the jutting branches like rungs

206

of a ladder, then pulled hard on the arrow holding the cape and it came away. The second it did so, the Oracle Spirit vanished, locked back inside the arrow, and just a wisp of grey hung in the air.

Moll jumped down from the tree, slipped the arrow into her quiver and swung it on to her back. 'Let's get going. Come on, Scrap, lead the way.'

They stepped out of the forest on to the path lining the riverbank. It was almost entirely overgrown by long grasses and wild flowers, but they followed it along the river's meandering course, south towards the coast. Moll felt for the leather strap of her quiver and held it tight.

After a mile of walking, Scrap stopped and turned to the others, her expression tense. Gryff craned his neck through the reeds towards the river, his tail slung low to the ground, his whiskers twitching. He'd seen something: Moll knew the signs. She reached for her bow and listened.

Something was stepping through the still waters lapping the reeds. The moonlight shivered. Then there was a splash, reeds shook and a large bird burst up from the riverbank and flapped off into the night.

Alfie breathed out slowly. 'Heron.'

They carried on walking and Moll was suddenly glad of the alder tree ahead, its long, thin trunk a familiar shadow in the night. It reminded her of the alders lining the river back in Tanglefern Forest. She'd spoken to Alfie for the first time up in their branches and she'd fished in the shallows below them for minnows with Siddy every summer for as long as she could remember. Moll tried to hold these memories close, anything to shift her mind from the danger they were facing.

But, as they walked beneath the tree, Gryff began to growl – quietly at first, like a rumbling engine far away, and then louder, as the noise grew in his throat.

'There!' Siddy screamed suddenly.

Tucked into the branches of the alder, two yellow eyes blinked at them slowly.

'The owl that Willow injured!' Moll yelled.

It shot out from the branch, no longer wounded, its steel blades glinting in the moonlight. Moll ducked and the knives skimmed past her skin. But her reactions were quick, faster than the others, and while they reached for their bows she had already ripped hers from her shoulder and set an arrow to it. She felt the moonbeam in the grooves of her fingers, pulled back until it was taut beneath her chin, then she thought single-mindedly, as Willow had taught them, and fired at the owl.

The arrow jammed into the bird and it reeled, screeching and twisting in the air. But the Oracle Spirit brought it crashing to the ground and, as Moll stood over it, she watched the owl crumple into a stack of knives and feathers. She spat on it, hard, as the Oracle Spirit melted away.

Alfie slung his bow back onto his shoulder and raised an eyebrow. 'Fast thinking, Moll.'

Moll shrugged. 'Got a-hold of my thought and didn't let it go.'

They carried on walking and, after a while, Scrap turned

to the group. Alfie approached her slowly and said her name, so she knew he was near.

'Are you tired?' he asked her.

Scrap nodded.

Alfie was silent for a moment, then he said, 'If you hold my quiver, I'll carry you on my shoulders.'

Scrap let the rucksack she'd been carrying with the blankets inside slip to the ground. Siddy picked it up and Alfie crouched as Scrap felt for his back. She had got used to Alfie now and somehow she was able to find him more easily, as if she could sense where he was, even without being told. She clambered up on to his shoulders.

Siddy grinned. 'You'll look like a girl floating in mid-air to strangers!'

They followed the river on, long into the night. It widened and quickened, its sound growing to a roar, and, as they came to a cluster of ash trees with huge boughs leaning over the river, Alfie turned to them.

'Let's rest here for a moment,' he panted, the weight of Scrap's body finally slowing him. 'It's sheltered enough.'

As they stooped beneath the trees, clouds folded over the moon and the night seemed to thicken. Moll glanced back towards the forest, willing herself to be braver than she felt, but, when the clouds slid away from the moon, her stomach plunged.

'On the path!' she hissed to the others. 'Look!'

Dark shapes, seven or eight of them at least, were slinking from the forest towards them. Moll tried to keep calm; she

209

knew these animals, even in the dark. They were foxes. But foxes didn't hunt in packs.

And then a howl split the night and Moll froze. Foxes didn't howl either.

These were wolves.

Chapter 27
Claws and Teeth

'The arrows!' Moll screamed, reaching for her bow. But she was fumbling this time, her fingers damp with sweat.

The wolves bounded towards them, a blur of grey limbs and fur. Their eyes gleamed purple against the night and Moll knew as she saw them that these were more than ordinary wolves: these were creatures conjured by Darkebite.

Alfie pushed Scrap behind him, then slotted an arrow to his bow and pulled. He fired at the same time as Siddy, and both boys' arrows lodged deep inside the wolves at the head of the pack. The Oracle Spirit ballooned out, snatching round them, and they groaned before slumping down dead. Scrap reached for her catapult and fired at the next wolf. Her stone struck hard and the wolf slowed for a moment, long enough for Alfie and Siddy to reload.

Gryff charged forward, dodging the snarling teeth and lashing out against the wolves with his claws. And, behind him, Moll set an arrow to her bow and fired just as a wolf leapt towards her. The beast crashed down at her feet: its

211

head was enormous, its jaw a cavern of razored teeth, and its claws were long, black and hooked, like the talons of a giant bird of prey. Moll tore herself away and took aim once more with a fresh arrow. Again and again the wolves advanced and the children whirled to face the threat, sending Oracle Spirits into the pack.

Then the wolves were fewer, just a handful bounding towards the children. Their howls shredded the night, then their muzzles bent low, purple eyes burning, and they stalked closer, snarling. Siddy leapt on to a low-hanging branch, drew his bow back and let an arrow fly. One of the wolves spasmed as the Oracle Spirit swelled round it, then it stumbled to the ground, dead. Alfie and Moll fired again until there was just one wolf circling them. All eyes were trained on it, every arrow poised, then a cloud rolled over the moon and the wolf disappeared from sight.

'Quick! Hide in the reeds!' Alfie shouted.

There was a scuffling of feet and panting breaths as Moll darted backwards with Gryff to where the reeds were tall and thick. But a heavy, hungry breathing followed them.

Moll saw the eyes first, a glower of purple in the dark, then the moon slipped out and she saw that the wolf was just metres from her and Gryff, its jaw dripping with saliva, rows of teeth gleaming in the moonlight. Too late to raise an arrow to her bow, Moll retreated, her face pressed against the reeds. She waited for the pain, her features twisted with fear. But it didn't come.

With a snarl, Gryff flew through the air towards the wolf.

Claws clashed, but the wolf tossed Gryff aside and made to leap for Moll. In a flash, the wildcat was on his feet again, pouncing on the wolf's back. The beast howled and staggered backwards. Gryff tore at the wolf's fur with his claws, then the wolf whipped his drooling jaw round and snapped centimetres from Gryff's face.

'No!' Moll screamed, reaching for her bow. Her thoughts ran in frenzied circles and even when the arrow was in place, she knew she was going to miss. It careered out of the bow and struck a branch above the fight, before dropping uselessly down. Moll's blood roared. 'Get back, Gryff!'

But she knew no amount of yelling would help. Gryff's instinct to protect her outweighed everything else; he'd fight for her life until the bitter end.

Alfie hesitated with his bow. 'Moll, he's got to let go. I can't fire!' he cried. 'If my aim's not perfect, I'll hit Gryff!'

The wildcat leapt from the wolf's back for a second and Moll stiffened. Gryff was tossing his head from side to side and as he turned to face the wolf again his growl seemed weaker, smaller. But, in that fleeting moment, Siddy took aim with his bow and released an arrow. It shot through the air, struck the wolf hard and the Oracle Spirit burst out. The creature slumped to the ground, dead, and Gryff staggered backwards.

Moll sprang out from the reeds and threw herself down beside the wildcat. She held him close while the others gathered round. Gryff's body shuddered inside her arms and suddenly Moll grew very still and her thoughts turned dark

213

and cold. There were no wounds on his body, no blood from any cuts. And yet . . . She pulled back from Gryff and, shakily, the wildcat stood up. In the moonlight, Moll could see that his whiskers had been sliced clean off, and her heart trembled.

'What is it, Moll?' Siddy asked.

Moll looked into Gryff's eyes, but they were glazed and distant, not focusing on her own.

'No,' Moll breathed, her throat closing tight. She wrapped her arms round Gryff and buried herself in his fur as all the hope she'd mustered drained from her heart. 'Not this!' she sobbed.

Siddy shook his head. 'I don't understand.'

Moll looked up, her voice almost swallowed by the tears. 'He's – he's blind!'

'But how?' Alfie asked. 'Did the wolf scratch his eyes? There's no blood . . .'

Moll ran desperate hands over Gryff's head. 'It's his whiskers. The wolf sliced them off! I knew that they were part of his strength – so did Willow somehow – but I didn't know what would happen, only that Gryff would be weaker without them.' Tears rolled down her cheeks and she held the wildcat's head in her shaking hands. 'It's not meant to happen this way; he's done nothing except protect us.' Moll's voice broke apart as outrage slipped into despair.

Siddy fumbled in the rucksack for the ointment they'd used on Gryff's paws, but, when Moll held it over the wildcat's eyes, he didn't even blink. This was a dark damage no simple herb could fix.

Scrap flung her arms round Moll and Gryff and wept, and Alfie and Siddy sat beside them, their heads hung low. Neither could think of words that would make anything better.

Eventually Moll looked up from Gryff. She felt for her quiver on the path beside her, then stood up and set an arrow against the moonbeam.

Alfie started forward; he could tell what Moll was going to do. 'Moll, Willow warned us we can only use the cocoons once. Shouldn't we save it for when we can't fight any longer?'

Moll pulled the arrow until the moonbeam was taut beneath her chin, then she looked at Alfie, her eyes brimming with tears. 'My fight's over without Gryff.' She turned back to the tree, thought hard of a land where the night didn't shatter into dark magic and animals like Gryff weren't stripped of their strength. She willed this world on, begged it to come close, then fired her arrow. A shining cape hung down from the alder branch and, without a word, Moll gathered Gryff up in her arms. Though his weight almost crushed her, Moll heaved him into the cape with Siddy's help, then she slipped between the silken fabric with him and folded them both into a place where they couldn't be hurt.

Chapter 28
Scrap's Part of the Bargain

Several hours later, Alfie woke inside the reeds. After keeping watch for a while, he'd smoothed down a resting place for him and Scrap and left Siddy on guard. But it was early morning now and the sky was pale blue over the autumn trees. Alfie stood up to see Siddy sitting on the path, his bow resting across his lap. He nudged Scrap awake.

'We should get going,' he said quietly.

He glanced at Moll's Oracle Spirit hanging from the alder branch like a large white chrysalis. Below it two mallards wove in and out of the rushes. Alfie leant out and touched the cocoon gently, then a moment later Moll slipped out with Gryff. She pulled the arrow from the bark so that the cocoon vanished, then she cupped her hands into the river and drank. The others did the same and though they didn't say anything they could tell from Moll's swollen eyes that she'd been crying. Even the way Gryff stood beside Moll was different now. Before, his eyes would be scanning his surroundings, his ears pricking towards near-silent sounds.

216

But now his shoulders hunched forward as he stared ahead with unseeing eyes.

'Is the Blinking Eye far, Scrap?' Siddy asked.

She shook her head.

Alfie squeezed his talisman, the knot of Raven's hair inside his leather pouch, and turned to Moll. 'Your fight's not over without Gryff. You've got us, Moll. And we're going to help you fix this.'

Moll sniffed. 'How? Everything seems to be falling apart.'

Alfie was silent for a moment. 'I don't know how we'll fix it, but you promised to undo whatever curse the Shadowmasks have put on me, and I'm telling you the same goes for Gryff. He's looked after us every single day since the day I met him in Tanglefern Forest; now it's our turn to look after him.'

Moll sniffed again and scuffed her boot against the grass, afraid to speak in case her voice should break.

'You've got to believe we'll help you, Moll,' Siddy said. 'Remember what Willow told us – together we've got a chance of beating the Shadowmasks' dark magic. You can't do this alone.'

Moll nodded, a flicker of hope kindling inside her at Alfie's and Siddy's words. They walked down the path and she trailed a hand across Gryff's back so that he could follow her, on towards the Blinking Eye. His steps were hesitant, as they had been when his soles were cut, but he followed Moll's every stride, never doubting her for an instant.

After a while, the river widened and fields patched together either side of them, some cut to stubble and filled with bales, others ploughed into trenches. Then sycamore trees with bright orange leaves curved up either side of the river and, further ahead still, two narrowboats, their hulls painted red and blue with green and yellow swirls, had been moored. The children hung back beneath a sycamore some way from the boats and Moll couldn't help thinking about her brightly-painted wagon tucked safely in Tanglefern Forest. How she wished she could curl up in her box bed with Gryff now.

Alfie pointed to the boats. 'We walk past as if nothing's wrong, OK? Nice and normal-looking.'

Moll raised her eyebrows. 'We've got quivers on our backs – and a wildcat. It's hardly like they're going to think we don't mean trouble.'

Alfie looked down at Gryff, then lowered his voice. 'Right now Gryff doesn't seem as wild as he normally does, and if we just walk on past it may look like we're kids out hunting pigeons.' He shrugged. 'You never know, the folk inside might be all right.'

They walked towards the narrowboats and Siddy began to hum.

'What are you doing?' Alfie hissed.

'Trying to sound casual.'

Alfie threw up his hands. 'That's not casual, Sid; that's just odd!'

Siddy shoved a hand into his pocket to commiserate about the situation with Hermit.

Then a door at the back of the first boat opened and a man came out, holding a mug of tea. He narrowed his eyes at the children as they passed, but said nothing. They walked on by the second boat in silence, their heads down, and Moll tried to ignore the smell of freshly-baked bread that came from it and the sound of her growling stomach. A woman was up early, wringing out clothes from a bucket in the stern of the boat. She looked up at the children, her eyes flitting over their dark features and dirty clothing.

She scowled at them. 'Hey! You're those dratted gypsies the village down the coast was talking of a few days ago, aren't you? We travelled by there and heard about the trouble you'd caused – bewitching crops and making them die.' She spat into the river. 'I suggest you stop snooping round our boats and get out of my sight before I set my husband on you.'

Moll glowered at the woman, but Siddy clutched her wrist. 'Please don't start a fight before breakfast. We need to keep moving and not draw attention.'

They carried on walking, but, as they reached the end of the narrowboat, Alfie leapt from the path into its bow. Moll's eyes widened, but beside her Scrap only giggled.

Of course, Moll remembered. *Alfie's invisible to them!*

While the woman's back was turned, he snatched up the loaf of bread set out on a tea towel, then jumped off the boat to rejoin the others.

He turned to Moll. 'There have got to be some advantages to being like this.' He paused. 'And anyway she seemed like a rotten sort.'

Moll nodded. 'Proper spudmuckers.'

They ate the bread as they walked, afraid of lingering any

219

longer than they had to, and, when it had been eaten, Scrap quickened her pace, every now and again blowing her whistle until Alfie managed to grab it from her lips. It seemed they were getting close to the Blinking Eye now – whatever it might be – and Scrap's excitement was growing.

They followed her over a wooden bridge, leaving the river behind, then they raced across a stubble field, in between the rounded bales. Moll's hand never strayed from Gryff's back and he went with her, wherever she led him. Moments later, the sea came into view again. It looked cool and grey under the morning sky, but the familiar cries of seagulls once more filled the air and a warmth spread out inside Moll; this place felt safer than the marsh and the blighted forest – and it reminded her of Little Hollows and everyone inside it. She thought of Oak lying in his hammock – had Willow been to see him yet or was Mooshie still tending his wounds?

Scrap's dreadlocks bounced up and down against her back as she hurdled the gate at the far side of the field and thumped down on to softer ground. Moll helped Gryff over, then looked around. Sand dunes rose and dipped amid gorse bushes before spreading out into bracken towards towering white cliffs. And in the distance, some way to their left, the river rushed out to the sea.

Moll breathed deeply. The Shadowmasks hadn't been here; the land was too rich and fresh. They were going to beat them to the Blinking Eye and perhaps everything would be OK. She bent low next to Gryff and stroked his head. His eyes, usually so bright, were dull and glazed and Moll felt the wildcat's sadness deep inside her. She clenched her fists. The Shadowmasks would pay for what they'd done.

Scrap stared through the bracken until her eyes rested on a sheep track wiggling towards the coast. She ran down it, the others at her heels, and it was then that Moll realised where Scrap was heading.

The track wound through the bracken a little way down the cliff, out on to a peninsula of land jutting into the sea, and there, on the furthest point, rising up at the cliff edge like an old, forgotten tower, was a lighthouse. Its circular base, once painted white, was now chipped and battered from stormy weather, and a rusted ladder climbed its length on one side. But, at the top of it, a light blinked out over the sea, roving over the waters.

The sun rose up from behind the horizon and its dazzling brightness drowned out the lighthouse beam.

But Moll finally understood. Scrap had kept her part of the bargain. Because this wasn't just a lighthouse: it was what the smuggler child had promised them all along.

This was the Blinking Eye.

Chapter 29
The Blinking Eye

Scrap shoved the whistle in her mouth and blew hard. A handful of seagulls squawked back at her from above, but Scrap didn't care. She blew the whistle again, even harder, and the others laughed with relief.

'You did it!' Alfie cried, the wind ruffling his hair over his eyes.

Scrap cartwheeled down the path and Moll and Siddy hurried to keep up with her.

'Thank you, Scrap,' Moll said.

Siddy nodded. 'We never would've found this without you!'

Scrap twizzled her dreadlocks in delight and Siddy lifted Hermit out of his pocket.

'Look, Hermit – the sea!' Two shaking pincers reached imploringly from their shell towards the coast. Then a set of eyes appeared, caught sight of the lighthouse and glazed over with dread.

Moll bent down to Gryff. 'We've found it,' she whispered. 'We're closer to the amulet now and it's going to help you,

222

I know it.' She stroked the fur beneath his chin and Gryff purred back, leaning helplessly into Moll's body.

The track skirted round the edge of the cliff amid the bracken and Moll swallowed as she took in the sheer white face of rock plunging down to the sea. Waves crashed against boulders and Moll craned her neck closer – because mingling with the rush of the sea there was a roar – constant and fierce. But there was no waterfall in sight, as Moll had expected from such a sound, so she kept on walking with the others.

Eventually the bracken petered out into grass and sea thrift and the children stopped a few metres from the lighthouse. Moll could just make out a lamp inside a glass dome at the top of the tower. It was turning slowly, sunlight glinting off it, but, other than that, there was no movement inside. Curtains were drawn either side of a latticed window halfway down and even the stone outbuilding to the left of the lighthouse, its whitewashed walls chipped and cracked, looked abandoned.

'Don't these things usually have keepers?' Siddy said. 'Someone to check the lamp keeps turning?'

Alfie shrugged. 'Doesn't look like there's anyone about.'

All of a sudden there was an almighty blast. The children jumped as a foghorn boomed out into the morning and, seconds later, the front door of the lighthouse flew open. An enormous man, clad from head to toe in yellow waterproofs, filled its frame.

'Will you shut up, Dorothy!' he shouted.

The man stopped in his tracks and stared at the children before him. Beneath his yellow rain hat was a bushy white beard, as large as a crow's nest, and blue eyes fringed with wrinkles. He took a step towards the children, reached a large hand into the pocket of his waterproof and drew out a telescope. Setting it to his eye, he stared at them through it, even though they were just metres away.

'What is the meaning of this little gathering?' he roared.

Moll and Gryff edged backwards, Siddy stood rooted to the ground and Alfie shifted closer to Scrap. But the smuggler child only grinned.

The man's eyes widened inside the telescope and he swelled up before them so that he looked even bigger than before. Scrap tried to hide her smile and look impressed, but, when the foghorn inside the lighthouse blasted out again, making everyone jump, she lost it and fell about laughing.

The man turned in the doorway and shouted up inside the lighthouse. 'Enough, Dorothy!'

'We – er – we're looking for something,' Siddy stammered.

The man looked from Siddy to Scrap and then from Moll to Gryff, missing Alfie entirely. 'With bows and arrows?' he shouted.

Moll squared up to him. 'We only put arrows in unhelpful people – the ones who don't give us what we're looking for.'

Siddy winced at Moll's words. 'We don't mean any harm. Please don't shout at us, we just—'

'Shout?' the man bellowed. 'Am I shouting?'

Siddy put his hands over his ears. 'Yes!'

The man cocked his head to one side and wiggled his ear. Water dribbled out. He did the same to the other ear. 'Better?' he said, his voice now at a reasonable volume.

Siddy nodded.

The man straightened his hat. 'It's this leaking lighthouse that makes me shout,' he muttered. 'Water trickling into my ears every second of the day and night and blocking off my hearing . . . I haven't been dry since last March!'

Scrap poked a head out from behind Siddy, took a few steps closer and blew her whistle. The man peered down at her over his beard and frowned.

'She – she can't speak,' Moll said. 'But she's fierce with a catapult so don't you lay a finger on her.'

The man bent down and Moll suddenly saw the kindness in his eyes. 'Well, fancy that. I don't often speak either,' he said to Scrap. 'Not many people to talk to out on the cliff edge; the Nibbled Head is a lonely sort of place.'

Scrap plucked at the hem of the tunic beneath her coat and Alfie edged towards her protectively, unseen by the man.

'But I shout a lot,' the man said. 'At Dorothy usually.'

'Is Dorothy your wife?' Siddy asked, desperate to keep the conversation light while Moll was so stormy.

The man shook his head and smiled. 'Dorothy's my lighthouse. She's a right pain, this one. Got a temper like no one's business – always mouthing off with her foghorn for no good reason and shining her beam in the wrong places.' He ran a hand down the door frame. 'But I love her, all the same.' He looked across at Gryff and let out a whistle. 'That a wildcat you got there, missy?'

Moll reached for Gryff's back; the fur was bristled.

'Didn't think there were wildcats down in the southern part of the country.' The man paused. 'Is he all right? I've not seen a wildcat up close, but he looks in a bad way to me.'

Moll felt a familiar lump slide up her throat. She raised her chin, but said nothing.

The man shrugged. 'What is it you're after anyway?'

Siddy waved a hand carelessly. 'Oh, well, this and that.' He scratched his jaw. 'Don't suppose you've got an amulet stored away inside?'

Moll shot him a look and Scrap turned and blew her whistle hard in Siddy's face.

'We – we . . .' Moll's words faltered. 'We think you might have something we need. Badly.'

'Just tell him the truth,' Alfie whispered in her ear. 'I don't think he means any harm.'

Moll looked at the man, willing him to be someone they could count on, someone they could trust. She thought of Willow's words – *You've got to search through the knots to find out what you believe in* – and took a deep breath. 'We're searching for an amulet – but not just any old amulet.' She looked at her feet. 'This one's magical. And if we don't find it then, well . . .' She shook her head; not finding it would mean not freeing her ma's soul or helping Oak and Gryff or saving the old magic . . . 'Well, that's not even an option. We *have* to find it.'

The man ran a large hand over his yellow cagoule. 'Magical, you say?'

Moll nodded. 'I know you might not believe us—'

'Believe you?' the man said. 'Oh, just because I'm older and out here with no one to talk to doesn't mean I don't believe in magic.' He swept a hand out towards the sea. 'You can't live beside something so wild and strong and not believe in its magic.' He smiled. 'The name's Big P.'

'What does the "P" stand for?' Siddy asked.

The man sighed. 'Puddle.'

The lighthouse was bigger inside than Moll had expected, and as Puddle had glumly pointed out: 'There are six floors and each one's got a leak. Even the bedroom.' A spiral staircase ran inside the stone walls and a circular room led off left from every level. The first two floors were storerooms housing casks of oil, metal flasks and bundles of rope – even Scrap wasn't much interested in those. But from the third floor there came delicious, warming smells.

Puddle paused outside the door of the kitchen. 'Got a bedroom up on the next level – the wettest of the lot – then it's the flag signalling and lantern room where it all happens.' He looked at the quivers the children were carrying.

Moll followed his gaze. 'Some people are coming to kill us,' she said matter-of-factly, 'but we're going to kill them first.'

Siddy gave Moll an exasperated look. 'Stop being so aggressive.'

Puddle half smiled. 'Unless you're planning to use those to catch breakfast, I suggest you leave them here on the steps.'

Reluctantly, Moll laid down her quiver with Siddy and

228

Alfie's, and Scrap put a foot on the step above Puddle. She looked at him with large, questioning eyes.

'You want to go up higher?' Puddle asked.

Scrap nodded.

'You can have a snoop round the flag room, but I think talk of this amulet is going to warrant a spot of porridge. Hurry down once you've had a look.'

Scrap raced up the stairs and Puddle looked down at Gryff who had edged behind Moll's legs. The wildcat had managed to walk alongside the river and through fields without his sight, but being trapped inside a stranger's lighthouse had made him fearful. His every instinct warned him to stay outside in the wild, but he didn't want to leave Moll, not now. He needed her, just like she needed him.

'Wait one minute, will you?' Puddle said.

He disappeared down the stairs and Moll turned quickly to Alfie and Siddy. 'Do you trust him?'

Alfie nodded.

'Me too,' Siddy said. 'I've got a good feeling about him and I never really had that with Ashtongue.' He paused. 'And he offered us porridge; I don't think that's a very Shadowmasky thing to do.'

Puddle emerged on the stairs, holding four dead mice. 'Hundreds of them in the outbuilding – thought your wildcat might like them.'

'Thank you.' Moll lowered the mice before Gryff.

He sniffed them nervously, but, on sensing the meat, set his teeth in hard. Puddle ducked beneath the door frame, leading Moll and Siddy inside the kitchen. But Alfie hung back by the entrance, unseen by Puddle, with Gryff.

'Make yourself at home,' Puddle said, pulling back two chairs tucked into the circular table.

Cautiously, Moll made to sit down.

'Oooh,' Puddle winced. 'Wouldn't sit there. Below the worst leak in the house that spot is.'

As if on demand, water dripped through a crack in the ceiling, straight on to Moll's face. 'Then why do you have a chair here?' she muttered.

Puddle shrugged. 'To catch the drops.'

Moll moved to the seat next to Siddy's, sat down and looked round the kitchen. The plaster on the walls was coming away in great chunks, the rug beneath the table was threadbare and the little wooden cupboards lining the room were chipped. But, despite all this, the lighthouse had a cosy charm. Between the curtains there was a vase of pink sea thrift, and beyond that a spectacular view of the sea. Puddle kept utensils in brightly coloured glass bottles that must have washed up in the tide and every surface was cluttered with jars, pots and bowls – most of them full to the brim with food: condiments, pickled vegetables, spices and dried fruits.

Puddle waved a hand over them. 'Dorothy likes her food well seasoned; she's got high standards.' He patted the wall and a cloud of dust puffed out.

Moll raised her eyebrows at Siddy. 'Who lives in the outbuilding beside the lighthouse?' she asked.

Puddle bent over the pot of porridge bubbling on his stove

and gave it a stir. 'I spend some of the colder months down there, but I like to be up here with Dorothy most of the time – got to keep an eye on the old girl.'

A piece of plaster crunched away from the wall beside the door and landed with a thud on the floor. Gryff leapt backwards.

'Dorothy, we've got company!' Puddle moaned. He rolled up the sleeve of his cagoule and, with fingers as chubby as sausages, he picked up a teaspoon and a pot of honey. Both were dwarfed in his hands, but he tried his best to decant the honey into his porridge. After several minutes, he shot a glance over his shoulder. 'Who am I trying to fool?' he muttered. 'I normally just tip the whole lot in.'

Siddy grinned. 'We're not known for our manners. In fact we haven't eaten a single meal with cutlery since April when Moll sank all the knives and forks in the river back in the forest. So don't mind us.'

Moll sat on her hands. 'It was a Tribe dare, in case you're wondering. And we've done way worse.'

Siddy settled Hermit on the table, but, on catching sight of the pan on the hob, the crab scuttled left, smashed into a pepper pot, then lay, upturned and stunned, in the middle of the table. Siddy wrapped him in a paper napkin and cradled him in his lap.

Wind rattled the window in its frame as Puddle handed out bowls of piping-hot porridge. 'A storm's brewing,' he mummered. 'I can feel it in my beard.'

Scrap skipped into the room, wrapped in a red-and-yellow

231

striped flag so that she looked more like a maypole than a girl. Perching on the seat with Moll, she gulped a few mouthfuls of porridge down.

Moll glanced towards Alfie; he was leaning against the door frame, his eyes glued to the floor. Puddle took off his hat to reveal a mass of wild white hair and Moll watched him tuck into his breakfast, hoping that the feeling in her gut was right. She could trust this man, couldn't she?

'What if I told you there was a boy in the doorway.' Moll's voice was low and full of challenge.

Siddy began concentrating extremely hard on his porridge and even Scrap seemed to shrink inside her flag.

Puddle leant against the wall. 'Like a ghost?'

Moll considered this. 'No. Not like a ghost. More real than that – and better with a bow and arrow.'

Puddle thought about it for a while. 'Has this boy got something to do with your amulet?'

Moll held his gaze. 'Maybe.' She paused. 'Yes.'

Puddle swallowed a spoonful of porridge. 'I always think it's best to believe in something until it's proved otherwise.'

Moll's eyebrows rose a little. People, she was beginning to realise, were surprising. You never knew what was going on inside their heads. This lighthouse keeper wasn't a gypsy and yet somehow he was willing to believe in magic and mysteries. And maybe that was all they needed. 'You really mean that?' Moll asked.

Puddle nodded and Moll stood up, walked across the room and gave her bowl to Alfie.

'Thanks,' he mumbled.

Puddle's eyes grew round as saucers. 'The bowl – it's disappeared!' He reached for his telescope and pointed it towards Alfie. 'There's nothing there, but – but I could have *sworn* I heard a voice.' He tutted. 'Well, I never. I wait three years for a visitor and I get two gypsies, a wildcat, an invisible child—'

'He's called Alfie,' Siddy prompted.

'And,' Puddle glanced at Scrap, 'a walking flag.'

'It'd be a dull old world if everyone was the same,' Alfie said.

Puddle gasped but Moll smiled. She remembered saying those very words to Alfie back in Tanglefern Forest – and it made her suddenly glad of the friends she had around her.

Scrap whistled in Alfie's direction, budging up on her seat to make room for him, and Puddle handed Moll another bowl of porridge. Scrap smiled as Alfie sat down then she patted him on the shoulder – she seemed to know where he was instinctively now.

Siddy grinned. 'Scrap's got a soft spot for Alfie. Don't you?'

Scrap nodded simply.

Alfie blushed. 'The porridge is good.'

Puddle rubbed his eyes at the sound of Alfie's voice. 'What a thing ... An invisible boy. I suppose you'd better tell me about this amulet then and how you happened across me and Dorothy.'

And so Moll, Siddy and Alfie did.

*

At the end of their telling, Puddle was silent for a long time, then he looked up at the window and listened to the wind battering against the glass. They'd been talking for so long clouds had now gathered and the afternoon had turned grey. 'There's been a strangeness in the wind and the sea these past few weeks.' He ran a hand over his beard. 'As if they're afeared – or angry.'

Moll nodded. 'The Shadowmasks' magic is slipping in fast through the thresholds. They've already turned our cove bad, rotting the gorse and killing the bracken, and on our journey here we found a whole forest sucked of life.'

'It makes sense now,' Puddle said. 'Even Dorothy's been playing up more than usual, but I never imagined something like this could be behind it.'

'It took Hermit by surprise too,' Siddy said gloomily.

Alfie bit his lip. 'We think the amulet might be able to make all this better though. Do – do you have it?'

Puddle was less startled by Alfie's voice now, but still his eyes flitted from place to place, trying to fix on a point.

'I'm sorry, boy. I've never heard of an amulet like the one you're speaking of.' Puddle sighed. 'I wish I had but,' he looked around at the crumbling kitchen, 'it's just Dorothy and me here.'

Moll said anxiously, 'But it *has* to be in the lighthouse. Scrap was right: this is the Blinking Eye!'

Puddle leant forward and collected up their bowls. 'There'll be a reason your Oracle Bones led you here. For one thing,' he looked at Gryff curled up beside Moll, his head buried beneath his paw, 'the lighthouse is known by many as a symbol of hope.'

'Hope for who?' Moll asked flatly. 'Lazy sailors?'

Puddle smiled. 'Hope for the blind.'

Moll felt her knees grow weak with longing – could this battered lighthouse somehow help Gryff?

Puddle placed the bowls in the sink. 'I don't know how or why, but there's a reason you've all come here. Magic isn't straightforward; we've just got to work it out.'

The wind outside picked up and whistled round the lighthouse, gusting through the cracks and crevices. Then the rain began, tapping against the window and smearing down the glass.

'It's going to be nasty out. I think you lot need some rest before we plan anything.'

They followed Puddle up another floor to the circular bedroom. Most of the room was taken up by a large bed which, on closer inspection, appeared to be a rowing boat lined with a mattress and laden with blankets and pillows, and on the walls hung different-coloured life rings and medals Puddle had been awarded for saving sailors. There was a round window, like a porthole in a ship's cabin, and a set of shelves piled high with books on tides, sea creatures and sailor's knots.

Puddle waved a hand. 'Sleep anywhere you like – in the boat, on the floor,' he pulled back a dustsheet and raised an eyebrow, 'on the sofa which I forgot I had ... Just get some rest and I'll start thinking about this amulet.' Dorothy let out

235

a foghorn blast and Puddle scowled. 'She's very particular about her bedroom – all sorts of airs and graces, this one. But just ignore her and get a bit of kip.'

Siddy, Alfie and Scrap flopped down on the bed while Moll led Gryff over to the sofa and scooped him up among the lumpy cushions. She curled round him protectively and listened to his purr rumbling inside her body. And though a storm was brewing outside – waves smashed against the rocks and whipped up into the wind – the children slept as soundly as if they'd been back in Little Hollows.

But not so far away, their heads bent down against the driving rain, a huddle of dark shapes was rowing out at sea, advancing slowly along the coast.

Chapter 31
Dorothy's Secret

'Will you stop it!' Puddle roared.

Moll's eyes sprang open. It was dark outside now.

'Enough is enough!' Puddle shouted again. 'You're going to get somebody killed!'

Moll tensed. The shouting was coming from higher up the lighthouse. She reached a hand down for her quiver, but remembered she'd left it outside the kitchen.

'I will NOT have this, Dorothy!' Puddle boomed.

Moll breathed a sigh of relief that it was the lighthouse playing up and nothing worse. She listened to the storm outside, still raging against the window and the darkness. Puddle had lit a candle while they were sleeping and its light flickered across the bed. Alfie stirred, then opened his eyes and looked at Moll.

'I'm going up to speak to Puddle,' she whispered. 'Stay here with the others.'

Alfie nodded sleepily and Moll turned to Gryff. His eyes were open, staring blankly, and when Moll saw them she squeezed her fists hard. 'Come on,' she breathed, helping Gryff from the sofa and grabbing her coat. 'We've got to work out why the bones sent us here.'

They climbed the cold stone steps up another level, past a room filled with spare lamps, until they reached the very last floor of the lighthouse: the lantern room. It was smaller than the rest, hexagonal in shape, and boxed in on every side by large sheets of latticed glass that were only just holding out against the rain. In the centre of the room there was a big, glowing lamp, surrounded by hundreds of pieces of beautiful, specially-cut glass, casting a beam of roving light out on to the sea – and, beside that, stood Puddle.

Moll watched from the doorway. 'What's Dorothy up to?'

Puddle jumped in surprise, then, on seeing Moll and Gryff, he smiled. 'What *isn't* she up to, more like ...' He rolled the sleeves of his cagoule up and placed a hand on a lever beneath the glass lens, then pushed. From the base there came a grinding sound, like a clockwork wheel turning. 'The lamp needs winding up every two hours,' Puddle muttered. 'She's high maintenance, I'll tell you that.' His muscles flexed and he kept pushing. 'Her lens collects light from the lamp as it turns and directs the rays out to sea as a single beam. Clever old thing, isn't she?'

Moll nodded. 'Oak would've liked to have seen this.'

Puddle looked up. 'Who's Oak then?'

Moll was silent for a moment. 'Someone who looks out for me, even when I'm annoying.' She picked at her coat. 'He

238

got injured trying to protect me and I'm hoping this amulet might make things better.'

She padded towards a window with Gryff. The storm outside was furious. Huge waves battered against the rocks at the bottom of the cliffs, hurling themselves again and again amid the rain and wind, and thunderclaps ground out from the night sky, shaking the whole lighthouse.

But still Dorothy's light shone out, scouring steady beams over the sea. And then her lamp began to flash on and off, not regularly as it had been doing before, but in a haphazard, stuttering way. Seconds later, it juddered to a complete stop, lighting up just one place.

'Dorothy!' Puddle hollered. 'Stop messing around!'

But Moll was only half listening. She screwed up her eyes against the windowpane, ignoring the rain that lashed against it.

'What's that just round the coastline – where the beam's shining?' she asked.

Puddle followed Moll's gaze. 'That there's Devil's Drop where the river spills out into the sea.'

Moll nodded. The roar she'd heard when they arrived at the coast earlier suddenly made sense. Because pouring over the edge of the cliffs in a bay just round from the lighthouse, and only visible from this height, was an enormous waterfall. Torrents of water cascaded over the lip and plunged down into the sea, sending up metres of foaming spray. Moll watched as the water fell, great curtains of white crashing down into the sea. The lamp flashed on and off again, jerking light then shadow over the falls, but it refused to turn regularly as Puddle wanted it to.

'No one ever goes near there,' Puddle added. 'A ship called the *Craggan* sank before the falls years and years ago. There are rumours that the dead sailors' bodies haunt the wreck so people tend to steer clear.'

Moll carried on watching, mesmerised by the gushing water. The lamp flickered again and again over Devil's Drop and Moll turned to Puddle. 'The Oracle Bones sent us to the Blinking Eye. Maybe – maybe – the lighthouse is trying to show us something.'

Puddle snorted. 'Dorothy? She's just having one of her moods.' He bent down to try and fix the lamp again and the rain beat harder against the windows, seeping in through unsealed cracks.

Moll frowned. 'But the way the lamp flashes on and off – it's not just random.' She gasped. 'Look, Puddle! There's some sort of pattern!'

Puddle stood beside Moll, his eyes squinting into the darkness. '*Is that . . .*' His voice trailed off into a whisper.

'Is that what?' Moll asked eagerly.

'Long long long, short, long, short, short . . . You might be on to something after all . . . This looks like a code!'

Moll's eyes grew large. 'How do you know?'

Puddle watched intently as the lamp flicked on and off over the waterfall. 'Because I recognise the patterns. I think it's Morse code – an emergency code sent through signals.'

Moll's breath misted up in a circle on the pane before her. She rubbed it away. 'Do you know what it means?'

Puddle reached behind him and grabbed an old parchment map rolled up on a table. Unfurling it and turning it over, he drew a pencil from his cagoule pocket and began to write. 'Dashes for the longer stretches of light, then we draw a diagonal line when there's a pause with no light at all, then dots for when it flashes in short bursts.' Before long, Puddle had scribbled a line of dashes and dots:

$$\_\_\_/.\_../../..\_/$$

'What does it mean?' Moll asked again.

'Each set of dashes and dots between a diagonal line is a letter.' Puddle ran his pencil over the symbols, then looked up at Moll. Her eyes were wide and green against the night. 'I've got a word,' he said.

Moll nodded, hardly daring to speak. Beside her, Gryff leant close.

'OLIVE,' Puddle said. 'The code reads: OLIVE.'

Moll raised two hands to the glass and watched the waterfall crashing down over the cliffs.

'Does that mean something to you?' Puddle asked.

The longing inside Moll ached. 'Olive was my ma. The Shadowmasks killed her.'

Puddle looked from the parchment to the waterfall, then back to Moll. 'Well, I never . . .'

Moll nodded. 'The amulet is my ma's soul . . . and I think

241

Dorothy's trying to tell me that it's trapped near Devil's Drop.'

The rain beat against the lantern room and thunder growled across the sky.

'There is a cave,' Puddle said slowly, 'behind Devil's Drop. Only no one's been in it since the *Craggan* sank.'

'Because of the rumours of the haunted wreck?' Moll asked.

Puddle nodded. 'Them – and the swell is so strong round the falls that any sailor would be mad to steer their boat towards it.'

Moll dug her hands into her coat pockets. 'That's where the amulet is; I just know it. We have to go there.'

'You'll be killed out there on a night like this!'

Moll bit her lip. 'I'll be killed anyway if I stay.'

A whistle sounded sleepily from the doorway and Scrap appeared, dreadlocks wild about her face, her striped flag knotted under her chin.

Moll looked at her. 'I think we know where the amulet is, Scrap.'

Puddle fiddled nervously with the zip on his cagoule. 'It's too dangerous. You're just a kid, it's the middle of the night and we don't even have a boat to—'

His words were cut short by three loud raps coming from further down the lighthouse. Knocks on the front door echoed through the building.

Moll glanced at Puddle. 'Are you expecting someone?' she said slowly.

Puddle frowned. 'No.'

The knocks sounded again, louder this time.

Alfie and Siddy appeared in the doorway behind Scrap. The storm and Puddle's shouting earlier hadn't bothered them too much, but knocks in the night – that meant trouble.

'We shouldn't answer it,' Alfie warned. 'It could be *them* – the Shadowmasks.'

The knocks didn't come again. Just the rain beat at the lighthouse, clawing at the windows with slippery fingers. The lamp flashed on and off, still repeating the pattern of Olive's name. But a feeling was growing inside Moll, whispering to her quietly. Whatever had been trying to get inside the lighthouse hadn't gone away.

Chapter 32
Night Callers

Puddle placed a protective hand on the lever before his lamp. 'The door's strong and it's bolted fast.' He scratched his beard. 'But in all the time I've been here no one has ever come knocking on it in the middle of the night.'

'We haven't got time to think on it,' Moll said urgently, she turned to the others. 'Listen, the lighthouse, it's been shining out a code—'

'—and Moll wants to go after it tonight,' Puddle finished. 'In the rain. Without a boat. To Devil's Drop.'

'What's Devil's Drop?' Siddy asked warily.

Moll raised her jaw. 'A waterfall that might or might not be a little bit haunted.'

'How haunted are we talking?' Alfie asked.

Moll tapped her foot impatiently. 'Dead sailors, I think.'

Siddy moaned. 'Only *you* would come up with a plan as mad as that, Moll.'

Ignoring them both, Moll spread out the parchment where Puddle had drawn the code. 'Puddle says it's something called a Morse code – emergency signals.' Her voice was a rush of breath. 'And it spells out OLIVE. My ma! Somehow we need to get down to Devil's Drop because that's where the amulet is. And we need to do it before the Shadowmasks find us!'

The reply didn't come from anyone inside the lighthouse. It came from the glass surrounding the lantern room – a tapping noise, scratching on a pane at the far side.

Scrap reached out to find Alfie and he took her hand in his. The lamp flickered off, and darkness fell, but when the light beamed again it shone upon a terrifying sight.

A crowbar gripped firmly by an enormous black hand.

Scrap screamed and Alfie held her tight. Before anyone could move, the crowbar slammed into the glass, the windowpane shattered to the floor and four smugglers, clad in long black leather boots and soaking shirts, piled in off the ladder that scaled the lighthouse: Barbarous Grudge, Smog Sprockett and the two older boys Moll and Siddy had seen back in Inchgrundle.

Moll plunged a hand into her dress pocket, but she'd taken the catapult and knife out before going to sleep – and the bows downstairs, even Willow had said, wouldn't work against those who knew nothing of the Bone Murmur. She backed up against the wall, shielding Gryff with her legs.

'Now – now listen here,' Puddle stammered, edging behind the lens. 'This is no place for smugglers. You and your lot aren't welcome so—'

Grudge raised his crowbar, all the while chewing hard

on the finger bone, grinding it between his golden teeth. He lunged towards Puddle and struck him in the stomach. The lighthouse keeper crashed to the ground, winded and groaning.

Moll leapt forward, but the two smuggler boys fell upon her, pinning her back. Smog cornered Gryff and, though he snarled and hissed, the street urchin could see the wildcat was now blind and he taunted and jeered at him as if Gryff was a harmless stray.

'Thought I wouldn't find you and your little friends?' Smog sniggered at Moll. 'I only had to ask around, then track your footprints . . .'

Grudge pushed his dreadlocks back from his face and pointed at Scrap with his crowbar. Then he crunched over the broken glass towards her.

'You!' he spat. 'You *helped* them? My own flesh and blood?' He looked at her with contempt. 'You're no daughter of mine any more!'

Moll's eyes widened. Scrap was Grudge's daughter! And yet she'd saved Moll from the kelpie and led them all to the Blinking Eye.

Grudge raised a pistol from his holster and Scrap raced round the wall to the door. But Grudge followed her with the barrel of his gun. 'Here's what I do to traitors, you little wretch!'

'Run, Scrap!' Moll screamed.

But it was too late. The gunshot roared. Scrap's legs buckled beneath her and she collapsed to the ground.

Moll bit the smuggler's hand fixed round her jaw, but it

held fast. Siddy darted towards Scrap, but Grudge advanced, his gun levelled at him. Siddy froze and Gryff growled from the corner, but Smog boxed him in. Only Alfie, unseen by the smugglers, could run to Scrap. He bent down, cradling her little body close. Immediately, he felt the blood leaking from her side.

His eyes stung. 'It's OK, Scrap, it's OK.'

The smugglers shifted uneasily at the voice coming from nowhere.

'More gypsy magic. Just like back in the port,' Smog muttered.

A smuggler boy shivered. 'It – it's a ghost!'

Grudge stiffened. 'Stay away from it, boys. Whatever it is.'

Scrap whimpered in Alfie's arms, her breaths shallow and fast. But in her eyes Alfie saw something different. She was looking at him, not around him, not in his general direction, but *at* him.

Tears rose in his eyes. 'You can see me now, can't you?' he whispered.

Scrap nodded, letting her eyes work their way over every curve of Alfie's face. She smiled faintly as if she was recognising him after a long time apart. Then she lifted her shaking arms up and wrapped them round his neck. She clung to Alfie, and he clung back, and then her body grew weaker and she slumped into his lap.

Gryff snarled and stamped on the floorboards. Alfie's jaw stiffened and he glared at Grudge. 'Murderer!' Still unseen by the smugglers, he picked up a shard of broken glass next to him and hurled it at Grudge.

Grudge may not have been able to see Alfie, but he spotted the flying glass and ducked just in time, his pistol swinging from Siddy to where the glass had come from. He shot once again into the room and Alfie ducked as the bullet skimmed the door frame.

'Keep back, spirit!' Grudge warned, training his pistol on Moll. 'Come close and I'll shoot your friends.'

Alfie looked down at Scrap and moaned. 'I promised her I'd keep her safe.'

From behind the lens, Puddle heaved himself up and limped towards the door. He glowered at Grudge as he passed. 'You can shoot me if you want,' he muttered, bending down to kneel by Scrap. He felt for Alfie and placed a hand on his back. 'It wasn't your fault, boy. There wasn't anything you could've done.'

Grudge grunted at Moll. 'It's you and your pal I'm after. We've come for that amulet.'

Moll blinked at Scrap's body, hardly able to take in what had happened. How could Scrap be dead? Tears pricked her eyes, but with Grudge there she wouldn't let them fall. She spat on to the ground by Grudge's boot as he advanced and the smugglers holding her tightened their grip.

'That's no way to cooperate, missy.' Grudge's lips curled back to show two rows of golden teeth.

Moll looked him square in the eye. 'How *could* you? She was your own daughter!'

248

Grudge ground the finger bone between his teeth.

Moll watched the storm swelling around them outside. Scrap was gone – and it hadn't even been the Shadowmasks who'd taken her away. She looked at the little smuggler girl and a lump swelled in her throat. Grudge would answer for this; she would see to that. And then, just as she was about to look away, Moll's heart beat faster. She could have sworn she'd seen a tiny, almost unnoticeable, flicker cross Scrap's eyelids. Moll's pulse hammered as Scrap's chest rose then dipped a fraction. She glanced from Puddle to Alfie to Siddy. They'd seen it too: *Scrap was still alive*. But if Grudge caught on he wouldn't show her mercy.

Thinking fast, Puddle scooped Scrap up from Alfie's arms and looked at Grudge. 'There's nothing you want from me. I'm taking her body; she deserves a proper burial. You owe her that much.'

Grudge scowled as Puddle left the room with Scrap lying limp in his arms. And then an idea began to form in Moll's mind. She didn't like it, but maybe, just maybe, it might work. She forced the words out, trying her best to turn her anger into a plan. 'You got a boat?'

Grudge nodded.

'Good,' she told him. 'Cos you're going to need it if you want the amulet.'

Siddy turned panicked eyes towards her. 'You're going to trust *them* to take us to the amulet?'

Moll glanced at Siddy, then at Alfie and took a deep

breath. She faced Grudge square on. 'We'll take you to the amulet – if you're man enough to brave Devil's Drop.'

Smog looked up from taunting Gryff, and the two smugglers glanced at one another uneasily.

'It's haunted, that place,' one of them muttered. 'There's not one sailor who's made it past those waters alive.'

The other smuggler nodded. 'I heard there are ghosts that drag you from your boat and drown you . . .'

Grudge snorted. 'Tall tales. There isn't a sea in the land I can't master if there's loot at the end of it.' He made a fist of Moll's coat. 'Whatever gypsy magic you have going on up here – whatever ghost you claim follows you – you'd better leave all that behind. Understand?'

Moll said nothing, wishing him dead. Then she dipped her head.

'One wrong move from you and I'll bury you and your friend alive. You've seen what I can do.' Grudge bared his teeth at Moll in an ugly smile. 'Well, we'd best get downstairs then, hadn't we? The boat's moored below the cliffs.'

Grudge flung Moll forward. She snatched at Gryff's fur, but Grudge shoved her in the back again and forced her on towards the door.

I'll come back for you, Moll said silently as Gryff reached out a paw towards her.

'We'll leave the cat,' Smog said. 'He's blind as they come, this one. No use to anyone.'

The smugglers grabbed Siddy by his arms and marched him to the door behind Moll. But, just before she crossed

250

the threshold, Moll stole a look at Alfie. 'Look after Scrap, then come after us,' she whispered. 'With Willow's quivers, in case the Shadowmasks are near. I've got a plan; I won't let Grudge get away with this.'

Chapter 33
Out at Sea

With his pistol lodged in the back of Moll's neck, and his smugglers gripping Siddy by the arms, Grudge led them behind the lighthouse, down towards the rocky precipice. The rain pelted against their clothes, but Moll could hardly feel it; her mind was swimming with images of Scrap. Would Puddle and Alfie know what to do to save her?

Grudge paused at the edge of the cliff and, as the lightning flashed, Moll and Siddy saw the chalky limestone fall abruptly away below them. At the bottom was the sea, a dark expanse of churning water, heaving in and out against the cliffs, dashing spray over the rocks.

Moll pointed to the left. 'Devil's Drop is in the next bay. Shouldn't we walk round?'

Grudge clicked the safety catch back on his gun and Moll swallowed. 'Our boat's down here.'

'Is there a safer way?' Siddy asked with a gulp. 'It's a sheer drop – the ledges can't be more than a footstep wide!'

Grudge shoved Siddy closer to the edge. 'You'll go down there; same way as we came up.'

Siddy shivered and Moll pushed her sopping hair back from her face. She thought of the trees she'd climbed in Tanglefern Forest, tried to imagine the cliff was just one of the giant elms. But, as the rain splintered down and the lightning shone on the drop, Moll's muscles jolted with fear.

The tallest of the smuggler boys climbed over the cliff edge first, then Smog followed, clinging to the limestone with nail-bitten fingers as the wind pummelled through his rags.

Grudge motioned towards the edge with his gun. 'Down you go.'

Siddy sucked the rain from his trembling lips, then followed Moll over the edge. Now and again small chunks of limestone crumbled away beneath their hands, but they clung to nearby ledges and felt for footholds, desperate to keep hold. And, each time the waves crashed below, Moll felt as if the limestone was moving, steered by powers far beyond her control. This wasn't just an ordinary storm: this was the Shadowmasks' menace. She could feel it.

Eyes blinking back the rain, Moll lowered herself on to a grassy patch covering a wider ledge.

'I can't stop thinking about poor Scrap,' Siddy said as he dropped down level with Moll. 'And after she got us all the way here.'

'Puddle will have bandages, won't he?' Moll asked. 'To stop the bleeding?'

Siddy bit his lip. 'I hope so.' He looked down. 'You'd better have a plan in all of this.'

Moll glanced up to check Grudge was a safe distance

above them. 'I do,' she whispered. 'We use their boat to get us in behind Devil's Drop—'

'Then what?'

'We get rid of them.'

Siddy gave a little whimper. '*That's* your plan? Any idea *how* we get rid of them?'

Moll glimpsed the lamp flashing out its Morse code from the lighthouse above them. 'Not yet . . . but we'll find a way, Sid. These rotten smugglers aren't taking the amulet from us – specially not after what they did to Scrap.'

She turned inwards to face the cliff again and carried on climbing down. The waves grew louder, filling her ears with their mighty roars, and once or twice Moll lost her footing on a slippery ledge. But her hands were like claws, gripping tight with fear, and they held her fast.

Eventually they stepped down on to the rocks and shingle at the foot of the cliff. The wind gusted against them and Moll and Siddy clung to one another, shivering. A small rowing boat knocked against the rocks, water buffeting it from all sides and spilling over the edges. The smugglers untied it and Grudge nodded at Moll and Siddy to get in. Shakily, they clambered into the stern. Moll sat on a wooden slat beside Siddy, and when the lightning flashed she saw the tips of knives bundled up in a roll of leather at the bottom of the boat.

Grudge climbed inside, pushing Smog up to the bow. 'Keep a watch for rocks as we pass round the Nibbled Head!'

The storm snatched his words away and the smugglers

began to row. Grudge turned to Moll and Siddy, thumped down on a slat in front of them and swivelled the barrel of his pistol in his hands.

Moll sidled closer to her friend while the smugglers heaved hard into the waves, and, with the rain beating against their backs, they inched forward along the coast. They were far enough from the cliffs now to warrant being smashed against the rocks, but, as Moll faced the storm head on, she felt the wildness of it and sensed its tormented spirit.

The boat edged away from the Nibbled Head and Moll watched Dorothy's light flashing on and off in the direction of Devil's Drop. *I'm coming, Ma,* she thought to herself. *I'm coming.* She imagined Gryff and Alfie inside the lighthouse. Would Alfie come after them? Would he risk everything – again – for the sake of a magic that hadn't even been able to make him real? And how would Gryff manage without his sight?

The smugglers rowed on, despite the water that sprayed over the edges and sloshed round their ankles, and then suddenly, as if someone had told it to, the storm seemed to ease. The rain pulled back, the waves quelled and the wind dropped to nothing.

Moll's insides knotted. The storm hadn't done with them; there was more in store – she could feel the dark magic all around them now.

And then another noise began and, with every stroke of the smugglers' oars, it grew louder. Moll clasped her boxing fist talisman as they rounded the headland.

Devil's Drop roared in the distance.

Dorothy's beam flashed upon it again and again and only then did Moll understand the full menace of the falls: a giant, writhing whiteness growling with an energy all of its own. Spray clouded up where the water hammered into the sea and, to the sides of the falls, great clumps of jungled weeds hung down from rocks. And every now and again the silhouettes of swifts dived into the falls, passing so easily to the place most sailors feared to go.

A mist had settled on the surface of the sea now, but it wasn't billowing and frothing as it was beneath the falls. This hung like a band of fog, cold and brooding, and it made Moll and Siddy exchange a nervous glance.

Smog looked at the others. 'Can you hear them?'

Moll strained her ears against the roar of water. And there, just at the very edge of her hearing: whispers. They were faint and hollow, like dying breaths, and they sifted through the mist towards them.

The smugglers stopped rowing and one turned to Grudge. 'G-ghosts.' His voice was trembling. 'Come up from the *Craggan* . . .'

The boat drifted into the mist and it twisted round them, cool and damp.

'Just the wind,' Grudge muttered, but he gripped his pistol tighter.

The smugglers rowed on and the whispers grew all around them, hanging in the air. There was something sinister in their call, as if they wanted to be heard, and, as the mist closed in round the boat, lit now and again by Dorothy's beams, Moll peered down into the sea. From the deep darkness there rose a mast draped in seaweed: the wreck of the *Craggan* – and they were right above it. Smog crouched lower in the bow, his shoulders bunched up. Then the whispers hissed louder and he clattered backwards and screamed.

Ten fingers – long, bony and grey – were curled round the edge of the boat.

Chapter 34
Saving Scrap

Alfie sat on the edge of Puddle's boat bed, chewing his nails. 'Will she be OK?'

Puddle tucked Scrap's legs beneath a blanket and looked anxiously at her torso, bound tightly in bandages. Scrap's eyes were closed and her breaths were so weak that her chest barely rose and fell.

'I don't know,' Puddle said quietly. 'All we can do now is wait.'

Alfie's shoulders slumped and, over by the window, Gryff whimpered helplessly for Moll.

'Nothing you could have done would've stopped Grudge,' Puddle said. 'You can't protect everyone, even if you want to. It's not the way the world works.'

'Kelpies, cursed owls, wolves . . .' Alfie threw up his hands. 'We led her into danger again and again.'

Puddle shook his head. 'You can't shield people from the darkness out there, but the friendship and loyalty you showed Scrap will have counted for far more than you realise.'

'But I wanted to make things right for her.' Alfie twisted his shirt cuff. 'She was someone I could've looked after – she had no one else. She didn't deserve any of this.'

Puddle walked round the boat and reached out a hand until he found Alfie's back. 'No, she didn't. But, even though life deals us the most almighty blows, we must never give up fighting for those we love.' Puddle paused and threaded his beard through his fingers. 'Whatever happens to Scrap, I don't believe this world is the end, Alfie. I think there's more after – a place where lives aren't snatched away unjustly and where goodness prevails.'

Alfie looked up to the ceiling to force the tears away. 'She could see me,' he said quietly. 'While she was in my arms – she could see me.'

Puddle nodded. 'I've been thinking and I wonder whether I understand a little better now. Perhaps you can only be seen by those who have grown to love you and trust you. Moll, Siddy, Gryff – the whole of their camp if what you've told me is right – and then Scrap. It makes sense.'

'But the Shadowmasks – they can see me too.'

Puddle's face darkened. 'Maybe that's because they were the ones who made you this way in the first place.' He was silent for a little while. 'But I know there's a certain fiery-tempered girl with a huge heart who won't stop until she's fixed it for you.'

Alfie thought of Moll charging headlong into danger for the amulet – for Gryff, for Oak, for her ma – and for him.

Gryff edged round the side of the room. His strides were

tentative and slow, but he found Alfie and stopped short of him, his ears cocked forward.

Alfie sat on the floorboards, his head in his hands. 'What are we going to do, Gryff?'

The wildcat padded forward until he was just in front of Alfie. The boy looked up and held his breath, then he stared into Gryff's distant eyes. The wildcat had got used to him, he'd understood Alfie meant no harm, but Gryff had never come this close before. This was something he only ever did with Moll.

Slowly, carefully, Alfie raised his hand. The wildcat took another step forward, then stretched out his neck as if searching for something. Alfie's heart quickened as his fingers met Gryff's fur. It was soft and warm, but the muscles beneath were firm and strong. Alfie ran a hand over Gryff's back and the wildcat purred, then nuzzled Alfie with his head, leaning in closer, like he always did with Moll.

So much was uncertain and broken, but somehow Gryff's presence made Alfie feel safe, even loved. And, for the first time since escaping Skull's camp in Tanglefern Forest, Alfie cried. Tears trailed down his cheeks and great sobs shook his body. But Gryff didn't move; he let the tears fall on to his head and over his nose. The wildcat's purr stirred something inside the boy, drawing out fresh tears, and then Gryff's muscles flexed, his back arched and he stepped back.

'Alfie,' Puddle said after a moment. 'Look . . .'

Gryff blinked yellow-green eyes at Alfie. But they were not

distant eyes glazed with fear as they had been a moment ago. They were Gryff's eyes: wild, alert and fierce.

The wildcat sprang up on to the sofa and snarled towards the window.

'His whiskers have grown back!' Alfie cried.

Gryff pounded his forelegs against the table, hissing and spitting.

'Your tears,' Puddle gasped. 'I could see them . . . And when they fell on Gryff's head his whiskers grew back. You healed him. He can see.' He grinned. 'Alfie, there's something special about your tears, about *you*. Not real?' he scoffed. 'You're as real as they come, boy.'

Alfie stood up, his fists clenched. 'Look after Scrap for me, Puddle.' He dipped his head towards Gryff. 'We're going after Moll and Sid.'

Chapter 35
Grim Whispers

Moll stared in horror at the fingers curled round the bow of the boat. The mist thickened, lit hazily from behind by the lighthouse beams, then through the fog a face appeared.

Grey skin, mottled with barnacles, stretched tight over a long, thin face. Limpets and sea urchins clung to the tendrils of kelp that twisted down from the scalp, and wild eyes swivelled above jutting cheekbones.

The smugglers gripped the oars tightly, Grudge raised his pistol and this time neither Moll nor Siddy tried to stop him. Whatever this creature was, it looked rotten to the core. The gunshot blasted straight through it, as if it was made of mist, then there came a hollow laugh and all around the boat the whispers stitched together into a web of hisses.

'We're the Grim Whispers,' the creature by the bow crooned, 'the ghosts of the *Craggan*. And you cannot kill the dead ...'

Moll peered over the edge of the boat to see dozens of heads protruding just a few centimetres above the surface.

There were no eyes yet, just strands of twisted seaweed floating on the sea.

Smog and the smuggler boys were rigid with fear, but Grudge whirled round to face Moll and Siddy. 'Is this more of your tricks?'

Moll shook her head, her eyes locked on the Grim Whisperer at the bow. It tilted its head at her and the limpets caught in its hair clinked together. Moll turned to Siddy. 'Feels like the Shadowmasks' magic.'

Siddy nodded shakily, then he forced himself to look at the creature. 'We – we want to pass through to Devil's Drop.'

The Grim Whisperer smiled, white lips clinging to grey skin. 'Devil's Drop?' His hands scuttled down the boat edge and he pulled his bare chest through the water until he was at the stern before Moll and Siddy. They cringed back from the creature's bony fingers. 'And why should I let you past there?'

Siddy forced the words out. 'An amulet; we think it's hidden behind the falls.'

The whispers around the boat rasped and hissed again and the creature pulled his chest fully out of the water and leant into the boat, his eyes wild and roving. 'But we've been called to keep you here. To hold you until others much worse than us come along.'

Smog huddled at the bottom of the boat, shaking with fear. 'We should've left these children back in Inchgrundle; they're cursed!'

Moll didn't need to ask who had called the Grim Whispers.

She could feel the Shadowmasks' magic, like a gauze of evil woven around them. And then her mind flicked back to a conversation she'd had with Cinderella Bull back in the cove when she'd told them all about the sea spirits. *Sea spirits love tricks*, she'd said. But what had the fortune-teller told her about ghosts from shipwrecks? Moll thought fast. And then she heard Cinderella Bull's voice so clearly it was as if she was speaking inside her: *Beat a mer ghost at their own riddle and their hold over you will shrink.*

'What if we played you for it?' Moll said, her voice level and low, despite the fear she felt rising inside her.

The Grim Whisperer blinked slowly. 'Go on.'

'What if you set us a riddle and we solved it?'

Siddy shrank further inside his coat. 'Oh, Moll. This is a terrible, terrible plan.'

Grudge seized Moll by the wrist. 'What are you playing at now, girl?'

Moll ignored them both and twisted her body against Grudge's hold so that she was facing the Grim Whisperer straight on. An unsettling coldness crawled beneath her skin as she met his eyes, but Moll willed herself on. 'Try us.'

The barnacles above the Grim Whisperer's cheekbones clung closer together as his eyes narrowed. 'I could flood your lungs with water,' he spat. The whispers around him quavered with delight. 'But I'll play you because I know I'll win.'

Moll turned to Grudge. 'If you want that amulet, we've got to beat these ghosts at their own game.'

The smugglers behind Grudge spoke in low, frightened

voices to one another, but Grudge spun round and smacked his crowbar on the side of the boat. 'If you lot even think about trying to steer this boat away, I'll send the knives into you one by one.'

The largest smuggler eyed Moll up and down. 'It's her,' he muttered. 'I don't trust the gypsy girl. She could be on the side of these creatures – trying to work her way free from us.'

Grudge spun the barrel of his gun into place, lifted it and set it against Moll's forehead. 'She won't be going free from us, boys.'

Fear snaked down Moll's throat, but she swallowed it back and tried to keep her mind alert. Getting the amulet was the important thing. She shifted round on the wooden slat to face the Grim Whisperer and Grudge's gun barrel settled at the back of her neck. The creature smiled, revealing a gum full of rotten teeth, and the heads floating in the water around him rose a fraction, until dozens of eyes stared at the boat, drinking in the fear that had settled there. Then the whispers grew, like a swelling wave, and the Grim Whisperer leant further into the boat. He raised a hand and the whispers died to nothing.

'A riddle you asked for, a riddle you'll have.' He smiled darkly, then every whisper joined as one, hissing round the boat: '*One Killed None But Still Killed Twelve.* Tell us how this can be.'

Siddy bit his nails. 'Moll, what've you done? There's no sense in that riddle. We'll never get the answer!'

Moll's mind whirred. *Think*, she told herself. *Think*. But

265

her mind was empty and all she could feel was Grudge's gun rammed into her neck.

Siddy reached inside his pocket and drew out Hermit. 'It's over; after all we've gone through, we're going to be drowned by the Grim Whispers.'

Grudge clicked the safety catch on. 'Think fast, girl,' he growled. 'Get us out of this mess and on to find the amulet.'

Moll slid a glance at Siddy, her thoughts skittering inside her.

The Grim Whisperer smiled with crusted lips, then he laced his fingers together. 'It looks as if your wits have failed you. So you're ours to keep.' The creatures around him rose higher from the surface, strands of gutweed floating on the water. Then the Grim Whisperer lurched forward, wrapping a cold, clammy hand round Moll's wrist.

She recoiled in terror, but the creature held her fast.

'Wait!' Siddy cried.

The Grim Whisperer clung to Moll, seaweed sliming over her wrist.

'I – I think I have it,' Siddy stammered, staring wide-eyed at Hermit. 'One Killed None But Still Killed Twelve. A crab eats a poisoned shrimp that's already dead. The crab dies too,' Siddy said slowly. 'Twelve men eat a stew made from the crab – and all of *them* die from the poison as well. The crab didn't mean to kill anyone, but it killed twelve men!'

The whispers around the boat crumbled away. Silence followed.

Moll turned to Siddy in disbelief. 'It – it works. Siddy! What you said works!'

She felt the grip of the Grim Whisperer weaken, then its bony fingers slid from her wrist and it dropped into the sea behind the boat. Dozens of sunken eyes burned with hatred at Siddy, then the whispers started again, threading together and weaving their way round the boat: *'For now you shall pass, but the Shadowmasks are coming and their darkness will crush you both.'* The whispers faded and the hideous creatures surrounding the boat slipped beneath the surface of the sea until just the shipwreck remained, strands of seaweed floating eerily round the mast.

Moll breathed deeply, pushing back her fear, then she hugged Siddy tight. 'How did you do it?'

Siddy shook his head. 'I have absolutely no idea; it was Hermit who got me thinking!'

For the first time, Moll was thankful for Hermit. 'I could kiss your stinky crab, Sid!'

Grudge nudged his pistol against Moll's arm. 'Shut it, you two. We've got *that* to get past now.'

The mist had faded and there, glinting in the beam of the lighthouse, was Devil's Drop. Water drummed into the sea, deafening the night, and the smugglers rowed on, striking hard against the current.

Moll felt the water in the air first, droplets of spray showering her face, then the roar grew mightier and a cloud of whiteness swallowed them up. There was no up or down, just walls of white shaking around them. The spray grew,

267

drenching their faces, then great thrusts of water poured over the boat and slammed into their bodies. Moll gasped as the water punched the breath from her lungs.

'Turn us back!' Siddy yelled at Grudge.

'He's right!' the smuggler boys screamed. 'We'll die going under this!'

The water tossed the oars from the boat and dragged it into the heart of the falls – into the froth and the spray and the churn. Devil's Drop thundered down and Moll and Siddy clutched each other tight. The water thrashed itself against the boat and the vessel spun wildly, hurling Smog into the sea. Another thrust of water hammered down.

'Hang on to me, Sid!' Moll screamed, yanking him over the side of the boat with her.

They tumbled into the sea just before the boat shattered in two and was lost in the maelstrom. Water pounded down beneath the surface, flinging Moll and Siddy upside down, but they clung to one another, their hands locked together. Hundreds of words raced through Moll's mind – conversations she wished she'd had with Siddy, things left unspoken. And though Moll couldn't say a word she held Siddy's hand tight – cradling everything that should have been said but hadn't. They let the water take them, their breath pent up inside as it hurled them in every direction. Then suddenly they were kicking out, free from the heart of the waterfall, and they burst through the surface, a roar of water clattering down behind them. They were through and inside Devil's Drop itself.

Choking out ragged breaths, they kicked away from the curtain of water that closed them in, towards the smooth rocks in front of them. As Puddle had said, there was a cave – and it towered above them, a giant mouth leading into the cliff. Despite the rumble of the falls, there was a stillness inside, and from somewhere further in a light was shining.

Moll put her hands on her knees as her breath sawed back through her. 'Thank you, Sid. For not letting go – and I know I don't say it enough, but for everything else too.'

'It's what the Tribe does,' Siddy panted, clambering up on to the rocks. 'Have we lost Grudge and the Dreads then?'

'We don't have time to worry about them.' Moll wrung the water from her coat and dress. 'The Shadowmasks will know we got past the Grim Whispers by now; we've got to get inside this cave.'

Chapter 36
Inside Devil's Drop

They crept over the rocks, glad of the solid ground beneath their feet. The cave walls arched around them, but, instead of the dark, marbled rock that lined Little Hollows, this was limestone, white and chalky. Stalactites hung from the ceiling like long, pointing fingers, and the light from somewhere further inside the cave cast shadows all about them.

Siddy wrapped his hand round his talisman and they walked on in silence, ignoring their echoing footsteps, until they came to a screen of ivy hanging down from the roof of the cave. Tentatively, Moll reached out a hand and pulled a creeper back. She gasped.

Beyond was an atrium four times the size of Little Hollows, and it was lit turquoise by thousands of glow-worms that clung to the roof and sides of the cave, glittering like a secret constellation of stars. Stalactites hung from the roof, but they weren't chalky-white like before: these were long shards of glinting crystals. And beneath them, filling the entire cave, was a lake – as still as a mirror.

Moll and Siddy pushed past the creepers and stepped out on to a downward formation of rocks leading to the lake.

'What is this place?' Siddy mummered.

The light from the glow-worms shivered, as if they weren't used to having visitors.

'I don't know,' Moll replied. 'But,' she fumbled for the right words, 'I know the amulet is in here this time. I can feel it.' A flutter of excitement prickled her skin. Any moment now, she might find her ma's soul. All those years of growing up without her – and soon she might be able to speak to her like she had with her pa, even if just for a short while.

They tiptoed towards the lake. The water in the middle shone turquoise beneath the glow-worms, but where it spread out to the edges it sank into a murky gloom and huge stalagmites rose up from the depths. Moll jumped as a droplet of water fell from the roof and pierced the skin of water, then her eyes were drawn to something else. On a boulder rising up in the middle of the lake was a large metal cage. Moll peered closer. From where she stood, it looked empty, but there was something about it that pulled at Moll, tugging her closer.

'That cage,' she whispered. 'I think we need to go over to it.'

'But how do we cross—'

Siddy's words were stopped short as two giant hands seized him and Moll by the scruff of the neck. They whirled round to a face of gold teeth and wild dreadlocks.

'Miss me?' Barbarous Grudge growled.

Moll jabbed her elbows into Grudge's stomach and Siddy struck out with his foot. But Grudge's hold was firm. Moll's eyes dropped to his holster and she saw that it was empty; the pistol must have been lost in the falls, but the crowbar was still hooked over his belt.

'The amulet's in that cage, isn't it?' Grudge spat. He glanced up at the shards of crystal, then smiled, his gold teeth gleaming in the glow-worm light. 'If that's what's growing out here, just think of the size of the amulet in the cage. It'll make me a fortune.'

Moll twisted beneath Grudge's grasp. 'It doesn't work like that,' she hissed. 'I'm not even sure if the amulet *is* a jewel.'

Grudge shook her. 'Whatever it is, it'll be valuable, I'll bet. And you're going to fetch it for me.'

Siddy strained against Grudge's fist, but the smuggler only smiled. Moll's mind raced. Where was Alfie? Had he tried to come after them or had he finally given up hope? She thought of the sheer-drop cliffs and the raging falls. Even if he had followed them, would he get past all that? She jerked against Grudge and her coat ripped, but he grappled for a stronger hold. She bit down on his fist, her eyes fierce slits, and the smuggler's hand shot back. Moll seized the opportunity and leapt backwards, but Grudge was over her in a flash, his crowbar raised.

'Moll!' Siddy screamed.

The crowbar hung in the air and Moll cowered beneath it.

'Wait!' Siddy spluttered. 'We'll get the amulet for you.'

Grudge lowered his weapon and Moll breathed again. 'See

those stepping stones leading out across the lake to the rock in the middle?' he snarled.

Moll and Siddy nodded.

'Cross them – and bring me back the amulet.'

Moll looked at the polished surface of the water; its stillness unnerved her. Although there didn't seem anything to be afraid of, she couldn't help feeling as if someone – something – was watching her.

Grudge threw Siddy forward, then jabbed Moll in the back with his crowbar. 'Off you go.'

They stood by the water's edge, the path of stepping stones laid out before them like half-made promises.

Siddy gripped Moll's hand. 'We can do this. There's nothing to be afraid of.' He paused. 'But, even so, I think you should go first. You're the brave one.'

Moll put a foot on the first stone. It held her weight and the lake remained still. She lifted the other foot out, wobbled slightly as she found her balance, then set both feet side by side. And, from the shore, Grudge watched every move. Moll raised her leg again and stepped on to the second stone and, although he groaned at every movement, Siddy followed. They stepped further into the lake, their breath bridled in tight.

Halfway to the cage the ripples started. Small ruffles over the surface of the water, nudging at the stones.

'What is it?' Siddy asked from the stone behind Moll.

Moll's arms wavered either side of her as she fumbled for balance. 'I'm – I'm not sure.'

Above them the glow-worms twitched, then dimmed a fraction.

Siddy gasped. 'There!'

Something large and dark was shifting in the gloom beneath the surface a few metres away. A ridge of fins arched, then slunk out of sight and the lake was once more still. Moll forced her breaths out, trying to keep calm, but she knew the darkness was out there, watching and waiting.

'Faster!' Grudge shouted from the shore.

Moll blinked back her terror and took another step.

Then, some distance away, the lake erupted. The long, shimmering body of an enormous eel coiled out of the water. Black-scaled gills flared, eyes glowered green and a blunt nose turned towards Moll and Siddy. They drank in its darkness, felt the Shadowmasks' magic seeping inside them, then the eel's head dipped low to the water and its great scaled length slithered towards them.

Chapter 37
The Monster in the Lake

'Moll, what do we do?' Siddy whimpered as the eel sliced a path through the water straight at them. Moll glanced to the shore where Grudge was edging backwards, then to the cage still six or seven stepping stones ahead. The eel loomed closer.

'I – I don't know,' she stammered.

Then from somewhere inside her, beyond the Shadow-masks' darkness, Moll thought of the Bone Murmur.

'There is a magic, old and true.' Her voice was little more than a whisper. 'That shadowed minds seek to undo.' The words seem to come from a power beyond Moll's own will and the eel felt their strength. It slowed slightly in the water and Moll spoke the words louder. 'They'll splinter the souls of those who hold the Oracle Bones from Guardians of old. And storms will rise; trees will die, if they free their dark magic into the sky.'

'It's working!' Siddy cried.

'Say it with me, Sid!' She clutched his hand. 'We need to call on the old magic together!'

The eel skulked close and thrashed its tail. Water sprayed

up around them, but Moll and Siddy kept their balance. Moll closed her eyes and thought of the Bone Murmur again – of the old magic that seemed to be unfolding around her. She took a deep breath and Siddy joined in: '*But a beast will come from lands full wild, to fight this darkness with a gypsy child.*'

The eel slunk beneath the water until just its blunt nose remained visible. Moll thought of Gryff and willed all of his strength to rise up inside her. Siddy's hand was a fist round hers, but his face was hard.

'*And they must find the Amulets of Truth,*' they shouted. '*To stop dark souls doing deeds uncouth.*'

The eel's slitted eyes closed, its nose slipped from sight and, once again, the water stilled.

Moll and Siddy looked at one another, too rattled to speak, but now the eel had disappeared Grudge was down by the shore again, shouting at them to hurry.

'Come on,' Moll whispered, and she leapt from stone to stone, further into the lake.

Finally, they reached the last stepping stone and jumped up on to the boulder. The enormous cage was perched on top of it, dome-shaped and rusted, like an old birdcage. Moll's heart thundered inside her. This was it. The second amulet waiting for them, just metres away.

Hands reaching for crevices, Moll and Siddy scrambled up the boulder and hauled themselves on to its flattened surface. They stepped up to the bars of the cage. Moll blinked. Bird feathers, hundreds of them, lined its bottom. She stooped down, stretched a hand through the bars and picked one up.

It was golden brown, like the others in the cage, and larger than any she'd ever seen before.

'It looks like a golden eagle's feather,' Siddy said. 'Only bigger. But why are they here?'

'What is it?' Grudge yelled from the shore. 'What've you found?'

Moll looked from the feather to Siddy. 'I – I don't understand. Was there something in the cage but it got out?' She shook her head. 'Where's the amulet?'

'Tell me what you've found!' Grudge roared.

Siddy walked to the edge of the boulder. 'Feathers!' he yelled. 'We told you that it wouldn't be what you expected.'

Silence. Then Grudge strode out on to the stepping stones.

'Siddy!' Moll gasped. But she wasn't looking at Grudge. 'There, tucked right up against the bars – it's an envelope!'

Grudge was moving fast over the stones now, his strides so big he only needed to stand on every second one. 'You're lying to me! You'll show me where this amulet is!' he spat.

Moll reached inside the cage and pulled the old brown envelope out. And there, in beautiful scripted writing were two words: *My Moll*.

Grudge loomed closer, but Moll stood up, the envelope clasped tightly in her hand. 'Stay away, Grudge!' she shouted. 'You've no right to anything!'

Grudge snorted. 'I'll take what I please.'

Suddenly the lake began to ripple, its stillness disturbed by a blunt black nose. It broke the surface and was followed by a scaled body that rose before Grudge, a terror of glittering

277

scales. The smuggler cowered beneath it, his body stalled by fear. And then the eel slid forward, opened its cavernous mouth and snatched Grudge from the stepping stone. Grudge howled in fear, thrashing against the eel's jagged teeth, but, a second later, his howls were silenced as the creature worked its jaws. It turned two green eyes towards Moll and Siddy, and Moll thrust her letter up in the air, hoping it might hold the same power that the Bone Murmur had. The eel blinked slowly and then sank back into the gloom until only a circle of ripples marked its presence.

Siddy let his head fall back, then he breathed hard. 'He's gone – Grudge is gone.'

Moll nodded. She expected to feel something, to relish in the sweet revenge of it, even if just for Scrap's sake, but there was a letter with her name on it in her hands. And feelings far greater than anger and revenge were brewing inside her.

'Open it,' Siddy whispered.

Moll peeled back the seal and drew out a piece of parchment covered in words. *Could it be?* she thought, hardly daring to hope. Could this be a letter from her ma?

'What does it say?' Siddy asked.

Moll opened it up and drew breath to read, but another voice cut across hers. It didn't belong to Siddy and there wasn't anyone else around them. But Moll recognised that voice – because it was the one that had soothed her tears and sung her to sleep as a baby and, though many years had passed since then, Moll had kept the sound of that voice locked inside her. It was soft, but there was a quiet strength to

278

it, as if it had been built from the embers of an unquenchable fire, and the sound seemed to cradle Moll in warmth. She followed the words in the letter as her ma's voice spoke them aloud.

'*My Moll,*

Oh, how I've missed you – more than this letter will ever be able to say. I remember you as a baby, with a shock of black hair and eyes just like mine. And now look at you, so much bigger than you were – so grown up. I wish I could have given you the childhood you deserved: we'd have climbed trees together, swum in the river, ridden cobs bareback through the forest . . . But, my darling Moll, what you've done – you and Gryff and your friends – is more than I ever expected. To have got this far when almost everything was against you fills me with a pride I want to shout from the sky.'

Moll felt a yearning in her chest for the mother she'd never known. It made her legs and chest go weak. 'They took you, took you when they had no right.'

'*The bones told me I would die – that the only way the Bone Murmur could go on was if your pa and I sacrificed our lives for it. We knew the old magic would stir and fight back, but neither of us could have understood the bravery that you would show – and the love and loyalty to your friends. The second amulet, my soul, was searching for a virtue needed for the old magic to win through. Moll, the second amulet stood for friendship.*'

Siddy gasped. 'The feathers scattered in the cage! Oak always told us brown feathers meant friendship!'

'Moll and Siddy, you have stuck by your friends – however hopeless things have seemed. You trusted Alfie when he came from a witch doctor's gang and held secrets none of you knew how to explain. You did everything you could to look after Scrap, the child of the man who sought to kill you. And Moll, there's no one out there who can break the bond you share with Gryff. My soul is trapped here, but in destroying the Shadowmasks' weapon you'll undo their power and I will be free. Remember this though: he who made the Soul Splinter will destroy it.'

Siddy glanced at Moll. 'We – we have to get the Shadowmasks to destroy it . . .'

The voice of Moll's ma came softer now, as if full of untold secrets.

'There are things I can tell you, things you've been begging to understand. I know you've been questioning why the Shadowmasks shaved my head and your pa's. It was for a reason, Moll – to use our hair, a symbol of the purity of the Bone Murmur, as thread. And, with it, the Shadowmasks plan to weave a quilt of darkness that will be carried across the land and used to smother children's dreams, poisoning their minds with evil. But there are forces stronger than the Shadowmasks' menace, and, if you set my soul free, as you did with your pa, the Bone Murmur will fight back and the ways of the old magic will be restored.'

The voice paused and, when it came again, Moll could feel it as a whisper in her ear.

'I love you, Moll. You were, and are, everything to me. And I'll always be with you – me and your pa – watching over you as stars from the Otherworld.'

Moll held the letter close, the words now smudged with tears. She wanted to rush into her ma's arms and hold her tight, but she was just a voice, a sound in a forgotten cave. 'That was her, Sid,' she sniffed. 'My ma – as real as you and me.'

Siddy nodded. 'That was her all right.' He looked at the parchment. 'And – and the amulet. Do you think it's her letter?'

Moll didn't answer. It had been niggling at her too. The first amulet had been a jewel more beautiful than anything she'd ever set eyes on before. But this – though it meant more to her than any ruby, sapphire or emerald could – was now a damp piece of parchment, blotted grey where words had once been.

'The feathers,' Moll said slowly. 'When me and Alfie spoke to Mellantha about the first amulet, she said something about birds when we were out on the heath.' Moll racked her brain. 'She said: *In a bird, we see our soul set free.*'

Siddy frowned. 'So you think these feathers are . . .'

His voice trailed off and Moll's face filled with dread. 'Are we too late? Perhaps there was a bird inside this cage once, but now—'

The glow-worms above them shuddered, splaying flickering turquoise over the cave walls. The lake didn't stir, as it had done before, but the curtain of creepers hanging down at the opening of the cave did. They swept aside and a throng of bats swarmed in, their screeches grating into the stillness.

Moll's insides convulsed with fear and Siddy's eyes grew large as the bats whirled together and merged to become one terrifying figure.

Darkebite had arrived.

Chapter 38
The Amulet

The Shadow Keeper landed with a crunch on top of the birdcage, her enormous leathery wings outstretched, her mask of charcoaled wood tilting down to the children.

Moll and Siddy backed away, to the furthest point of the boulder, but they could hear footsteps scuttling closer. Ashtongue was crawling on all fours towards them, his snakeskin mask glinting in the light, but he wasn't using the stepping stones to cross the lake: he was scampering over a length of glittering black scales. The eel had risen to the surface of the lake, bidden by the commands of the Shadowmasks.

Moll's blood roared inside her. There was nowhere left to turn; they were boxed in on both sides. And then a noise shattered the tension: an inhuman, blood-curdling shriek.

Ashtongue leapt up on to the boulder just as the eel reared backwards, hurling itself against the lake. And only then did Moll and Siddy see the silver-birch arrow lodged deep inside its gills. The Oracle Spirit billowed out, spreading the length of its body, and dragged the great beast under the surface.

Moll looked towards the shore, and there was Alfie, his bow raised to his chin, a second arrow poised.

'Alfie!' she screamed. He'd come for them, just as he'd done in Ashtongue's house. And Moll knew in that moment that she never should have doubted him.

Darkebite jumped down from the cage and landed in a crouch, her wings jutting out either side of her like claws.

Alfie drew back on his bow and fired again. The arrow whistled through the air, straight for Darkebite, but she drew the Soul Splinter from her cloak and the arrow clanged uselessly against the shard of black ice, before clattering to the ground. Ashtongue scurried round the cage behind Darkebite, and, hiding behind the safety and power of the Soul Splinter, he let his tongue flicker out from his mask.

Alfie raised another arrow to his bow, but there was someone else charging over the stepping stones now. Moll blinked once, twice, then again to be sure. It was Gryff! Not blind any more, but bounding towards her with every ounce of strength inside him, his teeth bared in a snarl, his claws splayed.

'It can't be . . .' Siddy murmured.

'Gryff!' Moll gasped. 'Gryff!'

Alfie released another arrow, but once again Darkebite raised the Soul Splinter to ward it off. Swift as light, Gryff leapt from the stepping stones up on to the boulder and flung himself against Moll. She wrapped her arms round him.

'You're OK! But how?'

Gryff looked back at Alfie and Moll's eyes widened. *Alfie had healed him? Just like he promised he would . . .*

The wildcat wriggled free of Moll's hug and sprang on to the cage, snarling at the Shadowmasks. Then he pounced.

'PAAAAAH!'

Ashtongue hissed and swiped with his hands, but Gryff was fighting with a new-found strength. He was bigger somehow, wilder, as if regaining his sight had made him stronger. Moll watched in awe as Ashtongue staggered backwards and Gryff tore at Darkebite's cloak with his teeth. Then Darkebite raised the Soul Splinter and Moll rushed forward to help Gryff, but the wildcat thrashed his claws at Darkebite's wings and the witchdoctor shifted backwards, the Soul Splinter still held high.

Moll's pulse quickened. Alfie and Gryff might be able to stall the Shadowmasks, but without the power of the amulet the dark magic would win. Grabbing Siddy by the arm, she rushed to the cage, her ma's letter clasped in her hand.

'Help us, Ma,' she whispered between the bars.

Something strange began to happen inside the cage. The feathers heaped on the ground started to quiver, as if brushed by a mysterious breath, then they floated upwards, shifting and twisting into unrecognisable shapes. Siddy's jaw dropped and he clung to the bars, and together they watched as an eagle larger than anything they'd ever seen, with shining golden-brown feathers, took shape.

This was the second amulet, her ma's soul.

Behind the cage there was a tangle of wings and claws. Then the bird, five times the size of an ordinary golden eagle, spread its wings and struck out. The cage groaned and the bars crashed to the ground.

Moll rushed towards the bird, somehow knowing what to do. 'Sid, get on! We won't last if we stay here!'

They leapt up on to the bird and Gryff skirted the cage, his strides more agile than Moll had ever seen. He leapt on to the eagle's back in front of Moll and the great bird dipped for a second, as if flexing its muscles after a long sleep. Then it launched itself off from the boulder, beating its wings towards the shore. Moll clung to the bird's back, her legs tucked beneath her.

'Come back!' Darkebite screeched, still wielding the Soul Splinter.

Siddy tightened his grip round Moll's waist as the eagle flew further and further across the lake. It swooped by Alfie, and Siddy stretched out a hand to yank him up on to the bird's back. The eagle faltered for a second under the extra weight, but didn't stop. It thrust its wings on, tearing through the creepers before flying on beneath the limestone stalactites.

Moll turned her head towards Alfie. 'You – you healed Gryff?'

'It was my tears,' he panted. 'I don't understand how, but they made his whiskers grow back.'

Moll didn't have time to reply because suddenly the roar of the falls filled their ears – and Devil's Drop appeared, thundering down, a wall of furious water.

'Hold on!' Moll shouted.

'Not through the middle of the falls again!' Siddy moaned.

The eagle flung itself into the churn. Water hammered down, clamouring in their ears, and the bird dropped several metres. Moll's stomach plunged and the water continued to beat down. Then the eagle burst free from Devil's Drop and soared upwards, into the breaking dawn. An orange sun hung above the horizon, casting shards of light through scattered clouds, and the eagle thrust with its wings, up and up, until it was circling above the falls.

This, Moll thought, *the fierce beating of wings and legs clamped hard round rippling feathers – this is what it means to fly.* And, in all her wildest dreams, Moll had never experienced anything so full of freedom. She gazed at the eagle's body, the tips of its wingspan flecked with white, the hooked beak releasing sharp, high cries. Two large brown eyes scanned the sea and its tail feathers rippled in the wind. This was her ma, somehow, and she had come to their rescue just when they'd needed her. Moll bent forward and stroked the golden feathers.

Down below, spray misted out from the falls. Siddy narrowed his eyes. 'Is – is that ... ?'

Beyond Devil's Drop was a small red rowing boat – the one from Little Hollows that Alfie had been waiting to take out – and, inside the boat, a man who built wagons and found secret coves.

'Oak!' Moll shouted, her heart flooding with relief.

Tucking in its giant wings, the eagle dived, and the children clung on. The wind whistled in their ears and their

287

stomachs rose into their throats, then the eagle's wingspan burst out and it swooped, level with the boat. Moll clutched at Oak's arms as they passed and he grappled for her hands, but the eagle had to circle to stay in the air.

'You're all right,' Moll gasped. 'You're OK!'

Oak smiled. 'I'm OK, Moll. It was Willow. After she left you, she came to Little Hollows and lifted the Shadowmasks' curse. She told me where to find you!' Moll's face dropped slightly as she noticed Oak's ankle was still bound in bandages. 'It'll heal in time,' he said.

'We've got the amulet!' Siddy yelled, stroking the eagle's feathers.

'This is my ma's soul!' Moll cried, her cheeks flushed with pride.

'I'm so proud of you all!' Oak shouted against the roar of the falls. 'You did it!' He glanced at Devil's Drop. 'Now what do we need to do?'

The answer was clear in Moll's mind already. 'Somehow I need to get the Shadowmasks to destroy their Soul Splinter. I think it'll help close the thresholds for a while and keep their dark magic back while we search for the last amulet.'

The bird circled again, but it was losing height, struggling under the weight of its load.

'There are too many of you on there!' Oak cried.

Siddy raised a shaky hand. 'I'll come off.'

As the eagle swooped once again, Oak grabbed Siddy and pulled him down into the boat. But, as he did so, a dark shape surged out of Devil's Drop.

Oak seized a quiver from the rowing boat and tossed it up to Moll. 'Alfie said you'd be needing this when I bumped into him before Devil's Drop.'

She caught it and slung it on to her back, then the eagle beat its wings harder and harder out to sea.

And, behind them, the Shadowmasks followed: Ashtongue, bent forward like a giant insect, riding between Darkebite's leathery wings.

Chapter 39
Sky Battle

The eagle climbed higher into the sky and Moll felt its soft, warm feathers beneath her and the strength of the wildcat in front. Eyes streaming from the headwind, she turned back to Alfie. 'Thank you. For coming after us and for healing Gryff.'

Alfie reached into his quiver for an arrow. 'I'll always come after you, Moll.'

She turned back to face the sun straight on. 'And I'll come after you – wherever you go and whatever the Shadowmasks might have in store for us.' Gripping the eagle's back with her legs, she reached for her own quiver.

'What's your plan?' Alfie asked.

Moll set an arrow against the moonbeam, only just visible in the daylight. 'To follow my gut.'

'And what's your gut saying now?'

Moll glanced back, the wind whistling in her ears. The Shadowmasks were gaining on them and Darkebite's screech hung in the air.

'Fight,' she answered.

The eagle soared higher and the sun-flicked waves grew small below them, but Darkebite's wings thrust on. Then the children pulled back on their bows and let their arrows fly. They hurtled through the air and Ashtongue ducked, but Darkebite raised the Soul Splinter in her hands and batted them away. She rose higher, climbing the air with her bat-like wings, the chin of her mask jutting out above them, as if thirsting for Moll and Gryff. And, before the children could reload and fire again, Ashtongue flicked his wrist.

A rope shot out from his sleeve, one end wrapping tight round Moll's arm, the other curled about Ashtongue's wrist. The eagle cried out and Moll felt her body being snatched upwards. In the nick of time, Alfie grabbed her by the shoulders and held her down. The eagle slowed, thrashing its wings against the strain from above, but the Shadowmasks drew closer as Ashtongue placed hand after hand on the rope, reeling himself in towards Moll.

And it was then that Moll realised what was really bound round her arm – not rope, but a snake. Her stomach lurched and she tried to wrench herself free, but the Shadowmasks loomed closer. Ashtongue's fingers grasped the brown-scaled reptile.

Gryff leapt on the snake, slashing with his claws. It writhed and hissed, then the wildcat's claws sliced through it and it split in two before tumbling from the sky. Moll yanked her arm in and Alfie raised an arrow to his bow. Darkebite had the Soul Splinter just metres from Moll, which left Ashtongue unprotected.

The eagle quickened its pace and Alfie released his arrow. It sailed through the air, a flash of wood, feather and moonsilver, then slammed into Ashtongue's chest. The Shadowmask howled as the Oracle Spirit billowed out and snatched him from Darkebite's back. Limbs scrabbling, Ashtongue fell through the air, his body crumbling into black dust as the Oracle Spirit brought it down.

'No!' Darkebite howled, reeling in the air. Her wings spread out either side of her, blocking out the sun, then she dived straight for Moll.

The eagle plummeted, wings tucked in like a bullet, and Gryff, Moll and Alfie clung on for their lives. Then the bird pulled up hard and swerved to the right. Moll grabbed another arrow and released it from her bow, but Darkebite ducked, then sped after them until both she and the eagle were side by side, speeding through the cloud-scattered sky.

'You want to know the truth about your past, Alfie?' Darkebite shrieked.

Alfie stiffened, but Moll reached for another arrow and set it to her bow. She fired again, but Darkebite flung it aside with the Soul Splinter. Then she threw back her head and laughed.

'Why you're broken inside? Why people treat you as if you don't exist?' Darkebite dipped her mask into the headwind and sped on through the sky beside the eagle. Then she looked at Alfie, eyes like coal burning behind her mask. 'You *created* the Soul Splinter, Alfie. The very weapon you want to destroy. *You* made it.'

Moll's body shook with hatred. 'Don't listen to her, Alfie! You're part of our camp and you've got the old magic on your side! You rescued me from Skull! You helped find the amulet! You cured Gryff! And you're real to every one of us!'

But Alfie was silent behind her and Moll could feel Gryff's fur stiffening with dread.

Darkebite laughed. 'We needed an innocent child's tears,' she sneered at Alfie. 'Skull stole you from a farm and it was *your* tears that helped bind our shadows inside the Soul Splinter.' Her dark wings beat on beside the eagle. 'You're a part of it, Alfie. A part of *us*.' She turned her mask towards Moll. 'So you see, if you destroy the Soul Splinter, then you destroy Alfie too.'

Moll shook her head, panic rising thick inside her. 'You're lying!' She spun round to Alfie, but his face was white, his eyes fighting back tears.

Moll blinked at him and Gryff placed a paw on the boy's foot. 'It's not true, Alfie. Don't believe what she says. Your tears healed Gryff – remember that! You're not like them!'

But the choice drummed inside her, as fast as her pounding heart. What if it *was* true? What if a part of Alfie belonged to the Shadowmasks? And what if destroying the Soul Splinter meant losing him? But doing nothing – letting the Soul Splinter exist – would allow the Shadowmasks' evil to spread and the Bone Murmur would be broken . . . They would lose everything. She bit down on her lip. It *couldn't* be true. She wouldn't believe it. She couldn't make that choice.

Darkebite raced along beside them, flying higher and

higher until she was above the eagle again. Then she raised the Soul Splinter in both hands and uttered a rasping chant:

'Below me now are the girl and the cat.
I soar above them, as fast as a bat.
Now the weapon is ready to poison them both,
To darken their souls. That's the Shadowmasks' oath.'

'Don't look up!' Alfie shouted. 'Don't let her do it, Moll!'

The eagle cried out and, as Moll buried her head in Gryff's fur, Alfie wrapped his arms round her. Darkebite smirked, then lashed out with her free arm, wrenching Alfie backwards.

Time skidded to a halt. Alfie tumbled from the eagle's back and Moll flung herself at him, grabbing him by the wrists. He dangled in the air, hundreds of metres above the sea, and Moll groaned at his weight, desperate not to lose him. She hauled hard, but Darkebite was circling again, wielding the Soul Splinter like a staff. Gryff lashed out splayed claws towards it, forcing the Shadow Keeper back.

'Let me go, Moll!' Alfie gasped. 'If your hands are on me, you've nothing to stop the Soul Splinter dripping inside you both.'

Moll winced under the strain. 'I'm not losing you, Alfie.' But her hands were sweating and the hold she had was starting to slip. She clutched him harder. 'I won't ever let you go. *You* were my impossible dream – to unlock the Oracle Spirit in my arrows. I wanted to make you real so that everyone could see you!' She struggled against Alfie's weight. 'I won't let you go!'

Alfie met her eyes, his jay feather fluttering against his neck, then he squeezed her hands tight. 'You don't have a choice, Moll.'

Darkebite swerved towards them and, as she raised the Soul Splinter at Moll, Alfie wrenched himself free from Moll's grasp and leapt on to the Shadow Keeper's back.

'If I made it, I can break it!' he shouted.

Darkebite reeled backwards at the weight of Alfie and, as he wrestled the Shadow Keeper for the shard of ice, Moll felt her world slide. It was just as her ma had said: '*He who made it will destroy it.*' Only she hadn't meant the Shadowmasks: she had meant Alfie.

'No!' Moll screamed. The eagle beat its wings towards Darkebite. 'No, Alfie!'

Alfie reached down and tore the Soul Splinter from Darkebite's clasp and, while the Shadowmask stretched out frenzied hands, Alfie looked at Moll with glassy eyes.

Then he snapped the ice in two.

It shattered into hundreds of black, glittering pieces before falling through the sky, like grains of dark sand.

Darkebite hovered in the air for a moment, her mask thrown back, screeching into the dawn. Alfie was poised on her back, his eyes locked on to Moll, then, as Darkebite's screech shrank to a moan, she crumbled into black dust, just as the Soul Splinter had done, and Alfie sprang towards the eagle.

Moll's heart leapt; Darkebite had been wrong: Alfie had broken the Soul Splinter, but it hadn't broken him.

But, mid-leap, Alfie's body began to fade, crumbling at the edges, growing dimmer where the colour and life had been. And, as Moll reached out her arms towards him, scrabbling through the air, she met with nothing but a wisp of white.

Alfie was gone.

The eagle didn't fly back to the others. As if it could sense Moll's sadness, it beat on and on towards the horizon, calling to her softly.

Moll buried her head in Gryff's fur, her heart breaking inside her. 'Alfie,' she sobbed. 'Alfie.' But only the waves answered, rolling on far below.

Moll closed her eyes. She had tried for so long to hold people at a distance and for a while she had managed to spread her heart so thinly she hadn't felt much of anything. And then people like Alfie had crept in and she'd learnt to trust. But, as the eagle flew further out to sea, Moll realised that Alfie hadn't just crept in – he'd stormed in and opened her heart up – and it felt as if he'd left a little part of his soul inside hers.

Moll's heart swelled and then ached and she clung to Gryff, letting the tears fall for the friend who'd followed her every step of the way since they'd met in the forest, even though there was nothing in his blood that tied him to any of this – only the Shadowmasks' curse before he was old enough to stop it. Gryff nuzzled into Moll, whimpering quietly, and they let the sea drift past.

It was sunset before the eagle flew Moll and Gryff back to the shore. The sky was streaked with pink clouds and, as the great bird swooped down towards the rocks beneath Puddle's lighthouse where the others had gathered, Moll was glad of the wind to dry her tear-stained face. The eagle's talons shot out and it slowed to a halt on the furthest rock.

Siddy looked up from where he was sitting, his eyes flicking from Moll to Gryff, the truth of things slowly dawning.

'Not – not Alfie . . .' He clutched his face and looked away.

Moll slid from the eagle's back with Gryff, and Oak limped over the rocks towards them, his head hung low. He drew close and Moll sank into his arms, closing her eyes against everything that had happened. Oak stroked her hair and looked up at the eagle. It dipped its head and Oak did the same, then he reached out a hand and ran it over the eagle's neck. Oak jumped as his fingers met with the feathers.

'The – the pain,' he said quietly. 'It's gone!' He bent down and wound the bandage away from his ankle. His leg was completely unharmed; there wasn't even a scar. 'The power of the amulet, as Willow said,' Oak murmured. He looked at the eagle. 'Thank you, Olive.'

The eagle turned its head to Moll and she noticed a single tear trickling down its beak.

'You have to leave, don't you?' Moll said, her voice small and cracked at the pain of things unsaid.

The eagle dipped its head again, then it nudged its beak against Moll's hand. *No one leaves forever, Moll. Have faith.*

Moll heard the words inside her, as if her ma was holding her heart and making it beat.

She leant into the eagle's chest and wrapped her arms round its neck. The great bird lifted a wing over Moll and for a few minutes they stayed like that, safe in each other's arms. Then the eagle ruffled its feathers, looked at Moll one last time, as if it was seeing right inside her soul, then took off into the setting sky. Moll followed the bird with her eyes, watching its wings beating out towards the horizon until it was just a dot. Then, when it disappeared completely and the sun dropped away, the first stars emerged, blinking brighter than they had in weeks, and Moll knew that her ma was safely home.

Chapter 40
Puddle's Bundle

U nder a starlit sky, Moll helped Oak and Siddy pile armfuls of driftwood into the rowing boat Oak had moored to the rocks. Then Siddy stepped inside it, his cheeks blotched by tears, and began rubbing two sticks until a trail of smoke appeared.

Moll had heard Oak and Mooshie talking about gypsy burial rites back in the forest: *Burn the wagon of the deceased with all their belongings so that their spirit doesn't come back to haunt this world.* Only Alfie hadn't owned a wagon – he didn't even have a body to most people – but this was the boat he had planned to go out in with Oak. Moll's eyes filled with fresh tears as Siddy set a flame to the sticks and sparks flitted into the sky. He climbed out, scooped up Hermit from a nearby rock, and Moll and Oak pushed the boat away from the rocks. Then they watched from the shingle as it floated out to sea, a glow of orange against a black satin sky.

After some time, Oak turned to them. 'Let's get a fire going with the rest of the driftwood. And I've bread, nuts and water from Mooshie for us all.'

Moll sat on a rock and, as Oak and Siddy heaped the sticks into a pile, Gryff nuzzled against her, rolling his head round and round her hand. She hugged him close to her chest and looked up at the cliffs, at the sheer drop she and Siddy had climbed to the bottom of. Then her eyes rested on a shape moving very slowly down the path towards them. Moll's hands shot to her bow, her heart drummed, then she squinted harder into the darkness at the large cagouled figure making its way down to the rocks.

'Sid,' Moll whispered. 'It's Puddle.'

They watched him draw close, then Siddy narrowed his eyes. 'And – and is that … ?'

His voice trailed off, he started forward and then Moll was on her feet too, scrambling over the rocks and rushing towards Puddle.

'Scrap!' Moll shouted. 'Oh, Scrap!'

And there she was – the little smuggler's child – wrapped in several blankets and huddled in Puddle's arms. She smiled weakly as Moll and Siddy gathered round her.

Puddle smiled. 'She's a fighter this one – especially after we had a visit from a very unusual-looking lady all dressed in silver.'

Moll and Siddy looked at one another. 'Willow,' they said in unison.

Puddle nodded. 'Scrap managed to eat a little porridge earlier and, after a bit of a rest, I think she's going to make a full recovery. We've even had a little talk about her moving into the lighthouse and making it her home. Dorothy and I could use a bit of company.'

Moll clutched Scrap's hand. 'It's good to have you back.'

Siddy ruffled her hair. 'It's not been the same without you.'

They made their way back to the campfire and, though Oak accepted Puddle straight away as he listened to what the lighthouse keeper had done for them all, Scrap wept silent tears when they told her about Alfie.

Before long, flames twisted into the night and they sat and ate around the fire. Moll thought of the last two Shadowmasks still out there, of the quilt of darkness they were spinning with her parents' hair. Was the final amulet going to be enough to destroy all that? And where had Alfie gone after shattering their Soul Splinter? He'd been there one minute – she could still picture his eyes, big and blue and full of hope – then he'd vanished. The sadness rocked inside Moll.

She bit off a mouthful of bread and swallowed it, then she looked at Oak. 'The amulet was meant to fix things – meant to make things better like the first one did.'

Oak stoked the fire with his boot. 'Things don't happen the same way twice, Moll, especially when magic's involved.'

Moll picked up a pebble and hurled it into the sea. 'But when I fix one thing something else seems to fall apart. It's never all as it should be – not ever.'

Oak turned his hat over in his hands. 'Often we don't realise how good something is until we lose it. It may not have been perfect before, but perhaps it was good enough in parts.'

'But losing Alfie ...' Moll looked away. 'I thought the amulet would keep us all safe – that we'd be sitting round this fire together.' She hung her head. 'I want to start again, a million miles from here.'

Oak was silent for several moments, then he stood up and went to sit on the rock beside Moll. 'Sometimes people leave us halfway through the journey – but what a journey this was, what things you, Siddy, Gryff, Alfie and Scrap achieved. You found the amulet and you set your ma's soul free. You broke the Soul Splinter and you destroyed Ashtongue and Darkebite. Don't forget all of that. The old magic is still turning because of what you did.'

Moll ran a hand over Gryff's back, then she glanced up at Oak. His deep dark eyes were shining – not with sorrow any more but with hope. Moll could feel the determination inside him, stronger than the Shadowmasks, like an ancient rock that could never be smashed.

'How can you go on hoping when things are broken like they are?' she said.

Oak looked into her eyes. 'Because no one leaves for good, Moll.'

She felt his words chime with her ma's.

Oak took her hand and clasped it tight. 'And I don't believe Alfie's dead.'

Siddy looked up from stroking Hermit's shell. 'You don't?'

Puddle fiddled with his beard. 'There's something about

302

that boy – I felt it when I was alone with him and Gryff in the lighthouse. Maybe I couldn't see him – maybe the Shadowmasks laid a curse on him that broke his "*real*" – but Alfie's not gone.' Puddle placed a hand over his heart. 'I can feel that much in here.'

Something inside Moll stirred with this knowledge, as if she too knew and believed its truth. 'Before we reached the lighthouse,' she said, 'Willow told us all to think of an impossible dream – a dream so full of hope it would fight back against the Shadowmasks' magic. Well, *making Alfie real* was my impossible dream. And although I didn't expect things to work out like this – maybe that's because this isn't the end.'

Moll reached for one of her arrows and ran a hand over the Oracle Bone symbol: *Hope*. She thought back to Alfie's words to her while they were on the eagle's back high up in the sky: '*I'll always come after you*,' he had said. Moll looked up at the others, remembering the promise she'd made back to him. 'Maybe there's more hoping and dreaming to be done.'

Oak drew her close to his chest. 'There's more hoping all right. You're not alone, Moll. Whatever the Shadowmasks have in store for us, we'll fight it together.' He reached for Moll's quiver on the rock behind her.

'What are you doing?' Siddy asked.

Moll took the quiver from Oak, pushed the hair back from her face and looked at Gryff. His yellow-green eyes blinked back at her own, his head dipped and she knew he'd understood.

Moll smiled. 'We're going after Alfie.'

Epilogue
The Turret in the Clouds

Many miles north of the lighthouse, past the knotted trees of Tanglefern Forest and the villages scattered throughout the countryside, the landscape grows wilder and fields give way to moors, lochs and glens. In the heart of this wilderness are the mountains, towering ridges scaling the width of the land. And carved into the rock face of the highest crag, almost lost in the clouds, is a monastery.

Night is at its thickest now; the mountain is dark and still. But there's a light coming from a room at the top of a turret, a single candle flickering on a window ledge. Inside sits a figure – cloaked and masked – before a spinning wheel. And the only sound to break the silence of the night is the slow tap of his foot against the treadle and the creak of old wood as the wheel turns.

Long, thin fingers pluck the fibre from a basket and feed it on to the wheel. The fibre is black and glittering and, as it spins round and round, it tightens into thread, shining like oil. And then the boot pauses. The wheel stops. And the figure looks up. Candlelight falls upon his mask: a canvas face – strips of tattered sack stitched together, rough holes cut for eyes and a jagged line for the mouth. There is no nose, but clumps of musty straw hang down beneath the hood where hair might once have been.

And there's another noise in the turret now, a sound so soft it might have been missed before. But it's there all right, a hushed kind of whispering, and it's coming from the fibre itself as if sounds have been locked inside it: muffled sobs, a gasp, teeth chattering, a faint scream. The fibre is almost a living, breathing thing and, although every sound it makes is different, each one tells of the same thing: fear.

The figure runs a curled nail along the fibre – slowly, thoughtfully, gently. This is something very precious. The sack mouth smiles and the eyeholes slant.

'You're almost ready, aren't you?'

Each word is precise, each syllable like a perfect stitch. The figure glances at an old wardrobe at the far side of the room. It is barred shut with a plank of wood, but, as the figure watches, the plank begins to shake. Whatever is locked inside the wardrobe knows it's being watched and wants to get out.

'All in good time,' the figure whispers. 'All in good time.'

Then the wardrobe doors are still once more and the figure pushes the treadle down with his foot. Again the wheel turns, creaking into the night, and the black thread gathers round the spindle.

THE DREAMSNATCHER saw the Tribe face the Shadowmasks in the forest. **THE SHADOW KEEPER** saw them battle the witchdoctors down by the sea. Get ready for the final book in the trilogy, where they journey to the northern wilderness to force the Shadowmasks back once and for all. Here's a little teaser for what to expect ...

An enormous thank you to creative superstar, Thierry Kelaart, for drawing me a world inside a feather.

Acknowledgements

The dream was to get one book published. But somehow, here I am writing the acknowledgments for my second book. There are not enough star jumps in the world to express the happiness, excitement and sheer magic of that. So here are some very special thank yous instead . . .

To the Salvesen Clan, thank you for the Norwegian adventures which helped shape a lot of the drama in the book: kayaking through the fjords, jumping off cliffs and diving for mussels. A big thanks to the De Lisle family for exploring beaches and lighthouses with me in Salcombe – Little Hollows grew out of that weekend. Thank you to Sam Allen Turner for an extremely bendy afternoon of Anti-Gravity Yoga, the inspiration behind the Oracle Spirits, and also to Huw Stephens and Kevin Higgs at Barbury Shooting School for letting me practise archery with a *real* Robin Hood bow so that the Tribe knew their stuff. And thank you to Fiona Bird for foraging tips and Pith and Bunga Heathcote Amory for advice on living wild.

Thank you to my wonderful agent, Hannah Sheppard. You've been there for Moll, Gryff, Alfie and Sid from the start and hearing your enthusiasm for this book when you read it out at sea a year ago made me stand on my chair and whoop. Your early editorial advice, together with your continued support throughout contracts I never understand, has been invaluable.

To Jane Griffiths, my hugely talented editor, you realised what was needed to make my characters stronger and the structure of the story tighter; your advice made me write a bolder book and your compassion for Porridge the Second and Hermit makes me smile. Liz Binks, you continually inject creativity and flair into the marketing and PR of my books – thank you (and Pete!) for all your hard work. Thank you also to Camilla Leask at Angel Publicity and Elisa Offord, Becky Peacock, Jade Westwood, Rachel Mann, Laura Hough, Stephanie Purcell, Sam Habib, Johnny Keyworth and Jane Tait from Simon & Schuster Kids for your enthusiasm, time and talent. Thomas Flintham, you've done a fantastic job on the book cover and the map – again. Huge thanks to you and Jenny Richards.

I also want to dedicate a paragraph of shouty-style praise to the incredible bloggers who have got behind me over the last two years: Jim Dean, Darren Hartwell, Michelle Toy, Clare Zinkin, Mathew Tobin, Joshua Aldwinckle-Povey, Vincent Ripley, Sarah Watkins, Hannah Weyh, Anne-Marie Carslaw, Carly Bennett and KM Lockwood. Together with Fiona Noble, Shelley Fallows and Aimee Layton, your kind words about *The Dreamsnatcher* on social media made my tummy flip and your continued support and encouragement throughout my writing *The Shadow Keeper* has made me feel a lot braver as a writer – thank you.

To the exceptional teachers and librarians who have championed my book – especially Helen Barker, Jo Clarke, Anna Tomlinson, Anne Thompson, Lesley Parr, Amy Kinross, Hannah Verney, James Malone, Kelly Tarrant and Guy Lucas – your enthusiasm, display boards and school visits have been among the highlights of my writing journey so far. Thank you. And a huge thank you to Mel Taylor at Little Star Writing for all her incredible support, to the following Waterstones booksellers who have pushed Moll and her Tribe out into the world so boldly – Jo Boyles, Stevie Connor, Amanda Jordan, Laura Main Ellen and Craig Hayworth – and to all the independent bookshops who have shown such fabulous support: Forum Books Kids, Topping & Company St Andrews and Bath, Storytellers Inc, A Bundle of Books, Haslemere Bookshop, Chicken and Frog, Mr B's Emporium, A Festival Of Books, Ottie and the Bea, Nutshell Studios, Tales on Moon Lane, Pea Green Boat Books and Mostly Books.

Thank you to all the awesome kids who have read my book, come to hear me speak and sent me lovely messages, drawings, stories and even raps – you guys are the best fans I could've asked for. A massive thank you to the Little Star Writers for their silvery advice on the cover, to all the brilliant kids at my Patron school – Whitchurch C of E

Primary – and to my Beanstalk gang at Essendine Primary for all their booky chat. And a special thanks to the children who read my book when it was only just tiptoeing out into the world: Corey Yuile, Seren James, Enya Eccleston, Sara and Tesa Getter, Annika and Ishaan Arora, Morgan Damiba and Pippa Bell. Tori Van Heerden – I bet one day we'll be signing books together. To all my wonderful friends, thank you for your continued love and support and huge hugs to Ed and Lizzie Webb for buying Edinburgh out of every single Abi Elphinstone book week in, week out.

And my family. The maddest, bestest bunch of the lot. I could never have written my books without you all – your love and support are unparalleled. Mum, I'm so proud of you in all that you do – how you manage to look after all the pupils in your school AND still find time to check I'm wearing a vest and see what Moll is up to is beyond me. You are a remarkable woman and the reason Moll is so brave is because of you. Dad, thank you for all our adventures – carving catapults, hiking the moors, watching salmon leap – you gave me a unforgettable childhood and whenever Moll and Oak explore, I imagine it's you and me. Will and Tom, thank you for bouncing down stairs on mattresses with me and scrambling over bales in the barn; the reason Moll has such great pals in Alfie and Sid is because you two were brilliantly reckless little brothers. Charli, thank you for all your incredible support and friendship – many a jar of Chazwinkle's was consumed during the writing of this book and I'll let Mooshie know she should be cooking with

310

it from now on. Matilda, you are too young to understand what on earth all this means but I want you to know Auntie Abi can't wait to go on adventures with you soon. Cruey, my little sis, thank you for that walk along St Cyrus beach where you named Scrap and helped me build her character. So much of you went into her. And Rosie and Tron, you're brilliant additions to Team Elph and I'm so grateful for all your support.

Edo. You get a whole paragraph to yourself. Hehe. Thank you for letting me stamp around the house when my stories aren't quite coming together. Thank you for your patience when I'm as impulsive and tiring as Moll. Thank you for charging up and down the county with me for events. Thank you for making me laugh when things go wrong. Thank you for being so up for any adventure that comes our way. And thank you for believing in me every single day. You're a very wonderful human being.

About the Author

Abi Elphinstone grew up in Scotland where she spent most of her childhood building dens, hiding in tree houses and running wild across highland glens. After being coaxed out of her tree house, she studied English at Bristol University and then worked as a teacher in Africa, Berkshire and London. THE SHADOW KEEPER is her second book (THE DREAMSNATCHER was her first) and a third book will complete the Tribe's adventures in 2017. When she's not writing about Moll and Gryff, Abi volunteers for Beanstalk charity, teaches creative writing workshops in schools and travels the world looking for her next story. Her latest adventure involved living with the Kazakh Eagle Hunters in Mongolia . . .

Website: www.abielphinstone.com
Facebook: www.facebook.com/abi.elphinstone
Twitter: @moontrug
Instagram: @moontrugger